About the aut

Sara Škrobo grew up in the small town of Županja in the East of Croatia. After getting a Master's degree in history from the University of Zagreb, she moved to London, UK. There she spent three years working different jobs and enrolled on a postgraduate programme in modern history at King's College London. Sara returned to Croatia and is currently living in Zagreb where she got the initial ideas for her debut novel, *Tayna Chronicles: The Secret City*. A relentless dreamer and bookworm, Sara enjoys fantasy novels paired with a cup of (Turkish) coffee, preferably at one of the terraces in Zagreb where she spent most of her adult life.

TAYNA CHRONICLES:
THE SECRET CITY

Sara Škrobo

TAYNA CHRONICLES:
THE SECRET CITY

Vanguard Press

VANGUARD PAPERBACK

© Copyright 2021
Sara Škrobo

A CIP catalogue record for this title is
available from the British Library.

ISBN 978-1-80016-125-2

Vanguard Press is an imprint of
Pegasus Elliot MacKenzie Publishers Ltd.
www.pegasuspublishers.com

First Published in 2021

Vanguard Press
Sheraton House Castle Park
Cambridge England

Printed & Bound in Great Britain

Dedication

To Nada and Marijan, the best grandparents a girl can wish
for.

Acknowledgements

First and foremost, I'd like to thank my parents for enrolling me on an English course at thirteen years old. They put me on a path that would eventually give me the tools without which this book wouldn't have been possible. Next, I'd like to give my warmest thanks to my aunt. She passed her passion for the English language on to me, always believing that one day I would visit England for real, not just through films and pictures. You were right!

This book wouldn't have been completed if it wasn't for my loyal and (extremely) patient friends, both in Croatia and abroad. Thank you for listening to my jabbering for hours on end – you know who you are! Your enthusiasm and support have been so very helpful, and I can never thank you enough. And to my sister and brother, who patiently commented on every stage of my writing, sharing their own ideas. I'm lucky to have you as siblings.

Next, I'd like to thank all those whose personality traits I 'borrowed' to create characters. I apologise if, in some cases, the characters modelled after you disappoint in the novel. They're only human!

Finally, I owe thanks to my friends who helped me through the extremely challenging period, which was the year 2020. Without your support and readiness to extend a helping hand, I wouldn't have been able to spend so much time telling Sofija's story. You're partly responsible for bringing her to life.

"Beautiful liberty, beloved liberty, liberty sweetly avowed, Thou are the treasured gift that God to us endowed,
    All our glory is thy true creation,
    To our home, thou are all the decoration,
    No silver nor gold, not life itself could replace
    The reward of thy pure and sublime grace."

Ivan Gundulić — A Hymn to Liberty, Dubravka

Prologue

My life never had any purpose to it, or at least that's how I've always perceived it. I existed for the pure sake of existence and made my peace with it a long time ago. Those I loved added some meaning to it, made it valuable; my family, my friends, were the reason I got out of bed every morning. But even they couldn't make up for the utter aimlessness of my small and unremarkable life. Or at least, that's how I always saw it. When I'm gone, nothing will be left, for I didn't believe I would ever create any sort of legacy.

I found my purpose now; most surprisingly, it happened as I went through excruciating pain, waiting like a promised ray of sunshine at the end of a dark tunnel. It happened when I lost whom I loved the most, when my only family was so violently taken away from me. That was, miraculously, when I found a new life for myself. That was when I fell in love for the first and the last time. True love happens only once in a person's existence; there are no second chances.

Now, as I was marching towards Kalemgrad, I couldn't bring myself to feel regretful. If I'd stayed where I was, I would've lived a life. A long but empty life, devoid of freedom. A life that was in no way mine. For better or for worse, I'd choose this new life, a hundred times over. For I was free to make my own choices, free to die in place of someone I love, in the place of something I believe in.

It occurred to me, as I listened to the thuds of my own footsteps hitting the cobbles of the abandoned streets of Agram, that I had not yet considered my own safety. How will I protect myself? My powers are useless here, and I cannot face Tanatos armed with nothing but my wits. He will crush me, and I will fade from this world, silently as if I'd never been here. Unremarkable, unimportant. Extinguished like a feeble flame.

But at least I'll see him one last time. In my mind's eye, I summoned the picture of his wide, emerald eyes, smiling down at me, his beautiful face alight with happiness. I'll carry that image with me, then it won't be so bad, will it? It cannot be. I let the memory linger in front of my eyes, shining light into the dark streets ahead of me, warding off the fear that, just moments ago, paralysed every centimetre of my body. With happiness came the sense of purpose, and I was free of my anxieties. Free to march on, for I knew what I had to do.

As I walked towards my end, I'd never felt freer.

Chapter 1
The Promised Child

(Tayna, the mage Danubia)

"That's just an old myth; you don't seriously believe it," said David, giving his friend a look of incredulity. "I always thought it was just an old wives' tale. Not a shred of evidence to support it."

"I don't need hard evidence for this one. I just know it. Call me a believer if you like," Tomislav answered calmly. He took another sip of his lager before adding in a low voice:

"You've got to have some faith sometimes. And a dash of imagination - an essential component you're clearly missing."

David burst into laughter, attracting the attention of other visitors in the spacious hotel bar.

"You really are a funny guy, Tom. Do you honestly believe some super-resilient, *promised* child with silver eyes and five gems is out there somewhere, waiting for us to call for his aid? Had that much to drink already?"

The way the word 'promised' came out of his mouth gave away exactly what he thought of the idea. David's bright eyes scrutinised Tomislav, who sat across the table, expecting him to admit the whole thing was downright ridiculous.

"No, I think the silver eyes are a bit over the top. In any case, that's what they say for Panmages, not the promised child. But the rest is possible; why not?" Tomislav answered confidently, and seeing David's smirk getting wider, he added, "Laugh all you want, David. You'll see soon enough."

Tomislav stood up, picking up his empty pint. "Want another one?"

"Sure. Maybe get a pint for Goran, too; he is on the way."

David watched his friend walk away from their table, mulling over what they'd just discussed.

Surely, there would be some evidence if the old story of a so-called 'promised' child was true, he thought to himself. David remembered well when he first heard the tale. It sounded ridiculous then, and it wasn't any less ridiculous twenty years later.

The war was lost, and the Rebellion was crushed. Everyone who hoped the mages still had any chance was downright deluded, he thought grimly. This insane story about some powerful, *promised* child (well, now it would be a twenty-year-old adult, he thought) was just giving everyone false hope. If we had a secret weapon up our sleeve, why didn't we get in touch already? Why didn't they? This person would allegedly have extraordinary skills, mastering more than three gems and being more resilient than the rest of us. If that's so, where is that kid? It was rare enough to come across mages who could control more than one gem, let alone three or — David scoffed at the thought — five!

He wasn't one for believing in myths, and this story about a promised child was exactly that. Having had the upper hand for so long historically, the mages couldn't accept the defeat. Out of self-pity, or perhaps self-justification, his fellow mages created a whole religion with this "promised" child in the centre. The number of its followers was still faltering, but Tom was a persuasive man. Soon, we'll see the creation of the Church of the promised child, David thought, scoffing in disgust.

"What a load of crap," he muttered to himself. He hoped Tomislav would let it go soon, as he ran out of ways to make fun of his friend.

"Here you go. Ah, there's Goran." Tomislav was back, placing three pints of lager on the table and sitting opposite David again. A moment later, a tall, bulky man, walked into the hotel and headed for the adjacent bar where the other two were sitting. His winter coat was covered in snow, which was an unusual occurrence in Tayna, even for January. The man hung it on a coatrack next to the entrance and joined the other two, taking several long strides until he reached their table, tucked in the back next to the fireplace.

"Good afternoon, lads. How're you doing? Thanks for the beer, by the way," the newcomer greeted them, taking the seat next to David and leaning closer to the fire, warming up his freezing hands. "All right, big brother? How's Sandra and my favourite niece?"

One large and burly, another skinny and bespectacled, Goran and

David didn't look like they're related at all. While Goran spent most of his life fighting the battle against the nemage government, either through Rebellion or combative journalism, his big brother preferred the confines of Tayna's Akademia of Magic. He used to teach Defensive magic there before the Wipe. After the Wipe, he was given a choice - serve at the Local Assembly, vote the party line and pretend to be one of the nemages *or* spend the rest of his life counting bricks in a prison cell. Like the others, he chose the former, hoping things would change someday.

The three friends clinked their pint glasses and took long swigs before David answered:

"They're both fine, sending their regards. It's Mila's birthday tomorrow, so Sandra is busy baking. You're both still coming, I hope?" He was looking from Goran to Tomislav.

"Yes, Natasha and I wouldn't miss it," said Tomislav, smiling. "Can't believe she's turning twenty already".

"Perhaps Mila's your promised child then, Tom? Ha-ha, wouldn't that be a blast," David provoked his old friend.

"Perhaps! We shall see," Tomislav answered confidently. "How are things in Agram? Any new taxes coming our way?"

The question was directed to Goran, who responded in a low, irritated voice.

"You know it. New taxes are the one certain thing these days." He attempted at the irony, but his face fell. "I'm not sure we'll stand to live like this for much longer. They're using us every way they can. If only we could still send our representatives to the Duma as we did before the wretched Concealment Act. We never used to hide from them; what happened to us?"

A grave silence fell over their table now. No one knew what to do or say these days when it came to Tayna's forced submission to the nemage government, Duma. They'd tried to break free twice and failed both times. The losses were too grave to even consider trying again, and magic was weaker and weaker each year. The fewer people used it, the less potent it was, that's just how it worked. And with the mages being shunted aside and forced within Tayna's boundaries, they had little hope of reviving the magical supplies in the rest of Danubia. It couldn't happen, they knew, until the mages were free again and at liberty to use their powers all around the country.

"Perhaps we could try a different way — by going to the nemages and refreshing their memories?" Tomislav asked, half-amused by his own suggestion.

"Sure, why not? They'd probably have us locked up with the Siva members. Mindless morons," Goran said gravely.

"It's not their fault, though. The non-magicals stood no chance against such a powerful spell, you know that," David told him, then went on under his breath, "Poor fools."

They sat in silence, drinking their beer and looking out the wide windows into the empty streets of their beloved Tayna. People were afraid to move around much these days, what with impromptu raids being an everyday thing now.

"How's Tanatos getting on? There's still no mention of him on the nemage news, not that I know of," Tomislav asked, glancing up at the other two.

"He's still there, the sneaky bastard. I bet he's waiting for the old guard to die out before he takes over the Duma," David replied, a disgusted expression on his face. "I wonder why he even bothered. Hiding in plain sight and biding his time, instead of just getting rid of them the only way he knows how." He spoke more to himself than to anyone else, his voice bitter.

"I don't know much about him, but you can't deny the man's got patience," Goran said in response to his brother. "If he'd just slaughtered the Duma representatives or thrown them in the Pit when the war ended, the nemages wouldn't trust his lies, would they? He's waiting for his time to come."

The other two looked up at him, nodding sombrely without speaking. Tomislav glanced around the half-empty bar, remembering how lively it used to be in his youth. It had been impossible to find an empty table without using his connections with Vesna, the waitress, he recalled with a smile. During the war, this hotel served as Tayna Defenders' League Headquarters, and he practically lived here. The upstairs rooms were full all the time, he remembered fondly, almost missing those uncertain times. They were in the war, that is true, but at least they had a cause, something to fight for.

And now, the hotel was barely making ends meet, still existing only thanks to the generous help of Tayna's citizens. Not that any of them had much money to spare, but this place — The Bayamonti it was called — was a sort of institution. Without it, Tayna wouldn't be the same.

Yet, it remained empty most of the time now. People were afraid to leave their houses unless it was absolutely necessary. Magic was no longer enough to protect them from the Duma, whose oblivious members had no clue a dark mage sat among them, hiding. It was Tanatos they all feared, not the nemages themselves, for he was the one pulling strings from the shadows. Tomislav suspected he was behind all the disappearances and accidents happening to the Tayna citizens. He did all this, Tomislav thought, to thin Tayna's ranks so that, when the time came, the magical community would be defenceless and demoralised.

"Well, Tom," David said with a sudden amusement in his voice, breaking the long silence, "I hope you'll introduce us to your *promised* child soon enough. Tell him to hurry up, will you? Could be a good match for Mila, I'd fancy a super-resilient son-in-law."

Chapter 2
The Outer Lands

Five years later (Velesh, the nemage Danubia)

There was no freedom in my country, at least not in the physical sense. The people had no control over who they were or what they did with their time in this life. The only freedom was that of the mind — our Supreme President's hand hasn't snatched that from us just yet.

Danubia was a place no one ever left or even thought of leaving. Everyone I knew (and I knew pretty much the whole of Velesh, not a difficult task since it was a small place) worked the same jobs from the day they reached adulthood. They all lived in the same house and followed the same path as their parents and grandparents. There were a few exceptions every year. For example, a person from a family of florists might go on to be a painter and decorator. Or someone from a family of bakers might become a butcher. But no one ever left Danubia; even if they wanted to, they couldn't obtain a permit unless they had a very good reason to venture over the border.

There were train and coach lines, but those could only take you as far as the next town. People rarely moved as they wouldn't fit with the new community easily, seeing as all their connections were in their hometown. It didn't make sense to most of them to try and make new connections. Why would you do that, they asked? You already have everything you need right here.

The people of Danubia travelled to the capital city of Agram in exceptional circumstances only. If you were sick or a family member required immediate medical care, you'd be given special permission to go to Agram to get what you need. Your return ticket would be pre-booked, and you'd be required to check-in upon return — no one left without authorisation. No one travelled for pleasure.

I wanted to leave to see what was out there, beyond the Great

Northern Border. I wished to venture beyond Danubia to learn about my parents, about their deaths in the Second Danubian War. To see what it was that the Biela caste worked so hard to hide from us. Since I was very young, I firmly believed travelling abroad would provide me with some answers — real, believable answers.

That was why, right now, I was queuing to the Velesh Library, hoping to use their computer station. Personal ownership of a computer was illegal, so I didn't have one. Using my work computer for anything other than work was risky at the very least, especially since I was surrounded by twenty other people in the office. Mobile phones were useless for anything other than calling pre-authorised numbers, which could be found in Danubia's Telephone Directory. Every aspect of our lives was being controlled, yet so many people chose to shut their eyes to it. *Sheep,* I thought to myself. *Do such cowards even deserve anything better?*

Velesh was a small riverside town set in the very east of the Federal State of Danubia. Most of its inhabitants were proud of what little it could offer. *Other towns of our size don't even have a library; you should be happy*, was what they'd tell me every time I passed a comment on a pitiful state of the library and its small collection.

I'd visited the library many times before, bookworm that I was. I'd never asked for permission to use the computer station, though, and my heart was about to come out of my chest any minute now. I wasn't sure this was going to work. *So many things could go wrong*, my best friend's voice echoed in my head. *Are you sure it's worth it?*

Yes, it was definitely and undeniably worth it. There must be a reason President Tanatos and the Biela members restricted all travel outside Danubia, why they wouldn't give us anything but vague explanations about what was in the Outer Lands. How come everything outside Danubia was a danger zone? What *is* dangerous? Was it some kind of war, or perhaps a nuclear attack? And how come the Great Northern Border is more heavily guarded compared to our other borders? Is there a war outbreak in the north? Is that the reason? If so, who started it, why and is Danubia at war right now? *So many questions and no answers whatsoever.*

We never got a straight answer and, to those paying attention to what was going on, it all made very little sense. If travelling beyond the borders of Danubia was as dangerous as we were told, how come the two highest castes — the Biela and the Cherwona — could leave whenever they pleased? Travel permits were issued to their members regularly, under the excuse that "They're risking their own well-being to protect our great country".

I came here today to find out more about the Outer Lands, hoping to not get caught in the process.

Ever since the war ended in 1955, Danubia has been gradually closing itself from the outside world, the explanation being that a country should be self-sufficient without having to rely on others. "We must believe in our own abilities. We don't need anyone else's help. Look at what happened the last time Danubians put their faith in a foreign power," the Biela members said over and over again when confronted with this question.

The "foreign power" they frequently referred to was the Eastern Empire. No one I knew actually visited there due to the travel ban. It was dangerous, like everywhere else, and why would you travel to the enemy territory anyway? That very intention put the person's loyalty to Danubia in question.

I scoffed at the thought, attracting the attention of two Zolta women standing in the queue in front of me. I thought their sunflower-coloured blazers looked pretty; it would be refreshing to be able to switch castes, even if it were only for a day or two. The navy-blue caste band on my right-hand wrist reminded me of an irritating itch underneath. It was such an ever-present sensation that I sometimes forgot about it; perhaps it was my mind's way to deal with the unpleasantness. A few months back, I developed a nasty rash underneath the satin band. For weeks, I've been trying every cream and lotion the local pharmacist could think of. The manager at work wouldn't allow me to take the satin band off and let the rash heal. The only thing I could do was wear it a little looser, or over long sleeves, to stop the pain for a while.

Lost in thought, I didn't notice the Zolta women were still staring at me. I smiled at them innocently, and the women returned to their conversation.

The Danubian government, namely the newly appointed President Tanatos, was determined to keep on digging up old animosities. Danubian provinces were a part of the Eastern Empire for nearly a millennia before becoming independent and, finally, united under the First Federal Republic of Danubia. Then the First Danubian Civil War happened, and the Second Federal Republic of Danubia was created from the ashes of an old republic, governed by our rotational presidency. I thought this was utter nonsense. How could we ever get things in order if every year a new president came into office? Granted, they were all from the same caste — the Biela, of course — but seemingly representing a different province in Danubia, so that "Every kanton gets their chance to govern". This was a blatant lie. The last representative for our kanton — the Stridon kanton — never set foot anywhere in Stridon. The rotational presidency was a sham. Well, I thought, at least they were now putting all their cards on the table. Tanatos took position early this year and put a stop to the rotational presidency. He is to be president for life — finally, an honest man, showing his true colours, no matter how vile. The strangest thing was people liked him and saw no problem with his power-grabbing intentions.

"He looks the part at least!" I remembered one of my colleagues saying and rolled my eyes at the memory. Yes, he looks like the exact reincarnation of evil if they asked me.

The queue moved forward, and it was my turn.

"Good afternoon," an elderly lady said, peering at me over the rim of her thick spectacles. She was familiar, but I couldn't place her. The town was so small everyone knew each other one way or another. "Could I have your library card, please?" she asked politely.

I produced a small card with my name and picture on it, handing it to her. She looked from the library card to me and gave it back with a nod. The featured photo was taken last year, and I hadn't changed much since; only my chestnut hair was a little longer.

"There are several empty tables in the reading area, Sofija. You're welcome to choose wherever you like," she said, waving in the general direction of the large reading section.

I smiled back, concentrating on what I was about to say, attempting to sound casual even though my palms were ice-cold, and I was jumpy with nervousness.

"Thank you, but I was hoping to use a computer station? Just for an hour if possible." She raised her eyebrows in surprise, looking me over.

"We don't generally allow computer stations to… lower castes," the lady said, visibly uncomfortable. I noticed she was also wearing the Plava satin band and a navy-blue blazer, same as mine — that should work in my favour, I thought.

I dropped my gaze to the floor, playing at her compassion.

"I know it's not a common practice, but, you see, I need to fill in the application for this course I'd like to enrol on; it's due today. I'd use the office computer, but my supervisor is very strict regarding non-work matters. I don't want to lose my job." The first part was a lie. The second part was, sadly, true. If I tried anything out of the ordinary at work, they'd dismiss me without thinking twice about it.

The queue behind me was growing larger, the people getting impatient. Some were craning their necks to see what was going on. I heard someone behind me loudly commenting that, "Someone from the Plava was chatting up the librarian."

The lady sat there, my ID in her hand, thinking. A few seconds passed, and I waited patiently, trying to keep calm, although my frantic mind was protesting. Taking a deep sigh, the lady finally said:

"Okay, but just this once. Come with me." She stood up and motioned for a library assistant who was stocking shelves to replace her at the reception desk. Then she headed for the computer section, and I followed her.

The computer section was a small room with no more than ten desks. The lady took me to the furthermost desk in the corner and, turning the worn-out computer on, she said:

"You have one hour. No illegal sites, no funny business. Okay?" She said sternly, and I nodded in understanding.

"Thank you so much."

The lady smiled at me.

"You're welcome, dear. Say hi to your grandparents for me." I watched her return to the reception before turning to the computer. I had no intention of letting anyone, least of all my grandparents, know that I'd been here. That could only put them in danger, I thought with a pang of guilt.

Looking around, I realised I was alone in the computer section; that was a good start.

The machine was on now, whirring loudly, and a small white window appeared. I was required to enter my ID number to gain access. Taking out my identity card, I copied the ten digits printed on the back of it and waited. After a few seconds, the white window disappeared, and I was connected to the network. So far, so good, I thought to myself.

Glancing both ways to make sure I was still alone; I took a small piece of paper out of my blazer pocket. Turning on the browser window, I pressed the buttons indicated on the note (reading #STIT), and a single grey field appeared at the very top of the screen. This was precisely what Anton, my colleague at work, said would happen, I thought with a sigh of relief.

Okay, now onto the second phase. I could feel my pulse accelerating rapidly as I grew more nervous with every passing second. My hands trembling uncontrollably, I made a mistake the first time, and the grey field flashed red. Hot flashes came all over me, immobilising me for a second. I closed my eyes and took several deep breaths. Looking up again, I re-entered the code jotted down on the piece of paper, this time more carefully. It was a long line of letters and numbers. Anton said the combination would provide me with a sort of shield while using the network. Finally, a small green tick appeared at the edge of the screen, and the grey line disappeared, along with the combination. With this on, no one could track my activity which is exactly what I needed. What I was about to look up was marked as illegal and "Highly dangerous for national security" under the Danubian Law.

No turning back now, I thought. I'd been hoping to have this opportunity for so long that it would be foolish to forsake it when I was this close. The shield was hopefully on, or so it seemed, so Armiya couldn't detect what I was browsing.

My hands trembling wildly, I typed in, "Outer Lands". I waited while the browser worked its way through backlogs of data, my eyes glued to the screen and wide in anticipation. One second... two seconds... three seconds... the time seemed to drag. Is it supposed to take this long? I've never browsed before; network search of all types was strictly forbidden. We could only enter approved sites that were pre-listed on all work computers and open our emails. That was all.

After half a minute, I was starting to panic. This couldn't be right; it was taking way too long. Just as I was about to turn the computer off and walk away, the search stopped. A large, white window appeared, filled with red letters. Startled at the brightness and size of the letters, I started reading, *"The search term you entered is ILLEGAL in the Federation of Danubia. If you pursue this further, you will be charged with Network Misuse and Terrorism under the Danubian Law. You are risking at least twenty years and possibly a life sentence in the rehabilitation centre."*

I froze in my chair; my index finger a centimetre away from the 'Enter' button. Slowly, I took my hands off the keyboard, turned the computer off and walked away, my heart pounding so loudly I couldn't hear anything else around me.

No one paid attention to me as I headed for the exit. The warm June day greeted me, and I sat on the steps outside the library with my head in my hands. I couldn't control the sobs when they came, nor my shoulders from trembling wildly. All I could hope for was that it would stop soon.

Chapter 3
Danubia

"Why don't you just ask your grandparents?" Helena suggested. We were having one of our after-work meetups. We'd always go to the same bar for lack of a better idea; it was cosy, offered relative privacy and good coffee. Despite being a little shabby, it felt like home. No wonder it did, since we'd been coming here for over a decade; we were a part of the bar's interior, as my grandma would always say. It wasn't far away from where I lived with my grandparents — situated in the Plava district of the city, it was mostly frequented by the members of the Plava caste. Occasional visits by other castes occurred here and there and would never go unnoticed. The centre of Velesh was an all-caste area; everyone, apart from the Biela, the elite, could be seen there. But here, the Plava ruled.

"They obviously don't want to tell me," I replied, ripping open a packet of sugar and stirring it into my coffee. Helena and I were sitting at one of the corner tables by the window, boasting views of an abandoned parking lot. Taking a sip of the foamy beverage, I placed the cup down and leaned back into the cosy cushion-laden chair.

"I've asked time and time again, but all I ever got was a stern look and a warning that 'I shouldn't ask too many questions'. The only thing I was ever told was that my parents died in the last war and that travel outside Danubia was not possible."

"Your grandparents are probably just protecting you. You know how *they* are," Helena replied pointedly, looking up at me from across the table. By 'they' she meant the Biela caste.

"I don't know. Could be. I've been trying to find out more. Anton told me about this person who can... *fabricate* travel permits." I said the last part in a hushed voice, glancing up expectantly at my best friend, knowing what's coming.

"Please tell me you're not thinking about forgery!" Helena hissed, frowning at me. "You could land yourself in serious trouble! And since when does Anton meddle in such shady business? I thought he was squeaky-clean."

"Not if I go to the best forger available, and Anton said this person is just that. You know he has access to all business listings in Velesh, and this one came off the black market."

Helena's expression was still suspicious. Trying to reassure her, I added, "It's just a travel permit, not an attempt to enter Kalemgrad. Don't worry, it'll be fine... I only want to find out more about my parents' lives. That's natural, isn't it? No one can blame me for being curious, not really."

I wasn't telling her the truth. Even though it's been a week since my unsuccessful attempt at the Velesh Library, I was still determined to learn more about the Outer Lands. That's why I hoped for a travel permit; to try and reach the borders of Danubia and see what's beyond. Learning about my parents would only be a bonus. But I somehow thought Helena wouldn't understand why I put myself in such danger. It was always safety first with her. I was the reckless one, the one who would just jump into new situations without much thinking beforehand. Obtaining an illegal travel permit was less risky than an unauthorised network search, at least in her eyes. Many people travelled on illegal permits these days; it wasn't unheard of. Still, what I was getting ready to do was a huge risk.

"Yes, well... I suppose you're right. Just be very careful, okay? I don't want you to end up in one of their rehabilitation centres," she said darkly before adding, her gaze dropping to the floor, "Not you, too."

I nodded in agreement. Helena was right to think a lot of things could go wrong. I could end up in the 'rehabilitation centre', commonly known as the 'RC'. The sentence probably wouldn't be too bad, two weeks at most, but why risk it? This would go on my record and scar me for life, potentially harming my odds at getting a better-paid job.
Then, another voice, one I'd been trying to hush, spoke to me. In some cases, family members were charged as guilty, too, just for being related to the person who committed the crime. An unwelcome image of my grandparents being taken to the Velesh RC lingered in my mind for a while, and I shuddered, shaking my head to dispel the horrifying vision. *I better do this right; there is no room for errors.*

"How's Igor doing? Have you been to visit him recently?" I asked, eager to change the subject.

"Oh, he's holding up. With a bit of luck, he'll be out of that place soon." Her expression brightened a little at the thought.

Igor was Helena's older brother who'd ended up in Velesh Rehabilitation Centre recently. Every major city across the Federation had its own RC; every one of them was nearly full of alleged enemies of President Tanatos.

Igor was a high school teacher by profession and a good one at that. Daring and bold as he was, he got out of the party line by getting slightly creative with an official class curriculum. He was charged with "anti-governmental agitation" and "poisonous indoctrination" of Danubia's youth. *Not very difficult to end up in the RC these days.* Preferring to keep the conversation as light as possible, I did not comment aloud.

"My family are throwing a welcome-home *soiree* on the day of his release. Nothing extravagant, just a few friends and relatives," said Helena, "you should come. Bring your grandma if she can part with your grandpa right now? How is he doing anyway?"

I averted my gaze, suddenly concentrating on the mug of coffee in my hands. *So much for keeping the conversation light.*

"Not well. He's entirely dependent on our help now. A nurse comes in every day, but I don't think grandma will want to part with him, even if it's only for a few hours. Thanks for the invitation anyway."

That was all I could muster to answer at that moment, without bursting into tears. Talking about my grandfather's worsening health was the most difficult topic for me lately. He was all I could ever think about and, in the rare moments when I was distracted by someone else's problems, I felt as if life were back to normal again. If only for half an hour. So, I was grateful when Helena changed the topic abruptly, perhaps sensing how I felt.

"Guess who I ran into at the RC when I went to see Igor?" she asked, her tone just a notch too enthusiastic about this piece of information. She was trying to make me not think about grandpa, I knew. So, I happily played along:

"Who was it? Someone from work?"

"Correct. It was Sandra, visiting her husband. What was his name

27

again… was it David? David Novak, that's right. You know he ended up in the RC last month after the elections."

"Oh, yes, that's right. Novak was accused of electoral fraud."

The image of a tall, bespectacled grey-haired man in his early sixties came to mind. He used to show up a lot on the Stridon kanton's news in the past several months, seeing as he was a member of the Local Assembly. *Must have done something to anger the Biela,* I thought to myself.

"If you ask me, it is more likely he *refused* to commit the fraud," I commented.

"Yes, I think so, too," Helena replied, and her face fell. "Sandra said he's on minus one, you know, with worse conditions where they place dangerous criminals. He seemed to have angered them seriously this time."

"At least he's not in the Pit; that would be far worse," I pointed out, trying to sound optimistic. "Is he getting out soon?"

"Should be, but only if he agrees to go with the party line from now on, at least that's what Sandra told me. If he doesn't comply, then he might be in for life."

"What is he going to do then?" I asked, now genuinely interested in the subject.

Helena gave me a surprised look, frowning slightly. Then she answered in a matter-of-fact tone:

"Well…" she started in a careful voice, "I hope he's going to comply. He has a family, and it's no good being a hero if nothing can be gained."

"Someone has to put a stop to their tyranny. How can that be done if we all put our heads in the sand?" I retorted, frowning at Helena.

It was all very frustrating for me. If what I knew about my parents was true, that they died in the Second Danubian War, then their deaths seemed pointless to me. Did they only die so that I can live under this dictatorship in disguise? And it wasn't even a very good disguise, I thought with a scowl. When did we become such servile people? Under this regime, we were nothing but worms hiding in the dirt so that our masters wouldn't pick on us.

"I don't know, Sofija, but I suggest that you don't go fighting the

Biela on your own," Helena whispered this last sentence. Surveillance measures were implemented more harshly these days, and one could never be too careful.

I went straight home afterwards, stopping only to buy some milk and flour to bake bread for dinner. That was all we could get from the grocery shops recently since the food shortage became more severe. Ever since their squabble with the Mursa kanton over some vital votes in the Duma, Danubia's food supply was cut in half. As one of the two solely agricultural kantons in the Federation, Mursa was exerting pressure this way to get their way in the government; or at least that's what the Biela said. An economic civil war, the media called it. *Mursa kanton undermining the Domovina, the motherland.*

I paid for both using food coupons and left in a hurry. The curfew was approaching and being caught out after hours was the one mistake I didn't want to make.

Our government did not know that, in their attic, my grandparents kept a small supply of preserved food. This habit was a hangover from the old days when every household prepared for long winters by making sausages and prosciutto and storing jars of pickled vegetables. This practise was banned under Tanatos' government, the official excuse being that such food is of dubious quality. But it was a feeble excuse; most Danubians knew this was yet another attempt to make the citizens entirely dependent on the state's mercy. I suspected that there was another motive to it, too; the domestic food production, along with traditional songs and folk tales, was a part of the Danubian culture. For some reason, the government worked very hard to erase any trace of it.

But if Danubians were good at anything in life, it was finding a way around laws and rules. Should an Armiya agent stop by, we would just say the attic had been boarded up for years, and we had no way to access it. All our neighbours did the same, and should anyone try and confirm the story, we all had each other's backs. The Armiya agents rarely investigated further, either due to lack of interest or laziness, we did not know. It was, in a way, a symbolic rebellion. It made me hopeful that things might change someday.

I still remembered vividly when I first attended the Commemoration of Danubia's independence. This was an annual event, the most important and most widely participated in our country. My grandparents took me when I was twelve; attendance wasn't mandatory before that age. I suppose they didn't want to expose me to hours of brainwashing unless it was absolutely necessary. The rule was that every Danubian citizen had to attend the Commemoration at least once every five years. Those who could not get the tickets watched the televised event from one of the public squares across the country.

The Commemoration took place in a massive stone amphitheatre, commonly known as the Arena, set on the outskirts of Agram. To be on time, we had to take an early morning train and then spend hours queuing at the entrance to the colossal ancient building. I remembered Grandma bringing salami-and-cheese sandwiches and homemade elderflower juice. We ate on the train, knowing the ceremony would be very long, and we would not have a chance to eat again until late afternoon.

The Arena had at least twenty levels, surrounding the central stage lit in the colours of the Danubian flag — red, white, and blue. We found our seats around the middle of the amphitheatre, with other members of the Plava caste. Like the rest of Plava, we, too, had navy-blue clothes. I was in my favourite navy-blue dress, and my grandparents wore their work clothes, topped with navy-blue blazers. All members of the Plava caste wore matching satin ribbons on their wrists. I smiled at the memory recalling how I tugged on my caste band that day, trying to take it off. It irritated me when I was a child, and I wasn't thrilled about wearing it now that I was an adult either.

Plava was the caste of administration officers, clerks, shop workers, nurses, and schoolteachers. Below us was the Zelena caste, consisting of field, mine, factory, and other manual workers. I could clearly remember the pretty emerald blazers on men and women from the Zelena caste who sat in a row behind us. I recalled Grandma chatting to the Zelena women while we were queuing. "They're almost as normal as us," I remembered her saying, "I could get used to being around them, you know," she said to Grandpa.

Only one caste never attended these events. At the very bottom of Danubia's social pyramid stood the Siva caste. The Siva gathered homeless people, prisoners and political dissidents, their clothes made of grey, dirty looking material.

"Clean clothing doesn't make a good person," my grandma used to say, "it is their behaviour and manners that matter." I thought that day how unfair it was that the Siva members were not present.

"Did they forget what day it is? Should we go get them?" I asked Grandma, thinking of all the Siva members I saw sitting in the streets on our way here. She gave me a puzzled look and answered quietly, so no one overhears, "I don't think they were invited, dear. Perhaps they'll be here the next time." I let my gaze drop to the ground, wondering why they wouldn't be invited but decided not to question my grandparents any further.

The very first row was filled with members of the Biela caste. I remembered glancing up towards them over the countless heads of eager Danubians attending the Commemoration. They looked somehow unreal, walking with such elegance that they were almost gliding. Each man and woman were dressed in impeccably white clothes. Intimidating and captivating at the same time, they attracted the most attention. When I asked Grandpa about 'the people in white', he just said:

"They are incompetent fools that make our laws and rule us, Sofi. Don't trust anything they say or do."

Biela was the ruling caste, including the President and the Duma members, all fifteen of them and their families. The clergy also belonged with them. There was no way to enter their ranks unless one was born into it. On the other hand, the Biela members could be degraded to one of the lower castes if they proved to be "harmful" to the "overall progress of our great country". I never heard of anyone being degraded from the Biela.

Behind the Biela sat the members of the Cherwona caste. I remembered thinking they looked smug and arrogant. The men were dressed in elegant, expensive-looking suits with crimson cravats; women were wrapped in extravagant bright-red dresses.

"The Taykuni. They own everything that isn't the state's property. A very uncomfortable bunch to be around, they are. Too self-centred and arrogant, you see," Grandpa explained in a low voice so that my Grandma wouldn't hear. Although I had seen some of them around the Velesh city centre, members of the Cherwona, or as I called them as a child — the red people — were rarely spotted in provinces. Their estates were scattered around the countryside, and most of them worked closely with the Biela in Agram.

Behind the extravagant men and women in red clothing sat a group of kinder looks and postures, mostly bespectacled. The women were wearing the most beautiful dresses in all shades of yellow. I thought they looked pretty and somehow powerful. Noticing my glances towards them, Grandpa said, "The Zolta caste. They're supposed to be our brains, you see." I recalled him saying this to me as we watched them taking the third-level seats. "Researchers and intelligentsia. Most of them are corrupted, the condescending idi—"

"Marin! Watch your language!" My grandma shrieked from her seat, cutting off her husband mid-sentence. The memory made me smile.

And then there were the Armiya members, all belonging to the Atera caste. The fourth caste from the top, they had seats behind the Zolta members. Dressed entirely in black and almost all men, their dark, unfriendly looks sent shivers down my spine. Grandpa said not to fear them, for they're here to protect us, but his words did little to reassure me.

I've learned later that most women born to the Atera caste choose to degrade to Plava or Zelena. While degrading by choice is possible, upgrading to a higher caste is a little more complicated. One can only "jump" one caste, usually by marriage. That meant that I had virtually nowhere to go — born in the Plava, I could only marry into Atera. Being an Armiya wife wasn't a goal I fancied pursuing in life, I thought as unpleasant memories came to mind. That was the life I narrowly escaped two years ago.

This was a relatively new rule — imposed after the Second Danubian War, the same year I was born. Before then, one could jump two or even three castes if qualified or recommended by someone in a powerful position. It was sometimes possible to go as far as Cherwona; only the Biela was unreachable; reserved for those born into it exclusively. However, the choice of a caste stayed with you forever; once made, the decision to change a caste could not be withdrawn.

For most of my adolescence, a part of me hoped that I would be able to surpass this new "one-caste-jump" rule and join the Zolta. Life proved me otherwise, deciding to stomp on my dreams yet again. *Dream simpler dreams, Sofija,* said the sarcastic voice in my head.

Brought back from my reverie, I stopped in my tracks as my grandparents' house came into view.

The house I grew up in stood at the beginning of a small, dead-end Birchtree Road. It had no more than fifty households (ours was at number four), all with carefully maintained front lawns and — as the name says — birch trees. The road had a circular shape, with a large green in the middle.

Number Four, Birchtree Road, was a large, one-storey house adorned with a colourful fence, now illuminated by a feeble light from the nearest streetlamp; it was nearly eight o'clock in the evening. Behind the house, there was a small garden with a garage and a barn that served as firewood storage. Rose bushes were in full bloom, and the narrow path surrounding the house was dotted with daisies.

Looks like we have guests, I thought in surprise, noticing a shabby bicycle parked outside the front door. Wondering who was visiting this close to the curfew, I made my way into the house.

As I entered the hallway, my grandmother rushed to me. "There you are! Thank goodness, I was starting to worry. I called you a couple of times, but something is up with the network again. Come, sit with us."

I found Grandpa in a small room next to the kitchen, as usual. He was lying on the hospital bed, seemingly lost in thought. His favourite song was blasting from the radio in the corner. *Dunav, oh my beautiful Dunav,* the male voice sang to the tender sounds of the *tambura,* the traditional Danubian instrument, *you stole my heart...*

The knot in my throat urged me to tears as I listened to the familiar verses, but I resisted somehow. Almost instantly, I was taken back to my childhood, to long afternoons in the sun and barbeque lunches with neighbours. The melody belonged to some old world I'd only known for a brief moment, evoking happiness that was lost in the whirls of time, now unreachable, unimaginable. As I listened, memories flew in my mind's eye. Grandma and Grandpa dancing merrily to this very song. Neighbours looking after me while my grandparents were at work. One of them, I remembered, didn't know how else to entertain me, so she showed me her collection of multi-coloured spatulas. I would play with them for hours, sorting them by size and colour, pretending they are people and playing out conversations.

All that was gone now, with Tanatos controlling every aspect of life in the Federation. We could probably get away with a small gathering once again, if only Grandpa were his old self. But he is not... and he will never be the same again. The knot in my throat grew larger as I struggled to remain tearless.

"If I could be reborn, I'd spend the entire life by the Dunav once more, watching the white boats passing by..."

The melody died away as another song started, and my grandfather turned his gaze upon me.

"How was work, Sofi?" He asked in a raspy voice, his frail hand reaching for mine in an enormous effort. He squeezed it once and smiled encouragingly as if trying to say *I'm actually fine. This is temporary.*

"Same as usual. So, extremely dull". I smiled and planted a peck on his cheek in greeting, motioning with my hands that he should not get up.

"Did the ladies expel you from the kitchen? They don't want you eavesdropping?" I teased, happy to see a grin stretching across his old face.

"Nah, I removed myself from their company. Enjoying the music."

I squeezed his hand again and walked towards the kitchen, taking off my work blazer and heels in the hallway. I couldn't wait for the weekend when I got to wear what I wanted — *anything but the blasted work clothes.* Still, a navy-blue satin band on my wrist was mandatory even on a work-free day. That didn't help the incessant rash underneath.

"What's going on? Did something happen?" I noticed a familiar woman sitting at the table with Grandma.

"No, dear, everything is fine. Come sit with us. Mrs Horvat from the hospital is here; she has some good news."

The small kitchen was bathing in the warm light emanating from a lamp in the far corner. Mrs Horvat was a chubby, short woman with a friendly smile and round face. She kept her blonde hair in a tight bun as most nurses did. She was still wearing her hospital clothes and a navy-blue satin band marking her caste; must have come straight here after work. Mrs Horvat was the only person I knew that jumped down the caste ladder — born in an Atera family, she chose the Plava life instead. Her husband was an Armiya agent, and we never saw much of him.

I took a seat opposite her at the kitchen table. Grandma placed a tray with a fresh pot of black coffee and some homemade honey biscuits in front of us.

I poured myself a cup of coffee and took a bite of a honey biscuit. Sweet and tasting of cinnamon, it was my favourite treat ever since I was a small child.

"Sofi, Mrs Horvat here says a medication that could help Grandpa recover is available now," Grandma said seriously. "However, it might be difficult to obtain."

Gulping down coffee quickly and burning my throat in the process, I said, "We'll do whatever needs to be done to get it!" I was peering at Mrs Horvat now, who had a concerned look on her face. Realising I might have come off a bit too intense, I relaxed in my seat and smiled pleasantly at her.

"I know you want to help your grandfather, Sofija, but this might get you in trouble with the Armiya. The problem is the medication in question is illegal, and... well, you'd have to travel to Agram. It isn't safe to send it by post; you know *they* open everything." She said all this in a barely audible voice as if scared the walls had ears.

"It doesn't matter. Where can I buy it in Agram?" I asked without thinking, my voice overly confident.

Mrs Horvat seemed surprised by my eagerness, her eyebrows rising. She spoke in a careful voice. "If you can get a travel permit, I'll put you in touch with my contact there who will deliver the medication to you."

My grandfather, who was quietly listening in from the adjacent room, suddenly bellowed:

"Sofi, you mustn't! You'll get caught!" His breathing was pained and slow, and so it took him a while to get these two sentences out. "Don't do it; you'll end up in the Pit! I forbid it, Sofija!"

"Calm down, Marin!" My grandma shot a look of warning in my direction before walking over to check on him, and I knew I had to lie.

"Don't worry, Grandpa, I'll be careful. I'll get the permit the regular way; all will be fine", I answered in a loud voice so that he would hear me. It felt terrible lying to him, but I had no choice.

"Can I have your contact's number, Mrs Horvat? I'll call them as soon as I have the permit," I asked in a hushed tone, grateful my suspicious grandparents weren't able to hear me.

"You can call me Vera, dear. And yes, of course, you can. When you are ready, just give him a call, and he'll meet up with you. I'll tell him which medication to get for your grandpa." I produced a piece of paper from my messenger bag and handed it to her. She scribbled a name and a number, thrusting the note into my hand. I placed it safely into my pocket.

"Zlatko is an old friend of mine; he works at the pharmacy somewhere in Central Agram. He'll help you," Mrs Horvat said, reassuringly. "Just make sure to go about this... you know, the right way", she said uncomfortably. When she continued, her voice turned to a whisper. "I mustn't even mention to my husband that I'm helping you. It could jeopardise his position at the Armiya".

I nodded in sombre understanding, and she nodded back.

Grandma soon returned to the kitchen, steering the conversation towards lighter topics. Not having to participate much, I tuned out, thinking.

I had to be incredibly careful and, well, now I finally get to contact that forger Anton recommended. Even though I knew what was at stake and getting to Agram will be no picnic, I could not help but feel the excitement rising in me. *I'm finally going to visit Agram! But only if everything goes well and I don't end up at the RC*, I thought with a shudder. I wasn't at all worried about getting the illegal medication; people frequently shopped on the black market because they had no choice amid the current shortage. It was the illegal travel permit that made me nervous. And I've just promised Mrs Horvat that I would get it the legal way — a promise I had no intention of keeping.

To get the permit through regular channels would be too slow and perhaps impossible. The only time when anyone who asked was allowed to travel to Agram was in the week before the Commemoration. That wasn't for another three months, I thought with a sigh.

The policy on travel permits changed, like many other things, when Tanatos assumed the presidency several months back. These days only the best-connected people were given travel permits without complications. As a low-ranking administrative officer, I wasn't exactly the most influential person, nor was my family. Besides, applying the usual way would put my grandparents and me on the radar and include thorough background checks. That was the last thing I wanted. One Armiya visit to our house might endanger my grandparents, who were storing too much food and medicinal supplies, way above their official allowance. I could not afford to put them in such danger.

Tomorrow night, I decided, I will visit Anton's contact. I knew where to go, the trouble was I could not leave work early, and I wanted to avoid being seen in the after-work rush. The fewer people knew of my whereabouts, the better. I will need Helena's help, I realised with reluctance. I'd prefer to leave my best friend out of this.

Chapter 4
The Dream

Mrs Horvat was on her way soon. I walked her outside, thanked her for helping out, and then went back into the house, entering the small room next to the kitchen. Grandpa was asleep now, the radio turned off. Grandma sat on a chair next to him, lost in thought.

"How is he doing? Is there anything I can do to help?" I asked quietly, careful not to wake him.

Her tired eyes averted mine as she answered in a hushed voice, "Oh... he's fine. Hanging in there, you know. The medication would help a lot, though. It's been weeks since he'd had any."

The small room featured a hospital bed with wheels on it. Grandpa was fast asleep, holding onto the bed remote control. It was wired to the bed's base, allowing him to adjust the frame's position at will. Along one side of the bed, high shelves were stocked with tiny bottles with blue and red labels on them, along with clean towels and medicinal supplies. The room smelled a bit like a hospital, with that pungent scent of ethanol in the air. An old, but still functioning TV stood on a wooden stand opposite the bed. This is where my grandfather spent most of his days now. One look at him was enough to bring tears to my eyes, and I stopped struggling, letting them roll down my face in silence. I was glad when Grandma walked over to the kitchen, leaving me alone with him. I wiped the escaped tears quickly and sat on a chair next to his bed.

Marin Filipov, the only father figure I've ever known, looked weaker with every passing day. His lined face was hollow, cheekbones silhouetted through pale skin. His arms lay limply next to his frail body, thinner than ever. Every day, he found it more difficult to move by himself or to eat regular food. He walked very slowly now, leaning against the walking stick. His meals consisted of stews and soups.

How did the wretched illness progress so quickly? I couldn't wrap my mind around it; it seemed too surreal. Somewhere deep, very deep in my mind, I knew no medication would make him healthy again. At the same time, I knew I had to try. Now would be about the right time to discover magic was real, I thought to myself, smiling a little at my own silliness.

Irma and Marin Filipov took care of me ever since I was a small child. They were the only family I had ever known, creating a warm and loving home for me, making sure I never lacked anything.

I was brought back to reality by my grandma's gentle knocking. She peered into the room and motioned for me to come closer.

"Come, Sofi, let's eat. Dinner is getting cold." She closed the door of my grandpa's room as I walked out.

That night I had my old dream again. The medieval old town's narrow streets were as familiar as ever, leading me into a tiny café opposite an ancient-looking square. An old well stood in the centre of the cobblestoned square, looking unused. A familiar smell of roast coffee and loud chatter greeted me upon entering the warm café, cosy with its mahogany walls and low, wooden coffee tables with ottoman chairs. There was a vase with fresh roses on every table. The roses were an emerald green every time I visited, a very unusual colour at first. Now, I was already used to it; I even expected it, so anything different than emerald would be alarming. I kept on walking past the full tables, not paying attention to the people occupying them or to their conversations. Pressing on, my feet led me past the long, mahogany bar, the same colour as the walls. I reached a small door adorned with a heavy brass knocker in the shape of a two-faced man wearing a Roman-like bay wreath on his head. For the umpteenth time, I grabbed the brass ring and gave the plate two light strikes, fully expecting to wake up without seeing what was behind the mahogany door. After all, that is what has happened every time I've been here before.

My unconscious mind was already waking up, now fully aware it was dreaming. In those last moments between waking and dream, the mysterious door opened, and the salty breeze flew through it, filling my nostrils and sending my long hair flying. I took one deep breath of salty air and woke up.

I could still taste salt on my tongue moments after waking. This has never happened before; the door always remained closed. For years, I had been walking those same narrow streets, passing the same ancient-looking square with an old well in its centre. I stopped counting how many times I had entered the same, inviting café with mahogany walls and the smell of roast coffee in the air. Ever since I could remember, I had been knocking on that door, striking the plate with a two-faced man on it, hoping it would finally open. But the door always remained closed, and I stopped expecting it to open a long time ago. Why did it open now? What did I do differently? The questions floated in my mind for a while, unanswered.

I shook my head, trying to get rid of them and started getting ready for work.

Sunlight was coming through the wide windows of my tiny room, illuminating a thick layer of dust on the windowsills, bookshelves and a small desk looking out the window. I did not have much time for tidying lately, what with Grandpa being sick and needing my help, and all the extra hours at work I have been doing to earn more money. Initially, the money was intended for my master's degree; ever since childhood, I wanted to be a researcher, but now it was mostly spent on food and medicine.

I soon learned that a career as a researcher wasn't an option for me. Coming from the Plava caste, I was two steps down the ladder from an academic career that was only open to members of the Zolta.

"Our heavenly Republic of Danubia gave life to seven castes living in harmony. This harmony can only be achieved if all the castes work together, under the ever-watching eye of our Supreme government, led by the Duma."

I still remembered these words as vividly as if I heard them yesterday. It was my first day of elementary school. I was seven years old, sitting in a class with thirty-nine other children. The tall, blonde teacher with kind eyes and crimson lips strolled up and down the classroom, telling us about our great country. The title on the chalkboard said, 'Introduction to Domovina'. Domovina, as it turned out, was (and still is) the main subject at schools. It teaches about the history of Danubia and its social and ideological system. As of early this year, it also teaches the children about the life of President Tanatos, who was given his divine right to rule by no other than God himself. I snorted at the thought, trying to get an unwelcome image of his cold, onyx eyes and slick black hair out of my mind. *He was no more than a power-grabbing snake.*

"By staying within your caste and contributing the best way you can, you are doing an admirable work which strengthens our great society. There is no progress without unity. There is no unity without order." At this, our kind-eyed, crimson-lipped teacher wrote the last two sentences on the chalkboard and told us to copy them into our notebooks twenty times. "No progress without unity. No unity without order". From that day on, we were asked to repeat the mantra every morning at school. It became a greeting. We chanted it at the beginning and end of every class. The mantra was written on the Danubian coat of arms and carved into every governmental building.

Soon after, we learned the names of all seven castes. Every child knew from an early age which caste they belonged to because everyone around them belonged to it too. Castes were divided by neighbourhoods in every city, and Velesh was no exception.

I worked a typical Plava job — an admin clerk at the local City Hall. They gave me a small desk in a huge room with twenty other people. I was lucky to have an hour-long lunch break and that coffee machines were free of charge. The Plava members worked nine hours a day, an hour more than the upper-half castes. It was tedious work, consisting of endless spreadsheets and repetitive phone calls. Keep the system running, we were told by our superiors. Keep it running smoothly, and don't ask too much. Tend to your own corner and do not look over the fence. Keep your head down. Do not ask for more. Ambition is bad.

So, I learned not to question things. I also learned not to hate my work uniform, consisting of a navy-blue pencil skirt and white shirt. I learned to arrange my hair into a boring bun and to wear the caste band every day.

I learned to do all this to protect my family, friends, and myself, but I never gave up hope that things would change someday, somehow. I never believed the state ideology was anything more than just that — ideology. I watched and occasionally attended the annual Commemoration because I had to, not because I enjoyed it. It was a frustrating way to live a life, but there was no point in constant whining about things I could not change.

After going through my usual morning rituals, I put on my uniform, then arranged my hair into the usual boring work bun. A pair of jeans and worn-out sneakers were packed in my brown messenger bag for after-work activities. Today, this meant getting in touch with an illegal forger without getting in trouble with the Armiya. *One thing at a time,* I thought to myself, trying to ignore the accelerated thudding in my chest — *one thing at a time.*

I concentrated on the girl looking back at me in the bathroom mirror. The stubborn under-eye bags were still there, looking dreadful against my pale skin. I applied some concealer, but it didn't help much. I was getting used to this drowned look anyway. An unusual turquoise strand of hair was tucked behind my right ear and fastened at the back with a hairpin. Although it didn't look bad with my long, chestnut hair and round, caramel-brown eyes, I've always wondered how it got there. My grandparents said I was born with it, a genetic anomaly of some sort. As a child, I was mocked for it a lot — any hair dye my grandmother tried didn't work. Now I rather thought the unusual turquoise strand added to my personality. I should count myself lucky because it was challenging to have any of that in this frigid society.

My grandparents were already halfway through their morning coffee when I descended into the kitchen. A cupful was waiting for me at the table, along with some freshly made *palachinki.* My grandmother was sitting at the kitchen table, while Grandpa's hospital bed was wheeled in from the adjacent room, put in an upright position. The scene made me smile a little. Even though he was now almost always bedridden, they still found a way to enjoy each other's company. She was feeding him something chocolatey that resembled baby food, and for once, he didn't complain. Careful not to drop it, he was drinking coffee from a takeaway paper cup, using a straw. After a few broken mugs, we decided this was a safer way.

"Good morning, Grandma, Grandpa," I said, giving them a hug each. "Thanks for making breakfast, Grandma. I'll have to make it quick, don't want to be late for work."

"You're welcome, dear. Come, sit with us." My grandma's kind eyes, the deep brown colour, scrutinised my face anxiously. She knew what I was getting ready to do that night, and it seemed my confident tone did not fool her the previous day.

We ate breakfast and drank coffee in silence, listening to the news on a small kitchen TV. The food shortage was getting worse, and the Duma had just voted for further spending restrictions. Until today, each of us was allowed two coupons a week to purchase necessary supplies. Each coupon was worth about a hundred dukats and could cover one day's worth of groceries for a small household. Now they have brought this down to one coupon a week only. This new restriction, the Duma said, applied to the lower-half castes, while the upper-halves were still entitled to their three coupons a week. The upper halves also had a higher spending limit, about four hundred dukats a coupon. The Plava belonged to the lower half, along with the Zelena and Siva castes. The upper half included the Atera, the Zolta, the Cherwona and of course, the Biela caste.

"Those rich bastards never have to ration! Instead, they feast on our earnings, the self-righteous, fat-bellied monkeys! Hope they choke on their lamb chops!" My grandpa was pointing at the television, agitated and angry.

I chuckled and said, "Yes, hope they choke on lamb chops — that is, if they can reach the plates from their fat bellies."

Now both of them started laughing with me, but the fit died out soon as the harsh reality hit us. This meant more rationing. The coupons already covered very little, and we had to use our thin cash savings to get additional supplies from the black market. How in the world will we survive on one coupon each per week?

"Right, time to go." I put on my work blazer and picked up the brown messenger bag. "See you in the evening; I'll try and get that travel permit after work," I said flatly, attempting at a nonchalant tone. Stepping into the hallway, I added, "Oh, and don't wait for me for dinner and call if you need anything from the grocery shop. I have one more coupon left for this week." I could hear the edge in my voice and knew Grandma did not miss it, though I hoped she would.

I was already at the door when she caught up with me.

"Sofi, a word before you go, please." She looked concerned. We stepped outside the door into the sunny June morning. She looked so much younger than she actually was, nearing her sixty-ninth birthday. Her curly hair was almost entirely white but combed back neatly into a loose bun. She absolutely refused to colour it. "I'm not ashamed of my age," she always said with a smile, "There is a look for every season, and I'm living the long autumn of my life."

Now though, she was looking at me suspiciously, and I waited for the rant to begin.

"How do you plan to get the permit?" She gave me a look that clearly meant, *don't you even think of lying, or I will know.* And I decided on the spot that I would tell her the truth.

"I'll use alternative ways. Anton from work put me in touch with this forger, apparently the best one in the kanton." I blurted this out very quickly, awaiting her reprimanding reaction. But it didn't come. Instead, she said, "Okay but take this. You might need it." She took a small black purse out of her cardigan pocket.

"No, Grandma, I couldn't. They're your savings; please keep them for something else."

She frowned at me, shaking her head vigorously.

"This isn't up for discussion, Sofija. Take it and use it if you must. And be safe, please. Call me when you're on your way back so that I don't worry."

I took the small purse and found two thousand dukats inside, the brown and blue notes carefully folded. I closed the zipper and placed the purse in my messenger bag.

"Then I won't object." I smiled at her, amazed by the determination and authority that didn't wane with age, not even a little. "I'll call you when I'm on my way, I promise. We'll get that medication for Grandpa, and he'll be fine." She nodded briefly, forcing a small smile. Leaning in, I hugged her goodbye and headed for the City Hall.

Chapter 5
The Travel Permit

I cycled to work. Most people drove, but I never had much interest in getting a driving license. Although my grandparents offered to pay for it when I turned eighteen, I asked them to put it towards my university fund instead. This was back when I still hoped I'd be able to have an academic career. That plan never panned out, I thought bitterly. The Federal State of Danubia had different ideas of what my life should be.

The City Hall was a large, red-bricked building in the Velesh city centre. It stretched over five floors full of offices with narrow, elongated windows looking out to Liberation Avenue. The street was a tribute to the day Velesh was liberated from its hostile occupants fifty-five years back, after the First Danubian War. Or so the political narrative said. Scarce texts that still existed about the old times didn't offer much evidence that those former 'occupants' were hostile in any way. Perhaps they just didn't go with the new party line, I thought with a scoff. But no one spoke of this any more. These were highly dangerous, reactionary thoughts, meticulously tucked under the carpet, covered with layers of dust. The newly established Tanatos' government frequently called for information on those talking or working against their policies. They gave out tempting rewards too — last I heard; one could earn a small fortune by turning 'traitors' in. It was difficult to trust anyone, with Tanatos constantly breathing down our necks, encouraging people to tell on their friends and neighbours.

I parked my bike in a small yard behind the City Hall and entered the spacious foyer with red stone tiles and a high ceiling. Heading for the reception desk in the middle, I grabbed the newspaper from the wooden stand next to the door, something I did out of habit every day. *New rationing measures introduced* screamed the headline from the front page, *Supreme President Tanatos: 'be brave and work together'*.

"Hard to work together when it's only us lower-halves being

affected, don't you think?" I looked up and saw Anton, the receptionist, beaming at me. Nerdy-looking and skinny, he always appeared a little unhealthy, or perhaps that's what administrative buildings made of people. My own dark undereye circles and drowned looks came to mind, and I refrained from commenting.

He was standing behind a large oak reception desk, the wall behind him covered in keys in all shapes and sizes, with satin ribbons in different colours on keyrings. Each colour marked a different caste. The higher the caste, the higher the person's clearance.

"Hello, Sofija, how are you this happy morning? Too bad our working hours aren't being rationed too," he said, referring to the newspaper headline.

I gave him a questioning look. "Since when are you so angry with our benevolent dictator, Anton? Thought you knew better than to speak so freely. Walls have ears, you know."

"Oh, I know you're a good one, Sofija; you wouldn't take it the wrong way. Hell, one might even say I trust you! A mad notion in these crazy times, mad!"

I laughed. Anton was a funny guy, just over a year younger than me. He always walked the fine line between joking and committing political treason, never quite crossing it. We had known each other for a long time and belonged to the same caste, so this was our standard exchange. But we had to be careful when talking to the members of other castes. People were eager to caste-jump, and what better way to do it than to tell on someone and take their place in exchange for information. The government was pitting castes against one another, and it worked. But this only strengthened internal caste relations; your caste became like family.

"Thank you, Anton; it's nice to hear that. I daresay that I trust you too." I flashed my best smile at him and signed the check-in sheet. "Have a great day."

"You too, Sofija! A pleasure to chat with you, as always!" I heard him shouting after me as I started climbing the steps to the administration office on the first floor.

My desk was in the middle of the large space with twenty-something desks cramped inside. Helena was already there, sipping her coffee and scrolling through emails.

"Morning, dear. How's it going?" I leaned in to give her a brief hug and waved at several other colleagues I sometimes hung out with. They all looked less than thrilled to be at work. I glanced around and saw that our supervisor just arrived, sitting at his desk at the front. Behind him was a board with the names of all employees. Each name had a green tick next to it, meaning all employees were present and on time. Blue ticks were for the lunch hour and red for absence from work. The large clock behind the supervisor's desk showed eight a.m. sharp.

"I'm all right. You? Did you get in touch with you-know-who yet?" Helena said the last part in a hushed voice. I knew she was worried about my after-work activity, but I didn't want to get into it right now.

"I'll tell you at lunch," I said, hoping that'd do for now. She nodded and went back to her coffee and emails.

Turning on my work PC, I had dived into the ever-growing pile of unread messages. I started adding information into spreadsheets and making calls.

About a hundred emails and fifteen calls later, I've set up meetings, answered queries about the current shortage crisis ("No, we don't know just yet how long it will last … yes, we are doing everything we can to solve the issues as soon as possible "… yes, you can file a complaint should you wish to…"). I'd forwarded complaints (knowing very well they'll just end up in the shredder), printed out letters, went through two cups of coffee and half a pack of the Dorina chocolate. Glancing up, I saw it was noon — time for lunch. Helena just turned her PC off and stood up.

"You ready? Should we go to the corner bakery again?"

"Yeah, great idea. Perhaps there's a free table at the café, so we can squeeze that in."

We walked to the small bakery just a few minutes down the street. After waiting in a short queue, we bought two chicken-and-mushroom bureks and a large Greek salad to share. There were no tables at the bakery; it was a small, kiosk-type space. So, we headed to the Park Café next door and occupied a table on a large terrace looking out to the busy street. Ordering two cups of coffee with milk, we took out our lunch and started eating.

"Ready to tell me what you're up to?" Helena looked up at me with a worried expression on her face. I added sugar into my cup of coffee and stirred it before responding.

"Actually, I have a small favour to ask of you. Can you collect next month's coupons for me tonight? I need to visit Nocturno after work, and if I do, I won't make it to the bank on time. Unless I want to risk the curfew, that is."

The curfew starts at eight p.m., and the coupon collection was set for five through seven p.m., on the first Wednesday each month. The bank was situated some ten minutes' walk away from the City Hall, so I could theoretically make it on time but didn't want to risk it. Queuing was inevitable as always, and I'll need as much time as possible for tonight's mission.

"Of course, I can, no problem. How do you know where to go?"

"Well... I asked Anton the other day," I said and, seeing Helena's surprised expression, continued, "he used to travel to Agram all the time for work before. You know he did a short internship there before Tanatos came to power. He said the safest way was to go through the City Hall, but that could take too long. So, he told me about this girl, Maya. Anton said I should go to Nocturno and ask for her."

"I've been to Nocturno countless times, never met a Maya," said Helena suspiciously.

"Me neither. Perhaps she works in the kitchen or something. Martina should know her; I hope to run into her tonight.".

"Okay, well... be careful. You know they track everything and everybody, especially with the curfew in place now."

I promised to be careful and to let her know how it went when we see each other tomorrow. We both knew it was best not to text or email about any of this — it was too risky. The conversation lightened up a little after this, as we started discussing Igor's coming-out-of- prison party. I promised Helena I'd swing by if I can and started wondering what to bring as a gift. A 'Thank God they didn't kill you' card? Or a striped shirt as a joke? Helena was my best friend, but I knew very little about her brother. He was five years older than us, and we were never a part of the same clique. Also, I remembered with a smirk, he always thought he was much cooler than us. True, he was very popular with his wavy blonde hair and blue eyes, same as Helena's. They were very alike when it came to looks, but I always thought Helena was more down-to-earth.

It was hard not to be cheerful on such a beautiful sunny day, twenty degrees Celsius and rising. We were both sporting our sunglasses, our blazers forgotten at the office. The café was packed, and the people around us looked happy. All were wearing similar uniforms; only the colours differed depending on caste.

Our lunch hour went by quickly. At one p.m., we were back at our desks and typing again. Only four more hours to go. An hour later, I started growing increasingly nervous, the tight knot in my stomach beginning to bother me. My palms were sweating, and I was jumpy. *Calm down,* I thought to myself — *one step at a time.* The first step is getting to Nocturno.

At five p.m. sharp, I stood up and collected my things, thanking Helena again for helping me out. She mouthed "Good luck" at me, and I walked out the door.

"Bye, Anton! See you tomorrow!"

"Bye, Sofija! Be a good girl," he said, winking at me. As if he knew what I was up to, I thought. Well, since the tip came from him, it didn't matter much. Arriving in the back yard, I mounted my bike, placing the navy-blue blazer in the front basket.

Just like Helena, I'd been to Nocturno many times. It was the most visited restaurant in Velesh, mostly due to its affordable and varied menu. Their house wine was cheap and sweet, and the servers were welcoming. Nocturno was situated by the river, near several small bars, off-licence shops and local produce stalls. A large terrace overlooked the vast Dunav, offering a romantic atmosphere in the evenings. Not something I'd experienced lately, I thought. Then again, maybe that's for the best. I had too much on my mind, and my last romantic endeavour didn't go as planned. I shivered at the unwelcome memory, pushing it out of my mind immediately.

A short ride away, I found myself standing in front of Nocturno. The blackboard outside read, 'Happy Hour 5 – 6 p.m. All cocktails 50% off. The offer was tempting, but margaritas would have to wait.

The sunny terrace was packed with people talking and laughing, enjoying their late lunches and discounted cocktails. They only had a couple of hours left before the recently enforced curfew kicked in, another 'necessary' measure by our new President Tanatos.

I parked my pony at the front and went inside. The bar area was deserted except for a couple of waiters and a bespectacled, tall barman I recognised from my many visits here. I've never learnt his name, but I'd spot him anywhere. Slightly disappointed that Martina, the waitress I knew fairly well, wasn't on her shift, I approached the bar.

"Hi," I said nervously, not sure how to go about this. Is this supposed to be a secret? Should I keep my voice down? Ugh, so stupid of me, I should have found out more from Anton. Now I look like an idiot, standing here struggling to think of something to say and not knowing how to say it. So, I decided to just blurt it out:

"Can I speak to Maya? Does she work here? Tell her Sofija Filipov would like a word, please." I could see the recognition in his eyes immediately. And something else — surprise, perhaps?

"Yes, I'll go get her. She's in the back." The bespectacled barman put down the glass he was wiping and headed behind the bar to the kitchen. So, Maya did work in the kitchen, then. I stood there, waiting, feeling conspicuous for some unknown reason. Technically, I wasn't doing anything illegal — yet. I was just asking to talk to this girl Maya, nothing else. Hoping to calm down, I started pacing, but it only made me more nervous, so I stopped and sat on the closest barstool. *There, better.*

The back door opened, and in came a tall, slim woman with dark curls around her face. She couldn't be more than thirty-five years old. She smiled widely at me and headed for the booth furthest from the bar, motioning for me to join her.

"Sofija, right? I'm Maya. Come sit here, it's more comfortable than that barstool. Would you like something to eat or drink?"

"Only a glass of water, thank you." I didn't feel like having anything else with my stomach still in the tight knot. Maya fixed herself a glass of elderflower juice and brought my water along with some honey cakes.

"On the house," she said, smiling up at me, and I thought something about her features was familiar. Perhaps I'd seen her somewhere before?

"How can I help you, Sofija?" asked Maya, her tone formal now.

"Anton, from the City Hall, told me to look for you. I need a travel permit to Agram, as soon as possible."

There was a pause as Maya beamed at me for a few seconds, her expression unreadable. Recovering quickly, she smiled widely and said, "He sent you to the right person then! Hope Anton is well? Do you work together?"

"Anton is... err... fine. Yes, we both work at the City Hall." I didn't know much about Anton's private life, but I supposed he was doing well. Come to think of it, I've never seen him in a bad mood, so I wasn't lying. "So, you can get the permit for me then?"

"No, I can't." I could feel my face fall before Maya continued, "But I can point you in the right direction."

And with that, she produced a small piece of paper and a pen out of her jeans pocket, then started scribbling. I sat there quietly, waiting. Another restaurant to visit. Who am I to look for now? For nothing better to do, I tugged on my caste band almost unconsciously.

Maya handed me the piece of paper. It had two short lines of text, reading:

KAIROS

Dunavska 56, Velesh

I read it over three times, confused. Looking up at Maya, I said, "I don't understand. Is this the person I should be looking for — Kairos?"

Maya chuckled a little at my question before answering:

"No, that's the password you'll need to enter the premises. You're looking for Goran, and that is the address," she answered, pointing at 'Dunavska 56, Velesh'.

"He'll tell you what the next step is. You better go straight away if the travel permit you need is urgent. Oh, and make sure to destroy the note once you're done."

I nodded in understanding and checked my phone clock — five-fifty p.m. I had another two hours at my disposal.

"Yes, it's urgent. I'll head out now then." I took the paper from her. "Thank you, Maya. Have a good week".

She smiled again and said, "It's nothing. Good luck to you, and safe travels." I was almost out the door when I heard her saying, "Oh, and Sofija… This meeting never happened," — she gave me a meaningful look — "understand?"

"Of course. Thanks again."

Chapter 6
The Task

Half an hour later, I was standing in front of the large house at Dunavska 56. Situated in a quiet neighbourhood at the outskirts of Velesh, it was surrounded by a large garden with a couple of apple trees in the back. A rusty looking, black Lada was parked at the front. It looked like a family house, not exactly where one would expect the most skilled forger in the Stridon kanton to operate from.

I knocked at the front door, waiting. The house seemed deserted; there were no sounds from the inside. Just when I was about to leave, thinking that Maya played some kind of joke on me, I heard footsteps and the key turning in the lock. The door opened, and a middle-aged, dark-haired man with a round face and a few days' beard growth peered outside.

"What do you want?" he barked at me. Taken aback by the unwelcoming reaction, I answered quickly, "Hi, I'm looking for Goran. I have the password, Maya—"

"Shhh! Not here!" The man cut me off mid-sentence and motioned for me to come inside. I followed him into a small hallway opening into a shabby living room. The place smelled of cigarettes and beer. The man took a seat on a grey sofa in the middle of the room, inviting me to sit on the armchair opposite him. I did as instructed, waiting for him to say something as I didn't quite fancy being shouted down again.

"Who are you, and why are you here?" he asked tersely. I made a mental note to let Maya know she has some shady friends if I ever saw her again.

"My name is Sofija Filipov. I need a travel permit. Maya from Nocturno gave me your address along with the password — Kairos."

The man stared at me for a few seconds, and then his features relaxed. He sat back on the sofa, nodding quietly. "Okay, then. Sorry for the cold welcome, but I didn't expect anyone today. Maya would usually let me know if someone was coming here, but I suppose she didn't get around to doing it just yet."

And as if on cue, his phone rang.

"That'll be her," the man said and answered his mobile, which sat on the coffee table.

"Yes, she's here now. Thanks for the warning!" Maya was saying something on the other side. The man thanked her for the call and hung up.

I looked up expectantly, eager to get on with the conversation as it was six-fifteen already.

"Do you want anything to drink? I have water and coffee," he asked politely.

"No, thanks, I'm fine. In a bit of a hurry, don't want to be caught out during curfew.

"Oh yes, that's a smart idea, unless you want to spend the night in the RC. Last I heard it wasn't a very comfortable place." He looked down, lost in thought for a while. I didn't have time for small talk.

"So... are you Goran? Can you help with my travel permit?"

"Yes, I'm Goran. And yes, I can help with the permit." He stood up, fetching a piece of paper and a pen for me. "Write down your full name, your date of birth, your caste and destination."

I took the paper and pen from him and started writing. "Where do you work? I see you're the Plava," he said, scanning my blue satin band.

"I work at the City Hall." He wasn't wearing a caste band or a work uniform, so I couldn't tell which caste he belonged to. This neighbourhood housed most of the Zolta, so he must have been one of them too. A researcher or journalist was my guess.

Once done writing, I pushed the paper towards him. He scanned the details quickly and set the paper aside.

"Thank you for that. So Agram, then? As soon as possible, I assume since you've come to me?"

"Yes, please. It's urgent."

"Okay, Sofija. I will get you the permit, and it will be valid for one week. Better make sure to return within that time frame, okay? We don't want to raise any flags and have one of them Armiya agents sniffing around."

"Yes, of course. A week is more than enough." I hesitated with the next question but knew it would come up soon anyway. "How much do I owe you?"

"I don't charge in money or coupons," he said. I looked up, raising my eyebrows in surprise and started getting up. I've heard of this before; the higher caste men offering all sorts of favours to the unfortunate women for certain services. *I won't sleep around for permits, nuh-uh. I'll just find another way; he can't be the only forger available.*

Goran must have read my reaction correctly and started laughing. "It's not what you think! Calm down, sit, let me finish." Relieved, I exhaled heavily and beamed up at him, suspicious.

"Explain then. What is it you need from me?" I asked in an edgy voice, sitting back down.

"Since you work at the City Hall, I'll need you to obtain some information." I was surprised by this. It almost sounded too easy, and I felt a surge of relief coming over me.

"I can do that, easy. What kind of information?"

"Hold your horses; it won't be as simple as you think. What I need from you is a classified file on a girl named Mila Novak. She disappeared last week, and the Armiya won't share anything with us."

I wasn't surprised to hear about yet another disappearance, though I felt sorry for this Mila person. She would be the fifth missing girl in the past month. The government had been ignoring the issue and dodging sensitive questions where possible. Sometimes, the missing persons just turned up after a few days, with a story that they've been visiting their friends without telling their family. A thin story for sure, but any excuse was good enough in a repressive regime. People rarely dared to question anything, so the Biela could afford to serve us weak explanations.

"Okay, it might take a while, but I'll find a way. Is Mila ... your daughter?" I asked carefully, not sure if I was crossing some sort of line asking this. Goran didn't seem bothered by my question. "No, she's my niece. My brother, David, is the father."

Something clicked, and I put two and two together.

"David Novak is your brother? He's in the RC, right?" I blurted out the last part without thinking and then added quickly, "sorry, it's not my place to ask."

"It's okay. Yes, David is in the rehabilitation centre for not voting the way they wanted him to. He's a research advisor at The Institute and a member of the Local Assembly." He explained in an aggravated voice. I recalled Helena mentioning David's wife, Sandra, visiting him in the Velesh RC.

"Hope he'll be out soon? Do you know if they took his daughter to pressure him to comply?" I asked next, trying to understand the situation.

Goran took a few seconds to think about my suggestion.

"Could be. It certainly wouldn't be below the Biela. Or it could be a part of some larger scheme, as many girls her age have been disappearing lately. Well… your age, actually. I see here you were born in 1985… same as Mila." He gaped at me, as if struck by a sudden realisation. His eyebrows were raised, and he was frowning, looking confused for some reason. I nodded, deciding to ignore the odd behaviour.

I didn't know Mila, probably because we went to different schools. I attended the First Gymnasium in the city centre, and she was probably going to the Third Gymnasium here at the Velesh industrial zone.

"I'll let you know when I obtain the file, then," I said, getting ready to head out.

"Just another thing, Sofija." He seemed reluctant to say it, whatever it was.

"You seem like a nice person and all, but my experience had taught me not to trust anyone easily." He gave me an apologetic look. "I need you to deliver the file within the next twenty-four hours. If you're late, our deal is off."

I gaped at him, shocked. How on Earth was I going to enter the City Hall's classified offices by this time tomorrow? It takes days to get the employee pass card to access these files. Even if I could go back to the City Hall tonight and apply for it, I wouldn't get it before the next week.

"I'm sorry, Goran, that's impossible. It takes days to obtain the pass card to enter the classified section. Can't you give me more time?" I could hear the desperation creeping into my voice and hated it. One of the things I hated the most was asking favours of people.

"I'm sorry, Sofija, I can't. That's my condition and the only way I can protect myself from whistle-blowers. Come by this time tomorrow with the file on Mila Novak or look for your travel permit elsewhere. The nearest reliable forger is in Narona kanton, last I heard."

He gave me an apologetic but firm look and I knew the terms were non-negotiable. So, I thanked him and promised to be back the following evening by seven p.m the latest.

"What happens if I don't show up on time?" I asked tentatively.

He looked up at me briefly, then shrugged. "Then I'll know you sold me out and will be on my way out of town. I'd prefer not to have to do that, see I quite like this place... so please be on time. And good luck."

Wondering how on Earth I would solve this one, I mounted my bicycle and headed home. It was getting dark outside, and I could see the Armiya agents patrolling the streets. There were two of them on every corner, checking the cars getting out of town. These checks were standard, even outside the curfew. Suddenly I was thankful for my bike — at least I didn't have to walk since it would take me ages to get home on foot.

As the city lights started lighting up, the streets seemed emptier. People retreated to the security of their homes, not willing to risk close encounters with Armiya agents. All dressed in black, they were a caste of policemen, soldiers, and intelligence agents. An unpleasant bunch, Armiya was doing the government's and Taykuni's bidding and receiving large sums of money for it. Glorified bullies and spies dressed in the mantle of protectors of the Great State of Danubia.

Chapter 7
Illness

At two in the morning, I was still wide awake and staring at the ceiling of my childhood room. The balcony door was wide open, a soft summer breeze cooling the air. The dark street was quiet and sombre, and the thoughts came rushing at me, interrupted by nothing but my loudly beating heart and deep breaths. I was scared. The plan I concocted earlier that evening was clear and simple enough in my head, but will it work out? What if anything goes wrong? What if I miss the deadline? Grandpa won't get his medicine on time. He will die because of me... because I failed.

Soon, I was walking down the familiar narrow street again, my feet leading me towards a small, ancient square with an old well in its centre. Someone was sobbing, their wails louder and louder, as I approached the crossroads with the square on one side and the small, cosy café with mahogany walls on the other. The sobs were getting more intense, and I was anxious to find that unfortunate person, to ask what was wrong, to help. But where are they? The sobs were coming from somewhere near the square, but I couldn't quite pin down the exact location. I should try the café; maybe they went through the mysterious door and are now stuck on the other side.

The sobs turned into loud cries for help, and my heart nearly stopped. I burst into the familiar café and headed straight for the back door. The place was as packed as always, and I couldn't understand why no one reacted to these cries for help. Have they all gone deaf? Or do they just not care at all?

The cries were now tearing my head apart, and I pressed both palms against my ears, trying to suppress the terrible, desperate noise. Passing the mahogany bar, I knew the person was on the other side of the mysterious door.

"I'm coming to help, I'm coming!" I bellowed, desperately trying to hush their wails.

I grabbed the brass knocker with a two-faced man on it and stroke the plate twice. Just then, I woke up, and the mahogany café was gone.

The sun was rising outside, covering my tiny room in the early-morning light. The cries were gone from inside my head, but I could still hear them somewhere further away. Did the person move away from the door? I was just about to get them, and they walked away? Why...?

Then I realised I was completely covered in sweat, and the cries were coming from downstairs, now receding into hushed sobs.

"Grandma! Grandpa?" I jumped out of bed and rushed down the stairs into Grandpa's room, my heart beating frantically.

My grandmother was sitting by the wheeled bed, where Grandpa lay, looking worse than ever. His breathing was pained and slow as he struggled to pull himself up against the large pillows. Grandma was trying to conceal her face behind the white handkerchief, but it was too late.

"What's going on? Were you crying?" I asked, bewildered, looking from one to the other. None of them spoke for a while, then Grandma said, "Sofi, please go back to bed. All is fine, we were just... having a conversation. Sorry we woke you."

I looked at her suspiciously, knowing she was lying. She never did that, and this simple realisation scared me more than her earlier sobs.

"What's wrong?" I asked again quietly, scared to hear the answer to my own question.

"He's just a little bit tired," she said and gave me the "Not here" look.

"Does anyone want some coffee?" I asked quickly, changing the topic. Even though it was still early, I knew I wouldn't be going back to sleep, not after this.

"Make some for me. I'll see you in the kitchen shortly," I heard Grandma answering quickly, sounding relieved.

I first went back upstairs, going through my morning rituals as fast as possible, putting on the usual pencil skirt, clean white shirt and heels. After arranging my hair into the tight bun, hiding the turquoise strand as I didn't quite fancy people staring at me, I made my way back to the deserted kitchen. I put the pot filled with water on the stove. Once the water boiled, I added two spoons of black coffee with some sugar and let it boil, creating a thick layer of coffee foam on top. Taking the pot off the stove, I poured two cups of black coffee and placed them on a tray in the middle of the kitchen table. It was only seven-fifteen, so I had some time left before departing for work.

Soon after, the kitchen door opened slowly, and Grandma came in.

"He's asleep now. Finally," she said, looking tired and worried.

"What's going on? He's looking worse than yesterday, and it's only been a day. Why were you crying?"

"Oh, Sofi... I'm so sorry we woke you. I didn't want you to see him like that," Grandma said and started weeping quietly. I fetched a kitchen towel from the counter and, handing it to her, pressed on, "What happened, Grandma? What's wrong?" My heart was pounding, fear rising in me like a storm. *Steady until you know what you're dealing with. Don't jump to conclusions; that never did you any good.* I sat down at the kitchen table opposite her, taking a sip of hot coffee, and waited.

Grandma calmed her breathing a little, struggling against a new wave of sobs. A minute or two passed before she managed to utter a sentence, quietly as if scared to say it out loud.

"He tried to choke himself," she said finally, "with the remote-control wire. He managed to wrap it around his neck somehow."

I sat there, staring at her as if she were insane.

What Grandma just told me can't be true; she must be wrong. My grandfather wouldn't try to take his own life. He's a fighter. A man who raised me, a man who taught me everything I knew wouldn't try to abandon us like that. I pressed my palms against my ears, elbows down on the kitchen table, shaking my head. *I couldn't believe it; I won't hear it. It isn't true!*

"It can't be. Grandpa wouldn't do that." I heard myself muttering, but the voice sounded unfamiliar as if belonging to someone else. My head was swimming with sudden dizziness, and I sat up straight, hoping to regain some clarity.

As I lifted my gaze, Grandma's deep eyes, swollen from crying, met mine over the kitchen table. I could read the truth from them as easily as if it were written out on a piece of paper.

"He did, Sofi... He is suffering a lot. Your grandfather was always very active, very able. Now he can't even feed himself at times, and it's getting worse. The wretched illness is progressive, so in a few months, he won't be able to... he won't be..." And she started sobbing again but added through tears, "He won't be able to breathe without aid."

I felt the shock coming over me, on top of fear that had already consumed me. Somewhere deep inside, I knew this was coming. I saw how it all started and witnessed the terrifying progress. At first, Grandpa started dropping things — car keys, spectacles, tools when fixing stuff around the house. Then he tripped a couple of times while climbing the stairs.

A few months later, he couldn't carry more than one thing at once as his grip wasn't as firm as before.

Half a year later, he couldn't walk without aid. Or hold a spoon. And now it was difficult for him to speak... soon, he will be trapped in his head, with nothing but his own thoughts for company. We won't be able to help him.

I felt tears rushing down my cheeks. I wiped them away quickly and tried to put on a brave face.

"Well, Grandpa's not going to attempt that again. Please can you take the remote from him? Cut the wire if you must, or hide it under the bed," I said, looking at Grandma seriously. She nodded, and I knew she already thought of the same thing. "I'll get him that medication, and he'll be well. There's still time."

I finished my coffee, skipping breakfast as I didn't feel like eating. Checking my messenger bag, I found a pair of jeans and sneakers for later, along with a small purse with money Grandma gave me the previous day. I nearly forgot about it as it was tucked in one of the side pockets. I thought of giving it back, as it turned out I didn't need the money for the travel permit after all but decided to keep it until tonight, just in case. Perhaps I'll have to bribe someone at the office to help me obtain the classified file on Mila Novak, I thought — it's best to be prepared. I'm not taking any chances, not now.

"See you tonight, Grandma. I should be back by seven." We were standing at the doorstep like we did every morning; me going to work, she heading to the garden to tend to her carefully looked-after vegetables and flowers.

"All right, dear. Have a good day, and be careful," she said, her eyes worried. "Don't forget to eat! You're so skinny."

Nodding, I mounted my pony and headed to the City Hall.

I headed straight for the reception desk, relieved to see Anton on his own. I wouldn't want to be overheard, so I arrived early.

"Morning, Anton. How are you?" I asked politely, hoping he'd cut the pleasantries short.

"Thrilled to be here, as always!" He laughed at his own joke. "Don't mind my sarcasm this early in the morning. Your signature, please," he said, pushing the check-in sheet towards me. I signed the sheet and then leaned in towards him, my voice low.

"I'll need another favour, Anton. Firstly, thanks for the tip; I managed to speak to Maya." I glanced around to make sure the hall was still deserted. "But I need the no-questions-asked favour now. Can you do that?" I looked up at him expectantly, hoping he'd be forthcoming.

"Depends on what it is, Sofija." Now he was looking at me with his eyebrows raised, curious.

"Nothing huge; I just need you to check me out during lunch hour. I need to stay in, have some… leftover work to do." I knew my excuse was weak and didn't expect him to buy it. It didn't matter as long as he didn't ask for a full explanation. I waited while he mulled it over.

"Okay," he finally said, "but you owe me a drink."

I smiled at him, relief washing over me. "Two, if you want. And dinner. Thank you so much."

Happy that the first step went well, I climbed the stairs to the first floor and walked into a half-empty office.

I could see Helena looking up as I approached the desk. "Morning, dear. How did it go?" she asked quietly.

"Well enough. I'll collect you-know-what after work." I decided on the spot not to tell her about the payment method required in exchange for the travel permit — the fewer people knew, the better. Should something go wrong (my stomach turned at the thought), Helena would be able to honestly say she knew nothing about it.

"Managed to get the coupons yesterday?"

Helena rummaged through her bag for a few seconds, producing a blue envelope.

"Yes, here you go," she placed the envelope on my desk.

"Thank you so much for that. I owe you one". I owed a lot of favours lately, I thought.

"You can repay me by baking that chocolate cake for Igor's party this Saturday," Helena said, "you know, the one you made for your last birthday? It was delicious."

Baking was one of my favourite hobbies. I didn't do it often but enjoyed it, nevertheless. Happy I'd have something to occupy myself with after returning from Agram, I agreed to bake the cake.

The check-in board showed everyone was present, and the clock showed eight sharp, so we both started typing, going through our morning coffees as we did so. There was a small kitchen on our floor with some cereal boxes for everyone to share, but I just didn't feel hungry. My mind was too occupied, and I felt too nervous to think about food.

I knew exactly where the classified files were stored. Everyone learned it during their orientation week, but we also learned that only selected personnel had access. To get through the large white door in the basement, I'd have to get creative and do it during lunch hour when the building is empty.

The next four hours flew by, and soon it was noon. Everyone was walking out for their lunch break.

"I'm behind a bit, so I'll just skip lunch today," I said to Helena briefly, "you go ahead, though". She gave me a suspicious look but didn't say anything. "See you later then."

As everyone cleared out and a small blue tick appeared next to my (and every other) name, I headed for the third floor. The managerial office took up most of the space. This is where our bosses worked, I thought, looking around. Each desk was considerably larger than those on the first and second floors where administration staff, coming from the Plava caste, worked. The fourth floor housed the Major's and the City Council members' offices. The managerial office was deserted as everyone cleared out for lunch hour. Glancing behind me one last time to make sure no one was around, I walked to the closest desk. Someone must have left their keys behind. Those things were heavy and difficult to replace, so most people preferred not to carry them around.

As quietly as possible, I checked the first desk. There was no sign of keys. They should have a black or yellow ribbon wrapped around the keyring, similar to those Anton kept at reception. Only selected members of Armiya and Intelligentsia were allowed into the Classified Files room. At City Hall, they worked on higher floors, serving as advisors for a local intelligence agency or directing the city's museums and galleries.

There was nothing on the next desk either. I tried the drawers too, but all were locked. Five desks later, still no sign of the keys. Finally, I spotted a yellow ribbon wrapped around a keyring on the floor near one of the desks in the middle of the room. I headed for it and picked up a set of keys. The large ribbon was made of yellow satin, the mark of the Zolta caste. Heading for the stairwell, I stopped dead in my tracks. Someone was coming; the sound of footsteps approaching was getting louder by a second. I looked around, realising I didn't have enough time to move, let alone hide. A few moments later, I exhaled in relief. It was only Anton. He was standing near the managerial office entrance, his arms crossed, smirking at me.

"Lost your way, Ms Filipov?" he asked mockingly.

"I don't have the time now, Anton — I'll explain later." I quickly hid the yellow-ribboned set of keys in my blazer pocket and headed for the stairs. "Thanks again for helping me," I said, passing him.

"Looking forward to those drinks! And dinner!" I heard him shouting after me.

A few minutes later, I was standing in front of the large white door in the basement. It, too, was deserted. I looked down, noticing five different keys laying in my outstretched palm. Having seen the Classified Files keys before, I recognised the right one immediately - the largest and the heaviest one should do the trick. The heavy door opened as I turned the key in the lock. I stepped inside, and impenetrable darkness embraced me.

I took the mobile phone out of my pocket and, under its weak light, managed to find a light switch.

The old, dusty room was large with a low ceiling and grey walls, long rows of wooden shelves stretching before me. The shelves were fully stocked with brown folders, bound only with thin bands made of white linen. Every row was labelled with a large white sticker. I approached the one closest to where I was standing and read the label. CFVL/6789/2008. Not sure what to make of it, I walked down the row and took out the first file. The name on the cover read CFVL/6789/2008-A. Looking through other files in the same row, I concluded the 2008-A part meant the year of birth, and A was the initial of a person's surname. Recalling my conversation with Goran, I remembered him mentioning Mila Novak was my age.

I walked through the long room, hoping to find a row with 1985-N files. The room was so large that after half an hour, I wasn't even close yet. The lunch hour was halfway through, I thought as my heart rate accelerated, and I felt beads of sweat on my forehead. *Calm down, Sofija. There must be a quicker way to browse these files.*

Ten minutes of fruitless search later, I spotted a shabby-looking wooden chair at the front of the room and sat down, my head in my hands. I have to find that file. I need the travel permit today. If I couldn't leave for Agram soon, Grandpa wouldn't get the medication on time and... I couldn't think of the consequences, not now. Hoping for a clue, I stood up and looked around. I must pull myself together and find that file soon.

A large wooden desk was placed just behind me. Since I entered through the back door, I haven't noticed it until now. Approaching it, I spotted a small desk drawer. Although there was no label or any indication of the drawer's contents, I somehow knew I'd find a list of files and their locations in it. The drawer was locked, but perhaps I could open it anyway. I rechecked my phone clock. Fifteen minutes left. Here goes nothing, I thought and pulled out the hairpin hiding the turquoise strand under the layers of brown hair. I started to pick the lock, fully aware that I'd never tried this before. Five minutes went by, and I was still trying to open the lock. Guess it isn't as easy as it looked on television, I thought to myself. Soon, people would start swarming into the building, and I'd be caught here, unauthorised to access and with a stolen key. *That means RC and, what's worse, no travel permit - an unwelcome voice in my head jeered. No medication. Grandpa will be gone, all because of my incompetence.* Trying to calm down and ignore the panic, I stopped picking for a few seconds and took a deep breath.

When my hands steadied a little bit, I tried again, but no luck. If only

I could pull my old trick again. It was a bit over the top and potentially dangerous, but I was out of options. Concentrating hard on the lock and clenching my sweaty fists, I reached inside my mind like I had done countless times before. Trying to imagine the lock open and forcing my mind to concentrate on its contents instead of the sounds of people getting into the building, I stood there, silent. The crowd on the upper floors was getting louder. I could hear the thudding of countless pairs of heels marching to their work positions. *Come on, I need this to work. It has to,* I pleaded with whoever might be listening.

And then, miraculously, the lock came off, landing on the floor with a loud thud. My nostrils filled with a strong scent of burnt wood. The top of the drawer where the lock stood only seconds ago was on fire. Shocked, I barely managed to muffle a scream when the fire died down as if extinguished with an invisible hose. Not daring to believe my luck, I pulled the drawer, and it opened with a creaking sound.

I wasn't surprised when my hands wrapped around a large, leatherbound catalogue inside. I took it out. The title on the front page read 'Velesh Classified Files — Index'. Opening it carefully, I then dived in, looking for a file under the name Mila Novak.

A few minutes later, I held a thin folder with Mila's name on it — the CFVL/6724/1985-N (77). People were swarming into the building, back to their positions in the basement and elsewhere in the City Hall. *Only two minutes left.* I quickly tucked the file underneath my blazer and walked towards the door, now pacing as panic took over. My hands were trembling, so it took a while to get the keys from my pocket and another few seconds to lock the white door of the Classified Files room. After that was done, I ran for the stairs, managing to get to the first floor without running into anyone. The administration office was full again, everyone back at their desks. I walked slowly now, breathing deeply to calm down, careful not to draw attention. Finally, I reached my desk and sat down, relieved. Carefully removing the folder from underneath my blazer, I slid it into the messenger bag under the desk. Then I replaced the hairpin, hiding the turquoise strand again.

"Where did you come from? You look like you were running!" Helena was beaming at me, questioningly.

"Oh, I... just went to the restroom. I lost track of time and didn't want to be late, so I ran back."

She didn't buy it. I was such a lousy liar. I braced myself for more questions, but none came. *Thank you, Helena,* I thought to myself.

Taking off the blazer as I was now hot from running, I felt something heavy in one of the pockets. Puzzled for a moment, I checked it quickly, and my heart nearly stopped. The keys! I'd completely forgotten to return them to the third floor! It was only a matter of time before the owner realises they're gone. My face must have changed colours as fear washed over me. I was grateful no one was looking my way, so I didn't have to explain anything.

I decided to leave the keys somewhere, anywhere, and hope the owner would find it soon enough. After all, I found them on the floor, so whoever owned them couldn't have been too careful.

I put the blazer back on, making sure the keys were still inside the pocket, then stood up, trying to remain calm. I climbed the stairs to the third floor, luckily meeting nobody. There was a small kitchenette just opposite the managerial office. I went in, facing two young women I recognised from company parties.

Smiling nervously at them, I said, "Just wondering if you can lend me some sugar? The first floor is out of it, and I cannot drink that instant crap unsweetened — it's too bitter". The women stopped staring at me and smiled politely, handing a few packets of sugar over.

"Thank you," I said and, leaving the kitchen, I dropped one of the packets on purpose. "So clumsy today!" I said in a light voice, bending down while carefully taking the keys out of my pocket. I glanced towards the women. They went back to their chatter, not paying attention to me anymore. I quickly picked up the sugar packets and placed the yellow-ribboned set of keys on the kitchen floor, out of their sight.

Thanking them for the sugar again, I darted out of the kitchen.

Chapter 8
The Escape

At five-thirty that evening, I found myself in front of Dunavska 56 once again. My bike was parked at the front like yesterday. Having changed into jeans and sneakers instead of a work pencil skirt and heels, I got there a little faster this time. Just one more thing to do, and then I could start getting ready for my trip to Agram. The earliest train was scheduled for six-thirty the next morning, and my plan was to be on it. If everything went well, I'd be back in Velesh by the following evening. I needed to remember to contact Mrs Horvat's friend that night and set a meeting with him. It was going to be interesting, finding my way around Agram, since I'd never visited a large city like that before, apart from attending the Commemoration but that took place outside the city centre.

I rang the doorbell, and Goran answered almost immediately. "Good, you're here. And ahead of time. Come in."

He seemed to be in good spirits today, I thought. Probably relieved, like I was, that I managed to show up before the deadline expired. He led me through the hallway into the living room, a cup of coffee already waiting for me and the TV blaring in the background. On the coffee table was a white envelope with my name on it.

"Thank you for the coffee. I got the file you asked for," I said, producing the thin folder on Mila Novak from my bag and placing it on the table. Goran took it, looking briefly through it, then glanced up at me.

"Thank you, you've helped a lot with this. Your travel permit is in the envelope. It is valid for one week, as promised. Don't lose it because I won't be able to get the new one to you. It's not advisable to send these in the post because the Armiya controls everything, and there aren't many regular travellers I trust enough to get it for you to Agram."

"I won't lose it and will most likely be back the same day. Thank you so much."

I gulped down my coffee, eager to get home as soon as possible as I was now experiencing sharp pangs of hunger. With everything that was going on, I had completely forgotten to eat. The news was on, and we listened as a government official read the latest decree directly from Kalemgrad. Another tax raise, I thought, listening in with very little interest.

"All intercity traffic will be suspended as of six-thirty this evening. The suspension will last until further notice. This is a routine exercise, ordered today by our President Tanatos himself."

I listened in disbelief, feeling Goran's shocked glare on my face.

"You have to go, now," he urged me, getting to his feet, "this isn't a coincidence; they know something. The Armiya must have been informed of a fake travel permit... or of the missing classified file. You must go, Sofija."

Goran stood there, looking at me with alarming urgency. Then, he walked past me and into the hallway, talking more to himself than to me.

"If you can get on the last train out of here, you'll be fine. Stay in Agram for a whole week until the dust settles. Yes, a week should do... unless..."

I stared at him, utterly confused, frozen at the spot. My eyes followed Goran as he darted to the door, peering outside nervously as if expecting a bunch of Armiya agents to wait outside.

Why would they stop the traffic just because I stole a file from the City Hall or obtained an illegal travel permit? Hundreds of people must be travelling on those permits and committing bigger crimes every day. Yet, the traffic was never 'routinely suspended' because of them. No, it must be something else, and this was just a coincidence; it must be. I'm too insignificant. Why would they go to all these lengths for me?

I checked my phone clock and noticed it was nearly six. I didn't have the time to go home; I'd just have to head straight to the station and hope to catch the last train. Were there any trains to Agram now? I didn't have the time to check or call the train station.

"You coming? Sofija, this is serious. You must go," Goran urged me once again, looking at me from the hallway.

I collected my things and walked over to him, my feet moving on their own accord.

"Yes, I'll go straight away. Thank you once again, Goran."

He walked me out, looking concerned. "Good luck, Sofija."

I waved at him one last time, cycling away from the Dunavska 56.

My mind was racing as I cycled to the station. Grandma was probably already worried sick; she must have seen the news. I decided to give her a call from the train and explain. I didn't have any spare clothes, only my pencil skirt and heels in the bag. That would do until tomorrow.

The Velesh Train Station was situated on the outskirts of the city. Built over a hundred years ago, it was a neglected, old building with dirty halls and rugged benches covered in ugly graffiti. When I arrived, the station was quiet, most people probably putting off their travels due to new restrictions. I parked my bicycle next to the main entrance, securing it with a lock. Hopefully, it would still be here when I returned, I thought. I was fond of that bike — it was originally Grandma's.

There were only four daily connections to Agram, used by the business travellers with travel permits. Most of them were wealthy members of the Biela or Cherwona castes; lower caste members rarely travelled. They didn't have much reason to go anywhere, and the travel permits were costly.

Entering the small, dirty hallway, I checked the departures board. *Please, let there be one more departure to Agram,* I pleaded with whoever might be listening. I'd had so much luck that day and hoped it didn't run out entirely just yet. The list was short, with only three departures left. Two were local connections for Mursa and Narona counties and just one for Agram. The Agram train was scheduled for six-twenty p.m.; in five minutes.

Not daring to believe my luck, I ran towards the check-in gate, rummaging through my messenger bag for the travel permit on the way. A stern looking Armiya member stood there, guarding the departures entrance. There was no queue, I noticed with relief. Approaching the man, I greeted him politely and handed him the travel permit. He took it without a word and then said:

"Your ID?" his eyebrows raised questioningly.

I nodded in understanding and took the ID card from my purse, handing it to him. He stood there, staring at my documents for what felt like an eternity. *Come on, man, I have a train to catch! Only a minute left now!* I could see the Agram train from where I was standing; it was right there, on platform number one just behind him.

"It says here you're travelling to Agram. What business do you have there?" he asked tersely. I had my answer ready.

"It's a business visit. The City Hall needs someone to attend a governmental seminar tomorrow morning, and I volunteered," I said, smiling innocently, hoping it would work. If he picks up the phone and checks with the City Hall, I'll be in serious trouble.

The man kept on scanning my ID and travel permit, beaming up at me suspiciously every now and then. *As if I had all the time in the world, instead of mere seconds.*

Trying to push him a little, I added, "In fact, my train is about to leave. My boss will kill me if I miss the seminar. Would you please let me through?"

He beamed up at me again, his brow furrowing as he was thinking something over. Probably worried he'd have to deal with an angry manager from the City Hall if his employee misses the train to an important business seminar, he finally let me through.

I heard the whistle as the train doors started closing. Running as fast as I could, I reached the platform and jumped inside at the last moment. Relieved that I made it without being crushed by the heavy door, I leaned against the glass partition and took several deep breaths to calm myself down. My whole body was shaking, and it took a while for the trembles to stop.

The department was half-empty; most seats were taken by solo travellers dressed in white and red blazers, the colours of Biela and Cherwona castes. I was right, I thought, in thinking that rich Taykuni and government members travelled the most. Trying not to attract too much attention, I walked to the back seat next to the window and took my mobile phone out to call Grandma. It barely rang once before she picked up.

"Where are you?" She said without a greeting, her voice high with panic.

"Grandma, I'm fine. I'm on the train to Agram. I'm sorry, but after seeing the news, I had no choice but to go straight to the train station; otherwise, I wouldn't have been able to leave at all." That calmed her down a little, and her voice was steadier now.

"You could have called! Please be careful, Sofi. Do you have enough money? When are you coming back?"

"Yes, I still have the money you gave me. I'll return tomorrow evening. Please don't worry." I said, trying to sound reassuring. "How is Grandpa doing?"

"A little better. I told him you're sleeping over at Helena's... didn't want to worry him with this whole Agram business." I was surprised to hear that because Grandma seldom resorted to lying. Perhaps with Grandpa this ill, it was a good idea not to trouble him further.

"Please, Sofi, promise me you'll return as soon as possible" she pleaded with me now.

"I promise. I'll speak to you when I've arrived in Agram," I uttered, the feeling of unease growing inside me.

I also promised, after her insisting, that I'd find a decent hotel to spend the night and reassured her that I'd eaten. Both were blatant lies. I didn't plan on spending a fortune on a hotel room, and I hadn't eaten at all today. Money was low already, and I'd need every dukat I can save. Perhaps I'd just find a bench somewhere at the Agram Train Station and spend the night. It wouldn't be the first time I slept rough, I thought as unwelcome images of my past came to mind. Once again, I pushed them away.

My next call was to Mrs Horvat's contact — she said his name was Zlatko and he worked at the pharmacy somewhere in Agram city centre. A deep voice answered after three rings.

"Hello, Zlatko speaking."

"Hello, sorry I'm calling this late. My name is Sofija Filipov; I got your contact from Mrs Vera Horvat, she's a nurse at the Velesh Central Hospital. I'm calling about the medication for my grandfather. She said you could help," I recited.

There was a short pause.

"Yes, Vera told me you'd be visiting Agram. Please can you meet me tomorrow morning at nine-thirty? Wait for me outside the Pharmacy at Tanatos Square. Don't be late."

"Pharmacy, Tanatos Square, nine-thirty. Thank you so much; I'll be there."

"Okay, see you. Bye." Mrs Horvat's friend hung up quickly, as if eager to finish the conversation as soon as possible. Well, at least now I knew where and when to go. If I got the medication in the morning, I'd have a good chance of returning to Velesh by late afternoon. Relaxing a little, I put the phone in my bag and sat back, looking out the window. The train was now leaving the town, driving past endless green fields below the orange skies in the looming sunset.

I was famished, and the prospect of spending the night on a bench somewhere didn't help elevate my mood. It would be so easy to find a hotel, but that would cost a lot. I couldn't risk spending the savings. I would sleep on the train back tomorrow, I said to myself. I can get through one sleepless night.

The unpleasant memories I worked so hard to forget overwhelmed my tired mind as I lost all will to fight them. As if it were yesterday, I could hear the sound of dinner plates breaking against the bright wall at our tiny apartment in Sopot. Even now, my heart started pounding as fear overwhelmed me. I wrapped both arms around myself, rocking back and forth as memories claimed my mind completely.

Davor, enraged and intoxicated with alcohol, stumbling towards the door to stop me from leaving. Davor, yelling insults at me, the contents of his wine glass spilling all over the floor as he tried to balance on his unstable feet. I, scared to death, grabbing my pre-packed rucksack from under the bed in the adjacent bedroom and quietly putting on shoes and coat with nothing underneath but thin pyjamas. Every time, I would lie fully dressed under the covers for hours, waiting for my opportunity to flee. Hoping he'd forget what he was yelling about and go to the living room so that I could eventually slip out. I could still vividly remember the relief I felt as I managed to get to the door after hours of waiting; feel the welcoming cold air on my face as I stepped in the night. Bewildered and scared, the only place that came to mind was the Sopot Train Station. I had no friends in Sopot, and even if I did, I couldn't bother them in the middle of the night. Or perhaps I could, but that wasn't an option for a person as proud as me.

The train station provided shelter and a full vending machine. Looking like a street beggar, dressed in pyjama bottoms, coat and boots, I felt like the biggest loser on Earth. I had to run from my own home nearly every week, as Davor had his drinking sessions. He'd reassure me to go to bed and promised he wouldn't get drunk, and then he'd do it again. Every weekend, his shouts and insults would wake me up from an already uneasy sleep. At first, I was completely unaware of the seriousness of the situation, caught up in a never-ending circle of fruitless attempts to reason with him. The more I talked, the more wound up and dangerous he became. Everything wrong in his life was my fault all of a sudden; He would tell me I didn't deserve anything else in life but to serve him. He'd force me to agree with him, and if I didn't, he'd threaten to hurt me. At first, I thought he was joking. He wouldn't really hurt me, I told myself over and over, trying to explain his behaviour away. Somewhere deep down, this man loved me.

The first time I ran was after he threw my clothes and books out of the door, onto the muddy sidewalk covered in rainwater. "Get out *now*! Get out, you disgraceful woman!" I could still hear his shouts in my head. I tried to plead with him, tried to reason, but it didn't work.

"Get out now, or I'll throw you out myself!" And I was out on the streets, again. After that, I always had my emergency rucksack ready under the bed.

I stopped counting how many times I slept on the bench at the Sopot Train Station, unable to catch a train to Velesh as there was no traffic after midnight. Well, not precisely slept. I couldn't sleep as, even with all the blankets and clothes I had, it was always too cold and uncomfortable. At least I was left alone, and no one ever bothered me. The next morning, I would return home, knowing it was safe now. Davor wouldn't remember anything and, when I told him how he acted, he'd call me paranoid and crazy. And so, the cycle continued, and I was its captive. Too weak to break it, I was the prisoner of my own fears.

The cycle finally broke when he hit me. Again, and again and again. I closed my eyes in anguish, remembering that night.

I was fast asleep in the bedroom when he came in, pulling the mattress from under me, shouting that I should get out and that everything in the house was his and nothing was mine. He forced me out the bed and hit me. I didn't remember how many times or where exactly the punches landed... I didn't even remember if it hurt. I was too shocked to notice the pain.

My mind was concentrated on finding the emergency rucksack in between the blows that kept on coming; I didn't want to leave the house without it knowing a very cold night awaits outside. Once my fingers wrapped around the rucksack handle, I ran for the door. He was coming after me, but he was too slow due to his impaired vision and delayed reflexes. Turning the handle, I felt the cold air on my face, welcoming and safe.

I didn't feel the pain until later that night, laying under blankets on the train station bench. Thinking it would pass if I just slept a little, I dozed off. The next thing I remembered was the bright lights of a hospital ceiling. I was told the street cleaners found me early that morning. They saw I was bleeding and took me to the nearest hospital. It turned out my lip was cut, so that's where most of the bleeding came from. I also had two broken ribs and bruises all over my torso.

My grandparents spent a week in Sopot, coming to the hospital every day, sitting by my bed. I asked them to thank the cleaners who brought me in. I owed them my life. Grandpa went to Davor's apartment to get my things; he said Davor wasn't there. I had no idea where he went and didn't care. Coming from the Atera caste, I guessed he joined the Armiya. I didn't want to press charges, although my grandparents urged me to. Tired and hurting, I somehow convinced them to let it go. At least I was now free.

And so, after six months with Davor, I went back to my grandparents' house in Velesh. This trip to Agram was the first one I had taken since. And tonight, would be the first time I slept rough... since then.

The train came to a halt, and I was brought back from my reverie by the commotion of people leaving the train and the newcomers getting on board. If only I had got something to eat earlier... the hunger pangs were getting more annoying now. I watched the new passengers coming in and placing their bags in the luggage department above seats. All were travelling alone, on business it seemed. The only exception was a middle-aged couple, both of them dressed in jeans and shirts, so I couldn't guess their caste. The woman had wavy blonde hair that reached to her shoulders, and the man was wearing a shabby-looking flat cap. They didn't have any baggage, I noticed. Perhaps they were only going away for a day, like me, I thought. The woman smiled at me as the couple took the two seats on the opposite side of the aisle. I returned the smile and quickly looked out of the window. There was a very small chance that the woman knew or recognised me. Still, it's best not to draw attention when travelling on an illegal permit.

A while later, an old, white-haired man selling coffee, juice and snacks came through the carriage. I bought a pack of crisps, some biscuits for later and a cup of black coffee from him, happy I'd have at least something to eat today.

The train came to a halt again. It was making a lot of stops, I noticed. The journey will probably last over four hours at this pace. The couple across the aisle started conversing quietly, pointing at something or someone out of the window. They looked alarmed, and I wondered what was going on. I couldn't see the town's name from where I was sitting, but it looked like a lot of people got on the train. Suddenly, someone was speaking to me, their voice alarmed.

"I know you don't know me, but I know you and need you to trust me, Sofija. You must come with us right now. The Armiya is looking for you and their agents have just entered the train a few carriages back."

The blonde woman from across the aisle was now sitting opposite me, speaking in a hushed voice, her face anxious. I shook my head slightly, thinking she'd mistaken me for someone. But didn't she just say my name? If she knew me, why didn't she say something earlier?

Her partner was standing next to my seat, glancing back nervously before saying, "Please, Sofija, you need to trust us. We'll explain in a minute, just get off the train. Now."

I was staring from one to the other, bewildered. What were these strange people talking about? Why would Armiya send their agents to look for me specifically?

But somewhere deep inside, I knew something was off all day. Goran said the new travel ban wasn't a coincidence. And now this. How come these people found themselves on the same train as me and just happen to know who I was? Not knowing why or how and hoping I wouldn't regret it, I decided on the spot to trust them. Most of all, I was hoping to finally get some answers. Taking the messenger bag and standing up, I nodded in agreement and followed them towards the back exit. One carriage back, five or more men dressed in black and carrying guns were moving among the confused passengers, asking for their IDs. The train was still unmoving, and the engine roar died down.

"Just act normal. Like you're looking for the toilet or something," the woman advised me. I followed her quietly down the aisle, scared to glance back. It looked like the Armiya men were still one carriage away.

Finally, we reached the exit doors.

"Shit," the man muttered to himself. "Shit, shit, shit." He motioned for us to stay behind him, and, pulling his flat cap over his forehead, he hurried further down the train. Then I saw three Armiya men standing outside every train exit. They anticipated this — they expected me to try to run away. Fear rose in me as I followed the man, the blonde woman at my heels, directing me further down the train.

We reached the last carriage and had nowhere to go but out. The three Armiya officers outside the door were looking away from us, smoking and apparently bored. We had no choice but to walk past them, I thought as my eyes travelled from one officer to the other. Each of them carried a gun, I noticed as my heart rate increased in response to the fresh rush of fear.

The man pressed the red button, and the double train doors opened.

"Hey, assholes! Take this," he bellowed, taking something small out of his pocket and thrusting it their way the moment the heavy train doors opened.

We broke into a run, as far away from the station as possible, into the warm summer night. Whatever it was the man threw at the Armiya agents, seemed to have temporarily incapacitated them or at least slowed them down. I heard the agents swearing and yelling obscenities from a growing distance. Then the gunshots came, breaking the evening lull of the small town we found ourselves in. Too slow, I thought with relief. Those shots will have been fired in vain, as we were long gone from their range.

"Damn it! That's bound to alert the whole town. Hurry, we don't want to be seen!" I heard the man yelling back at us.

We ran past the small park next to the train station, continuing down the narrow alley that led further from the unfamiliar town centre. The streets were empty, and we kept going. Only when we found ourselves in the forest, surrounded by dark oak trees, did we stop to take a breath.

"We weren't followed," the man said, sitting down on the nearby tree stump, "that was the last marble I had on me. It was only half-potent, lucky it worked."

I had no idea what the man was talking about; it all sounded like gobbledygook to me.

"Have you heard from anyone?" he asked. The question was directed to the blonde woman, who shook her head *no* while rummaging through her shoulder bag. A few seconds later, she took out a mobile phone and started dialling. I was looking from one to the other, waiting for an explanation that didn't come.

"What is going on? Why did we just do that?" I could hear panic seeping into my voice. Did I just make a massive mistake by trusting these two?

"We'll get to that, I promise," the man said reassuringly. "Right now, we need to get the hell out of here".

Again, even though not knowing why, I trusted him. I stood there, waiting for the woman to finish the call.

"All right, we'll be waiting at the Rustica. Call if there are any delays. To Agram, yes. Thanks."

She hung up and placed the phone back in her shoulder bag. I looked questioningly at her.

"There's a restaurant a few minutes' walk away from here. We'll go there and wait for the transfer to arrive." As I opened my mouth to fire more questions, she said, "And we'll answer all your questions then."

Chapter 9
Tayna

I followed them to the edge of the forest. A small restaurant came into view, surrounded by tall oak trees and flower beds. A wooden sign at the front read 'RUSTICA'. It looked like a wedding venue, though a bit neglected. With the Danubian economy worsening, people couldn't afford extravagant restaurant weddings, so the place probably remained unused. The rich castes were the only ones who could afford it, and they hosted weddings in their mansions.

The restaurant was warm and welcoming, with bright walls and dark oak tables covered in red-and-white chequered tablecloths. I noticed a small reception next to the entrance; so, this is a hotel, too. That explains why it's open during curfew; the new rules didn't apply to hospitality units offering accommodation outside urban areas. The Biela and Cherwona members had to sleep somewhere during their business travels — and enjoy lavish parties, of course.

We sat down at the table closest to the entrance and waved at the waiter who was busy polishing glasses. Apart from ours, only one more table was occupied. A five-member family was enjoying dinner, laughing and joking.

The waiter arrived, and we ordered three cups of coffee and three portions of whatever was on their daily menu. Looking forward to eating something, I relaxed a little in my seat.

"Time to introduce ourselves, I think." The man was smiling politely at me, taking off his flat cap. Brown curls surfaced from under it. "My name is Tomislav, you can call me Tom. This is my wife, Natasha. We were sent to your train tonight just in case you ran into trouble."

I stared at him; fully aware it was impolite but not caring much about etiquette.

"Why? Who sent you? I don't understand." My head was spinning. Were they playing some sick joke on me? Was I really that easy to mess with? *Yes, you are, said the sarcastic voice in my head. You could be a little less naive.*

"How much do you know about your parentage, Sofija?" I heard the man asking. He was speaking to me as if he knew me. How is this possible? We just met half an hour ago, and they talked to me as if we were old friends.

"My parents died in the war twenty-five years ago. My grandparents brought me up," I replied, baffled by an odd question.

"And where do you think your parents lived before the Rebellion? I mean... before the war?" the woman asked, her voice soft and careful as if she was talking to a mentally ill person. That only wound me up.

"What do you mean, where do I think they lived? In Velesh, of course!" I replied hotly, my voice high with frustration. "Look, I don't know what is going on, but I was on my way to Agram before you dragged me out of that train. I need to get there tonight; it's important."

"We'll get you to Agram, don't worry. I thought you wanted some answers first." The woman seemed very patient and calm, and I felt a surge of embarrassment washing over me.

I hated this. These people acted as if they knew something I didn't but wanted me to force the information out of them. Feeling agitated, I crossed my arms and looked away from them. We sat in silence as the waiter served our food. He placed three large portions of beef stew with dumplings on the table, a bowl of cabbage salad and a breadbasket. I started eating, famished.

"Sofija, we knew your parents. We were friends. Your father's name was Luka Filipov." I stared at the man, shock showing on my face. The woman added:

"Your mother's name was Alina Bayamonti, and they both died twenty-five years ago. You look exactly like her, and I bet you're hiding a turquoise hair strand somewhere underneath that bun, just like she did." She smiled softly at me, and I forgot my anger for a moment.

"But I've never seen you before. Are you from Velesh?" I asked, swallowing a spoonful of warm, delicious stew.

"We're not from Velesh. We're from somewhere else... from the city called Tayna. And so was your mother. Your father lived there most of his adult life," the man said carefully, finishing the last sentence in a low voice.

"Tayna? I've never heard of it. That cannot be; my parents were from Velesh." *What a load of crap. You're being played again, Sofija, the sarcastic voice said.*

"Shh, keep it quiet," the woman pleaded with me, her voice soft. She looked around the half-empty restaurant before speaking again.

"Look, I know this is all a lot to take in. But we're telling you the truth. We'll show you Tayna tomorrow but, for now, please just know that we wish you well. We boarded that train tonight to keep an eye on you and help if you get in trouble. Those Armiya people were looking for you specifically. Someone tipped off the government earlier this evening about your illegal permit. We just wanted to get you out of there, and I think you prefer being here rather than in the RC?"

I looked back at her, biting my lip in frustration. I didn't know what to say. It seemed like they were telling the truth, but the truth sounded insane. My parents were not from Velesh but from somewhere called Tayna? And these people — Natasha and Tomislav they said their names were — knew them? How come my grandparents never mentioned Tayna? They told me my parents grew up and met in Velesh. Too tired to argue further, I decided to let it go for now and listen to their explanation.

"No, you're right. Thank you for getting me out of there. Do you know who tipped them off and why is the government so interested in finding me? There must be dozens of people travelling on fake travel permits every day."

"We have... a theory. But it would be best to discuss the details tomorrow when we get to Tayna. Just trust us on this, please. You've done well so far." Tomislav was speaking now, smiling at me fondly. Almost like a parent. I felt embarrassed under his protective gaze and concentrated on eating.

My mind was racing as I thought of the possible traitor. The list of suspects was very short. Only Anton, Goran and Helena knew about the illegal travel permit, and I doubted they'd tell anyone else. Helena wouldn't tell; I just knew it. I trusted her. Goran would land himself in trouble, too, if he turned me in since he provided the permit. Anton... why would Anton do this to me? What's in it for him? I thought he was a friend. My head was spinning again, and I pushed the thought out of my mind. I'd worry about it the next day. Hopefully, getting to Tayna (if that place even existed, I thought) would shed some light on all this.

Feeling slightly better now that I'd eaten, I remembered the reason for my trip to Agram.

"I didn't plan on staying long and would like to board the return train by tomorrow afternoon. I have some... business to attend to in the morning, and then I'm off. How are we getting to Agram now? Is there a coach or something?"

Natasha and Tomislav exchanged worried looks.

"I don't think you'll be returning anytime soon, Sofija. You're in their database now, and your name is flagged. Unless you can change appearances, you cannot go back until they forget about you," I heard Natasha explaining in a careful tone.

A feeling of dread washed over my body. Grandpa needed his medication. If I cannot get it to him, his condition will worsen, and he will die. I'd promised Grandma I would return the following day; I promised I'd be okay. Then I remembered Goran's words: *the permit will be valid for one week... better make sure to return within that time frame.* What if I can't return within a week and then get stuck in Agram... or this Tayna the strange couple speak of, forever? Not knowing what to do, I put my head in my hands and sat there, staring at the chequered tablecloth.

"My grandfather is ill. I need to get him the medication he needs, or he'll die," I uttered quietly.

"Is that why you were on that train today? Marin is ill?" Natasha asked in a surprised voice.

"Yes, and getting worse by the day," I explained, looking up again. Something in her green eyes, full of sympathy, prompted me to keep on talking. "I'm meeting this pharmacist tomorrow morning... He'll give me the medication. It's impossible to buy in Velesh, especially with the current supplies shortage."

"I see," Natasha said, "we'll find a way to get the medication to your grandpa. But you'll have to hide for a while." I nodded, agreeing with her again for an unknown reason. I trusted them both so quickly, and that scared me.

"How did you know my grandpa's name?" I asked, suddenly remembering she called him by his first name earlier.

"Oh, we knew your grandparents when we were younger. Irma always made the best birthday cakes," Tomislav said, grinning widely. "And Marin had the best stash of plum rakija."

Chapter 10
Agram

I stared at them in disbelief. How come I've never heard of these people? I shook my head as if trying to rid my tired mind of the hundreds of questions currently spinning inside yearning to be answered. Tomorrow, I said to myself. Tomorrow I'll find out everything.

"Looks like our transfer will be here in five minutes," Natasha said, getting to her feet. I reached for my purse, but Tomislav already placed dukats on the table.

"That ought to cover it," he said before putting his flat cap back on and heading for the exit. I followed the couple out of the restaurant into the peaceful summer night, wondering what lay ahead.

A black Skoda was parked outside the restaurant entrance. Someone was leaning against the car, smoking. Approaching the dark figure, I saw it was a young man, around my own age, tall and skinny with dark hair that fell over his forehead. Getting closer, I noticed he was unusually, almost unnaturally, handsome with angular facial lines and high cheekbones. I'd never seen him around either. Where did all these people come from?

"Good evening, Ivan," Natasha greeted the man politely. "Thanks for arriving here so quickly."

Ivan threw the rest of his cigarette on the floor, stomping on it, so the light faded. "No problem," he said in a pleasant baritone that echoed through the silent night, "I was in the neighbourhood anyway when you called, doing some work down in Sopot."

I glanced up, surprised that he mentioned Sopot. I'd never seen him around there either, but then why would I? I lived there for no longer than six months and didn't socialise a lot.

"Well, thank you anyway. Can you get us all to Agram? To our place?" Tomislav asked him.

"Sure, no problem. I'm finished for the night and headed home too.

All three of you going to your house then?" He asked and, as if noticing me for the first time, extended his hand to me. "I'm Ivan, nice to meet you."

I shook his hand and said in reply, "Sofija. Nice to meet you too."

I liked him instantly, without even thinking about it. I wasn't given a choice in the matter. It was as if my mind — or heart, I didn't know which — made a decision before I was even aware of it. His eyes were wide, arched by the dark eyebrows; under the feeble streetlight illuminating the night, I noticed they were of stunning emerald-green colour. The shade reminded me of the deepest forest after rainfall, soothing and vibrant. His cheeks were hollowed, but this didn't make him look too skinny. His straight, white teeth looked stunning in contrast with his slightly tanned skin. His clothes were casual, just a pair of jeans and a black t-shirt; no hint of a caste, just like Natasha and Tomislav.

A strange, overwhelming notion of familiarity washed over me the moment our hands touched. Somehow, I felt as if I knew this beautiful man already, even though I was perfectly aware I'd never seen him before in my life. It was like we both knew, at that moment, that our relationship — whatever its nature might be — would start from the middle, instead of the very beginning. For one brief second, as our eyes met, I knew he felt the same way.

It's just another odd thing, add it to the list, I thought to myself. *Get a grip*, Sofija. Pushing yet another strange occurrence out of my tired mind, I followed Natasha to the back seat.

Soon we were driving down the winding road among dense forests towards Agram. Tomislav sat at the front with Ivan, while Natasha and I shared the spacious back seat. It was nearly ten p.m. now. Time to call Grandma, or she'd be worried sick. I took out my phone and dialled.

"Sofi, thank God. Are you okay?" She sounded livid.

"Yes, I'm fine. Just arrived at the hotel room and going to bed. I'll give you a call tomorrow again."

"Okay, dear. Sleep well. We love you."

"I love you both, too."

I could feel Tomislav's and Natasha's glances on my face. Ivan was looking at me in the back mirror, his eyebrows raised in half-amusement.

"Just arrived at a hotel room, huh? The Esplanade or the Palace?"

He asked, smirking. I averted my glance, blushing.

"It was my grandma. I didn't want to worry her with the whole 'ran out of the train' business. She has enough on her mind as it is." All three of them nodded in understanding and dropped the subject immediately. A rush of gratitude washed over me; the day has been too long, and I was exhausted.

As the darkness surrounded us, I felt my eyelids drooping and my head falling. Soon, I was walking the familiar cobbled streets, heading for a small café with emerald roses on tables, set opposite the little square with a well I passed so many times before. Shortly after, I was knocking on the familiar small door with a figure of a two-faced man on its brass knocker. As the door opened, I heard someone calling my name from somewhere far away.

"Wake up Sofija… wake up, we're here."

My eyes opened. Natasha was tugging on my arm, gently, waking me up. "We're nearly at our house. Welcome to Agram," she said, smiling down at me.

I propped myself up on the car seat. By the looks of it, I had been sleeping bent against the window and could feel subtle pangs of pain in my neck. The dark streets of Agram were eerily empty in the late-night hours. The car clock said it was one in the morning. Looking out of the window, I couldn't make out much. We were now passing a large park to our right, old art-nouveau buildings to our left. A few minutes later, a grand yellow building came into view, set in the middle of a large square adorned with a large, circular fountain at the front.

"That's the Danubian National Theatre," Natasha said, noticing I was peering at the building. "And the one opposite the street is Law University." I leaned forward to look through her window and saw a tall, regal-looking building with a bright facade and two flights of stairs approaching the entrance from both sides. A large statue of a woman sitting Indian style was set at the front, right in between the two flights of stairs. She was holding a large stone tablet in her lap.

"The statue is called *the history of Danubians*. Don't ask me why; I suppose the woman is a personification of Danubia or something. I'm not big on the history of art," Natasha explained.

"It looks even better than I imagined," I said, looking around as we drove further into the city centre. We passed by countless old buildings surrounded by large, green surfaces, restaurants and cafés (although closed now). The elevating feel of a grand, bustling city made me cheerful after the long and tiring day. I couldn't wait to have a better look around the next day, maybe visit a museum or two or have a walk by the river. Perhaps I could squeeze it in before catching the train back.

Then I remembered my predicament. I might not be able to go back that soon if what Tomislav and Natasha told me was true. What would happen to my grandpa? How would I explain my absence at work, and what would Grandma say? Overwhelmed by sudden worry, I pushed the thought out of my mind and concentrated on the night scenes of Agram out the car window.

Soon we were stopping in front of an old but handsome art-nouveau building in the city centre.

"This is where you live? It seems very central," I asked, impressed.

"Yes, it's a great location. We've just passed the Zrinjevac park, and one street away is the Main Square," Tomislav explained, with a hint of pride in his voice.

"Ivan, you coming with us for a nightcap?" Natasha asked.

Ivan shook his head, looking drained. "No, thank you, Natasha, I think I'll cross back, today's been very long."

Then he turned in his seat and looked at me. "Nice to meet you, Sofija. Good luck and see you soon."

He gave me the most beautiful smile I've ever seen. *Don't melt, Sofija* — I thought to myself — *or they'll have to mop you off the car floor.* That would be beyond embarrassing.

The three of us bade him goodbye and walked into the building. Tomislav and Natasha's apartment was on the second floor. There was no lift, but we had no luggage, so it didn't matter.

The apartment was small but very cosy, with bright walls and cream-coloured furniture. The small, narrow hallway opened to a large living room, a wooden coffee table and a soft couch loaded with pale blue cushions in its centre.

"Look, I don't want to intrude. I'm happy to go and find a room for the night," I said, thinking my actual plan of finding a comfy bench at the train station wouldn't go down well with the pair of them.

87

"That is out of the question. You're staying here with us. It's too late for you to be wandering around Agram on your own. You're welcome to sleep on the sofa," Tomislav said firmly. I knew there was no point in arguing and, in any case, I preferred their couch to a bench.

Natasha fussed around, looking for spare pillows and blankets, showing me the bathroom and the small kitchen.

"Sorry for the mess, we haven't been here for a while," she explained. Seeing my baffled expression, she added, "We were in Tayna for the past few days, took sick leave at work. I was a bit worried that going out without caste bands and clothes would be pushing our luck, but it all went well in the end." It seemed she was talking more to herself than to me, so I didn't question her further or made any comments. Somewhere in the back of my mind, I still thought that this Tayna Natasha and Tomislav kept on talking about was just a figment of their imagination. Still, I wasn't going to tell her that.

"Help yourself to anything from the fridge," Natasha went on, peering at me over the kitchen counter, "there isn't much, but I'm sure you'll find something edible for breakfast. We leave for work at eight-fifteen a.m., but you don't have to go that early — the Main Square is just a few minutes' away. We'll leave you a spare key on the coffee table."

"Thank you, Natasha, I'll be fine. I'm very grateful for your help. Go to sleep now, you must be exhausted."

I had to repeat several more times that I had everything I needed before she and Tomislav finally retreated to the bedroom.

I woke up early the next morning, feeling fully rested. I must have dozed off on the couch, as I didn't even change into pyjamas Natasha laid out for me. My hosts' muffled voices were coming from their bedroom. Having gone through my morning rituals, I knocked on their door softly. "I'm up, you don't have to whisper! Good morning."

A second later, Natasha opened their bedroom door, smiling widely. She was fully dressed, wearing a yellow pencil skirt and a white shirt, a yellow caste band on her wrist. Tomislav waved at me from a small balcony adjacent to their bedroom. So, they're in the Zolta, I thought. Researchers, perhaps? Or doctors?

"Morning, Sofija! Did you sleep okay?"

"Yes, it looks like I didn't move a centimetre all night. I must have been dead tired."

Natasha fixed me some coffee and showed me once again where everything was in the kitchen ("Please, make yourself at home... don't forget to eat...") I agreed to meet them at a bistro in the city centre at noon.

"You mustn't leave while the travel ban is in place. They are looking for you now and won't stop anytime soon. Please just trust us on this and don't attempt to go anywhere, at least not before we talk again," Tomislav was pleading with me.

They were so kind I had no choice but to agree, especially after seeing how worried they both were. I still felt like Tomislav and Natasha knew me somehow and that I should know them too, but I couldn't remember. It was a strange sensation, one that made me trust them.

They were almost out the door when Tomislav turned and said: "Oh, and bring your things with you, we might not be coming back here tonight." I had no idea what he meant but decided not to dwell on it for the time being.

After my hosts left for work, I enjoyed sitting at the kitchen counter, taking in the view out the small window. Countless Agram roofs spread upon me, the sounds of early morning chatter filling the room.

Since I hadn't brought any clothes with me, Natasha offered her wardrobe. We were about the same size and everything she gave me fitted well. I chose a pair of jeans and a beige t-shirt. It was warm outside, so I put the navy-blue blazer in my messenger bag for later.

My hair was falling limply against my shoulders, the turquoise strand combed down neatly to one side. I didn't want to conceal it today; it felt wrong to do so somehow.

At nine a.m., I was out the door and walking towards Main Square. The narrow streets leading to the square were packed with colourful little shops, souvenir stalls and bakeries. Delicious whiffs of freshly roasted coffee and pastry filled the air as people sat outside, enjoying their morning cupful before departing for work. Five minutes later, I was standing on the Tanatos Square, dominated by a giant statue of President Tanatos in the very middle of it. On one end, a large circular fountain was surrounded by people sitting on the steps around it, sipping their coffee and chatting animatedly. On the other end, a tall clock showed it was now ten past nine. I could see the green-and-white pharmacy sign just behind the clock. Since I still had some time left, I walked to the small bakery in a narrow, cobbled alley behind the pharmacy and purchased a chocolate croissant.

A few minutes later, I found myself standing underneath the large clock, leaning against its stone pedestal, and enjoying the warm croissant. It was such a pleasure watching the people passing by, hurrying to work, or taking their children to school. Just behind the square was a small market, bursting with colourful flowers and fruits. Even though I had no idea what this day would bring, and though I was dead scared of being stuck here on my own, I couldn't help but feel slightly happier now. I'd always wanted to see Agram, and now here I was — though under unfortunate circumstances. Perhaps I'd be able to return to Velesh within a week, after all, surely the government will forget all about me and my illegal permit. Maybe they'd think the tip was incorrect or something, I thought with a surge of hope. I wish I knew who told on me, and why.

The most important thing right now was to get that medication to Grandpa as quickly as possible. Tomislav said a safe delivery could be arranged.

At nine-thirty, I was waiting outside the pharmacy at the edge of Tanatos Square. I could see a tall, older man walking in my direction. He was wearing a blue work blazer, like mine, and carrying a small paper bag with a green pharmacy logo on it. Somehow, he recognised me straight away and, approaching me, he said, "Good morning. Thanks for being on time. This is for you." He handed me the paper bag and added, "It would be best to put it away for now."

He glanced around nervously as if expecting to see spy cameras on top of the surrounding buildings.

"Thank you. How much do I owe you?"

"It'll be four hundred dukats, please. This stuff is costly, and I managed to get it at a discounted price." I looked up, surprised. That was a lot of money. Taking out my purse, I counted four hundred dukats and paid him.

"Thank you," he said, "hope your grandfather gets better soon. I have to go now if you don't mind."

"Not at all. Thanks again!" And, with not so much as a backward glance at me, he disappeared behind the pharmacy entrance.

I stood there, staring inside my half-empty purse. That was a whole week's worth of money. Opening the paper bag, I found a small bottle with tiny yellow pills in it. Hopefully, this would last at least a month. If I had to stay there, then finding a job would be a good idea, especially if Grandpa would need more of the pills to get better. And with that thought, I took out my phone and called Helena.

"Hey. What's up?" she answered after one ring.

"Morning, dear. Listen, I had to leave for Agram yesterday to get Grandpa's medication. I'm still here and will have to stay for a while."

"What, why? Did something happen? And how did you manage to get there yesterday with the travel ban in place?"

"I took the last train. I'll explain everything when I see you. Can't do it over the phone." There was a short pause before I added, "I know I'm asking a lot lately, but could you please just cover for me until the end of next week at least? Tell them I'm sick or something... anything."

I listened, prepared for more questions to come. But once again, Helena refrained, and I was thankful.

"Okay, Sofija. I'll cover for as long as I can," she said.

"Oh, and... I won't be able to make it to Igor's party. Sorry," I added in a sad voice.

"Don't worry about that," she replied quickly, and I assumed she was cutting it short for the supervisor's sake.

"Thank you so much. Talk soon. Bye."

I checked the clock; it was a quarter to ten. I had just over two hours at my disposal before meeting Natasha and Tomislav in the Old Town. The address was written on a piece of paper in my purse.

Having had breakfast already, I decided to do some sightseeing. There was a small street sign opposite the pharmacy where I was standing, pointing to the left. It said 'Agram Old Town'. I headed towards the sign and turned left as instructed, grabbing a city map from the tiny tourist office on the way. The winding stone steps led upwards, to the medieval tower perched on the hill. I started climbing, enjoying the picturesque view over the red rooftops rising before me. Halfway through I noticed a funicular on the other side of the small hill but was glad I took the stairs instead. I enjoyed walking, especially in such beautiful weather. Reaching the top, I found myself at the beginning of a narrow promenade with a medieval-looking tower at its far end. The walk was deserted, with most people working in the busy downtown. I took the right turn at the tower and ended up in the middle of a small, cobbled square with a Baroque church on its far end. My eyes narrowing against the morning sun, I noticed a little café opposite the church with several people sitting on the terrace.

"It is the Blue Queen! The truth will out! It will!"

Startled, I turned around and saw a street beggar sitting on the ground, looking at me with his bulging eyes and pointing with bony fingers. He seemed upset and somehow excited at the same time.

"I'm sorry, did you say something?" I asked, not sure if I heard him correctly.

"The truth will out, my queen!" he bellowed again. Then, as if looking for something, he stood up and searched the pathway around the spot where he was just sitting. "Have you seen my gems? My precious gems!"

I had no idea what the man was talking about. He was middle-aged, wearing old, ripped jeans and a faded grey t-shirt. His hair was untidy and greying, his face expression insane. I wasn't afraid of the insane. Instead, I felt sorry for them and had the need to help if I could. Experience taught me to beware of those who concealed their weaknesses, rather than those who showed them openly, like this poor man. I took out my purse and gave him some change, but he started shaking his head and backed away.

"Don't need the money, my queen. Only my gems. Where are my precious gems?!"

"Good luck finding your gems, sir," I said before placing the money in a small metal cup next to him. "In the meantime, take this — it's not much but could buy you a coffee," I said, nodding towards the small café at the edge of the square. He stared at me, eyes wide. Then he nodded and, picking up his cup, walked away, towards the Baroque church.

Our Supreme President Tanatos didn't care about the Siva caste, I thought bitterly. He only cared about the powerful and the rich, knowing they will help him keep the presidency in return. The whole caste system was utterly ludicrous and only serving his power-mongering goals. By dividing the people into seven artificially created castes, he pitted the groups against one another. Everyone stayed exactly where Tanatos wanted them to be, both in life and otherwise.

There was no freedom in Danubia. But it always astounded me how many people didn't realise what was right in front of them. They had no idea that they were no longer free. Most Danubians somehow missed the fact their freedom of speech and expression was limited, if not non-existent. Instead, they chose to ignore the blatant ban on local customs and any type of cultural expression. 'We are one', goes the mantra, 'and as one we shall strive'.

But Danubia wasn't always "One". Not so long ago, it consisted of autonomous regions, each with its cultural heritage. Older people still whispered of old patriotic songs, of local fairy tales and folklore. Now, these regions were replaced with artificial kantons, each excelling at one particular industry. Local customs were banned under Tanatos' recently formed government. They served us the excuse of "Removing any reason for competition between the kantons of Danubia".

Unfortunately, most people bought the feeble excuse. It seemed he was trying to kill any individual spirit to pave the way for an easier rule. The communities grew stronger where local customs were present, and that was precisely what he wanted to avoid. A strong community would recognise his foul motives and his lousy rule. A united people would have replaced him and his minions with someone better.

Tanatos appeared in every newspaper, on every television and looked down on us from every billboard. The pale, pointed face with eyes as black as onyx, dark beard and slicked-back hair were all too familiar. His velvety voice made me shudder every time I heard it. It was so very dishonest and malevolent. Even his eyes looked evil, or at least I thought so. Some of my female colleagues found him handsome and told me I had poor taste. Even though Tanatos was around fifty years old, he looked remarkably 'well preserved', as Helena mockingly called it. The man didn't look a day older than thirty-five.

I checked the clock and saw it was half-past eleven already. I would meet Natasha and Tomislav in half an hour. Taking the piece of paper Natasha gave me this morning out of my purse, I saw the name of the bistro was Kairos. I recognised the word immediately. Wasn't that the password to Goran's place too? It might be a coincidence, I thought, although I wasn't too sure any more. Looking up the address on a city map I picked earlier, I saw the place wasn't far, only a ten-minute walk away. Noticing it was situated by the river, I headed there straight away, hoping to have some spare time to visit the riverbank.

Chapter 11
Kairos

Walking towards the bistro, I took out my mobile and called Grandma. It's best to get it done now since I had no idea what Natasha and Tomislav had planned for today.

"Morning, Sofi. Are you all right?" She sounded as anxious as yesterday. Attempting to calm her down, I said:

"All is fine, I got the medication and will send it to you shortly. I might have to stay here for a day or two due to the travel ban. I've been told it might not be smart to travel back while the restrictions are in place."

I waited for a few seconds for her reaction, silently. Then came a deep sigh of relief. Puzzled, I asked:

"Grandma? Is everything okay?"

"Yes, Sofi, it is. Might be best that you stay where you are for a while, I agree. Please don't travel just yet. How's the hotel? Do you have enough money? Stay at least until the end of the week, sure you can fix it at work."

I was surprised at her willingness to agree with me on this. She was so insistent that I should return as soon as possible yesterday. Was this travel ban really such a serious issue?

"Okay, I'll send the medication as soon as I can and stay here until the restriction is lifted. Don't worry about the money, I have enough." The last sentence was a lie, but since I wasn't paying for the hotel room anyway, I didn't have to worry just yet. In any case, I wouldn't accept any more from my grandparents, knowing how thin their savings were already.

I bade her goodbye, told her to kiss Grandpa for me and hung up.

Not paying attention to my surroundings while I was on the phone, I now stopped in my tracks, frozen. This was the exact same street I always walked down in my dream. I was standing in the narrow, cobbled alley, opening to a small square with an old well to the right. I must be dreaming, I thought, fighting the urge to rub my eyes awake; except that I wasn't dreaming. I was standing in the middle of my dream setting. Turning left, I saw the small café, loud chatter coming from the inside. A large, wooden sign was placed above the door, reading 'Kairos Café'. Now trembling head to foot with anticipation, I approached the entrance and opened the door.

Unusual, emerald roses stood in vases on low, wooden tables with ottoman chairs. The walls and the long bar were a vibrant mahogany colour, just like every time I dream-visited. Nearly every table was packed with people talking animatedly. No one paid attention as I entered and headed towards the back of the café, looking for the small door with a two-faced man on the brass knocker. And there it was, just like always. What is this, I wondered? How come I dreamt of this place so many times, and I've never even been here before? *I must be losing my mind.* Just like that street beggar who kept on calling me his queen. There was no other explanation.

"Are you okay, dear?" A plump waitress with kind, round face and blonde hair arranged in a tight ponytail was beaming at me questioningly over the counter. "Can I get you something to drink?" she asked.

"I'm fine, thanks. This place just looks so... familiar," I managed, still in shock and staring at the small wooden door with the familiar brass knocker on it. What was I supposed to tell her? 'I visited your café many times in my dreams? She'd call the ambulance to have me examined probably. I might as well go back and make friends with that beggar, at least I'd know someone when I'm degraded to the Siva.

Fighting the overwhelming urge to open the door, I took a seat at the nearest empty table and ordered a glass of elderflower juice. Natasha and Tomislav should be here soon, hopefully, ready to finally answer my ever-growing list of questions.

"One elderflower juice," said the blonde waitress, setting the tall glass in front of me. "Is this your first time in Agram?" She seemed friendly, though a bit too chatty for my taste.

"Yes, it's my first time here. Not the last, too, I hope."

"It is a pretty place, lots to do and see. Well, enjoy your stay. Let me know if you'd like something to eat, our food menu is excellent," the waitress said, walking back to the bar.

I was halfway through my drink when the door opened, and two familiar figures came in. Waving at Natasha and Tomislav, I motioned with my hands that they should join me.

"Good morning! You all right? Got everything done?" Natasha asked. She meant had I received the pills.

"Yes, all is done. I walked around a little, it's a beautiful city," I said, hoping that'll do for small talk. I was eager to get to the point as soon as possible.

"So... what are we doing? Will we go to Tayna? Are we taking the train or something, 'cause I'm not sure if that's clever while the travel ban is—"

"We're not taking the train, no," Tomislav interrupted, for some reason amused by my question, "we'll be walking in shortly."

"Walking in? From where? What are you talking about?" I asked, puzzled and confused. I hated feeling this way and could already sense the frustration building up.

"No point putting it off any longer," he said, sighing deeply with a worried look on his face.

But he wasn't talking to me. Instead, he was looking from Natasha to the plump waitress I just spoke to. The waitress nodded in understanding and disappeared through the door behind the bar. *I might as well get used to not having a clue what's going on,* I thought. *That's how things worked around here, apparently.*

"Sofija, this question might sound strange, but is this café at all familiar to you? Like you've... been here before?" Tomislav asked, whispering the last sentence. I stared at him. Does he know of my dreams? But that cannot be! I had no idea what to answer, so I just stood there, my mouth half-open, staring from Tomislav to Natasha.

"I'll take that as a yes," he said, and then went on, reading my bewildered expression correctly, "You're not going crazy. Everything will make sense soon."

His words were meant to calm me down, but they just aggravated my paranoia. Were they just as insane as I was, or worse? I didn't even know these people, yet here I was, agreeing to travel with them to someplace I've never heard of before. Fear froze me on the spot, and I nodded, feeling beyond stupid. I didn't have anywhere else to go, and nothing better to do so might as well see this through.

The blonde waitress was back, carrying something small in her hand. It looked like a key, and I somehow knew exactly what she was about to do. At last, I was about to walk through the wooden door with a brass knocker in the shape of a two-faced man.

"In you go. See you later and good luck," said the waitress, smiling warmly at me.

"Thank you, Lydia. Until next time," I heard Natasha saying to the waitress.

The wooden door stood ajar, and I looked through it. Right on the other side of the door was a sunny street. I could only see a tall palm tree and a stone bench next to it. It was so curious; the stone bench stood no more than two metres away from the dark café floor.

I followed Tomislav and Natasha through, no longer scared despite the loud thudding in my chest. After all, this was where I had been hoping to go for as long as I could remember. This door only recently opened in my dream, but I woke up before walking through it. The sensation was so strange, I had to pinch my hand to make sure I was still awake.

Chapter 12
Magic

"Welcome home, Sofija," said Tomislav, a broad grin stretching across his face.

I looked around. We were standing at the beginning of a long promenade paved in shiny, white stone. I glanced behind, but the cosy café was gone; instead, all I could see was an opening between tall cypress trees that led to what looked like a park. To my left, a large water surface of stunning, deep-blue colour was glinting in the sun. Several small boats were parked in the marina, slowly swaying in the mild wind. To my right, palm trees and benches lined the empty promenade, a Gothic bell tower rising on its far end. Countless bars and restaurants lined the footpath, all closed and deserted even though it was midday. Behind the long line of bars and restaurants stood tall, ancient-looking walls of what looked like an old town.

"Come, we better move on," Natasha urged, towing me towards the ancient walls. I stared around as she directed me, amazed. How come we had just walked into a seaside town? The nearest coast was hundreds of kilometres away from Danubia. Not knowing what to think, I concluded it must be a dream and let Natasha lead me towards the old town.

We crossed the promenade and went through the narrow passage between a deserted ice-cream parlour and an expensive-looking restaurant. Soon, we found ourselves in a basement-like construction, featuring empty stalls on both sides. Walls and the vaulted ceiling were made of dark brick, the only source of light coming from narrow openings at both ends. On the far end of the structure, I could see the stone steps leading up. Natasha and Tomislav motioned for me to keep on walking, and I followed them up the steps.

"Where are...", I started, puzzled.

Natasha interjected quickly, "Not here."

I closed my mouth shut and followed them in silence. The steps led us from the basement into a spacious square surrounded by magnificent stone buildings that looked like they've been around for at least a millennium. To my right, a large stone terrace took up half the square. Its front was adorned with pretty red bricks and giant half-lion, half-human statues laying on both sides. Sphinxes, I realised.

The square was stunningly beautiful, oozing with history. But the overall feeling was that of sadness, looming over the unnaturally empty streets, bars, shops and restaurants. Where were all the inhabitants, I wondered.

Soon we arrived at the entrance of an old hotel, looking deserted and neglected. It was tucked behind the beautiful ancient square and housed in an old stone building with pretty green windows. It didn't seem there was anybody inside though, or that it was even open. For the umpteenth time, I looked from Natasha to Tomislav, puzzled. What were we doing here?

Both of them were rummaging through their pockets, searching for something. A moment later, Tomislav produced a stick of sorts, short and made of metal. On top of it was something blue and brilliant, glinting against the afternoon sun. Natasha was holding a necklace adorned with a similar sort of thing, only glinting in emerald light. I soon realised those were gemstones. Curious things to carry around, I thought. I watched them silently, as they pressed the gems (Tomislav using the tip of the strange metal stick) against the small, circular dent just underneath the doorknob of the rundown hotel. Almost as if the stones were card keys, like those you get at hotels.

The door handle turned, clicked, and Tomislav pushed the heavy door open. He then looked both ways, making sure the street was deserted, and a moment later, he disappeared inside. Natasha encouraged me to follow, and, for the second time that day, I stepped into the unknown.

Fully expecting to walk into an empty room, I was surprised when loud chatter and the smell of coffee greeted me on the other side. At least a dozen unfamiliar people were sitting around circular coffee tables and conversing or playing board games. I stood at the entrance, unsure of what to say. The hotel didn't seem neglected at all from the inside. It was only a little shabby, as if in desperate need of renovation. Nevertheless, the place looked lived in. I noticed lots of fresh flowers (the unusual emerald roses stood on one of the coffee tables), colourful curtains and a large fireplace on the far end of the spacious lounge.

"Welcome to the Tayna Defenders' League Headquarters Sofija," Natasha said softly, "come, meet our friends."

I had no idea what the Tayna Defenders' League was but decided not to ask just yet. Natasha led me towards the only unoccupied table at the back of the hotel bar, next to the (now unused) fireplace.

As we were passing the tables, Natasha introduced me to some of the people in the lounge. Weirdly enough, most of them nodded in understanding, as if they knew who I was. A tall, blonde man with shoulder-length hair and beard exclaimed, "Ah, Luka's daughter! Nice to meet you, young lady," before he shook my hand a bit too enthusiastically. I gave Tomislav a questioning look, but he just smiled at me.

Finally, Natasha and I arrived at a small coffee table in the corner. The large armchair was cosy, and I sat back, trying to remain patient. I had no idea what was going on, again, but somehow getting used to the constant feeling of bafflement.

Tomislav joined us soon, carrying a large tray full of sandwiches. He put it down, and the petite, short-haired woman with a heart-shaped face we met by the door brought a bottle of white wine, a jug of water and three glasses.

"Is white wine okay, Sofija? I thought this calls for a little celebration," Tomislav said.

I raised my eyebrows, lost as always. "Yes, white wine is great. But what are we celebrating?"

"Your return, of course," said the short-haired woman, whose name I thought was Vesna. She gave me a wide, warm smile, poured three glasses of wine and walked away from the table. I saw her engaging in conversation with other people in the lounge and realised she was a waitress here. Or perhaps a hotel manager.

"Look, I don't mean to be rude, but I have no idea what is going on. Would either of you care to explain please?" I said, barely controlling my frustration.

Tomislav and Natasha sat on the sofa opposite me. After taking a sip, Natasha said:

"What we're about to tell you will sound insane. You might not believe us, but please wait until we're finished, and then you can walk away from here if that's what you want."

I gaped at her, baffled. Then after a few seconds, I nodded, taking a sip of wine and relaxing in my chair. The wine was sweet and delicious, like nothing I'd had before.

"We told you earlier that we were childhood friends with your parents, Alina and Luka. Your mother was born and raised in Tayna, and your father moved here in his twenties, to attend university. Tayna used to have the best university in Danubia," Natasha said.

"Wait, what do you mean? Surely, we're not still in Danubia? We're by the coast!" I protested.

"And that's the first thing you might not believe us. Danubia is a coastal country, and Tayna is its northernmost province. We arrived at the Tayna promenade, and what you saw earlier was the Adriatic Sea."

I sat upright in my chair now, gaping at her. What in the world...?

Tomislav took over, his voice composed. "The government separated Tayna from the rest of Danubia after the last war. The Great Northern Border was built to keep anyone from getting to us. Our representatives were removed from the Duma, and all the new rules and laws were forced on us. We had no say in anything. This division is called the Rift — I'm not sure if it's mentioned in the official Danubian history nowadays."

"You mean the Second Danubian War in 1985?" I asked, happy I finally knew what he was talking about.

"No, that was the Rebellion. I mean the First Danubian War, one which ended in 1955." I pressed my lips tight to stop myself from correcting him, nodding briefly. My frustrated expression didn't escape Tomislav.

"We call the... *war* in 1985 the Rebellion around here since that's what it actually was. The Tayna Defenders League organised it. We tried to break free of our isolation and be recognised as equals with the rest of Danubia once again like we were for centuries. As you know, your parents died in the Re... the war. So did many other people, most of them our friends and family."

Tomislav looked down, lost in thought for a while, his expression sombre.

"After we failed, Tanatos shunted Tayna aside once again, but this time he used a more *effective* method. You see, he erased any memory of Tayna and its magical community, which is why no one in Danubia — mage or nemage, with very few exceptions — knows we exist anymore. This only affected those who found themselves south from the Great Northern Border at the time; Tayna was exempt from it. We're not sure why he spared us. Perhaps he didn't think we'd stay unaware of our abilities for long, even with memories changed." Tomislav shrugged and took a sip of wine before continuing.

"That is the reason you had no idea Danubia had access to the Adriatic coast; Tayna is its only coastal province, and Tanatos made everyone in the rest of Danubia forget about us." He paused for a while, staring at his wine glass. Natasha looked up at him, encouraging him to continue. He spoke again, this time in a slightly angry voice.

"To be more exact, no-one knows of us *apart* from Tanatos and his tight circle, I assume. We call that... *event*" — he spat out the word bitterly — "The Wipe. By taking the nemages' memories about mages and Tayna, he paved the way for an autocratic government."

I only now realised I'd been staring at him, open-mouthed, for the last few minutes. I wasn't at all sure I heard half the things he said correctly. Memories wiped? Magic? *Ne*-mages?

Natasha spoke first this time.

"Tanatos wiped everyone's memories by the use of magic. And he's keeping us subordinated and hidden, knowing we're too few to fight back. You see, the First Danubian War was primarily a conflict between Danubia's magical and non-magical communities. The former community... well, us" — she said, looking around the room — "lost. And then we lost again, as Tomislav pointed out, in the Rebellion twenty-five years ago. Tayna is sometimes referred to as mage Danubia, while the rest of the country belongs to the nemage Danubia. This division happened after the Rift in the fifties, of course."

There was a pause. I gaped from one to the other for a few seconds.

"Magic? Like wands and all that?" I asked finally, starting to laugh. Soon, I couldn't control myself and was nearly choking with a howl,

Tomislav and Natasha along with several people from nearby tables staring at me. When the fit died out, I looked up and said, appreciatively, "Very funny. Ha-ha."

"Glad we made you laugh. I think it's time for a little demonstration," Tomislav said, smirking at me. Natasha nodded at him, like a skilful sidekick, signalling she was ready for the performance.

Tomislav took the small metal stick I saw earlier out of his jeans pocket, sapphire glinting on top of it, radiating in blue light. He pointed the stick at the water jug and gave it a little twitch.

The jug's contents disappeared before my very eyes. Something wet and cold touched upon the back of my neck, then the top of my head. I flinched from the cold, gasping and shifting in my seat in alarm. Looking up, I saw large, white snowflakes coming down from the tall bar ceiling. Natasha's and Tomislav's heads were white with snow that came from nowhere, and I started shivering, more from shock than cold.

"Not that again, Tom! Turn the damn thing off, it's the middle of summer!" the bearded, blonde man who spoke to me earlier shouted over from the other side of the bar.

"Just doing some convincing here, Marko, it'll stop soon!" Tomislav shouted back, still concentrated on the spell he was performing. He put the metal stick down on the table, I noticed, but the snow didn't disappear. He then made a swift hand gesture, mid-air, as if scooping something invisible. The next moment all the snow was gone. A second later, my wine glass was filled with ice cubes, top to bottom. The wine had, by the looks of it, turned into ice as well.

"Elemental magic. Water is one of the elements, of course, and with a little bit of practice, you can control it like this… to a certain degree of course. All magic has its limits," Tomislav explained.

Another scoop mid-air and the ice was gone from my glass. The wine was back, unfrozen, in its previous state.

"Now I've just undone my previous spell. It works sometimes, and only for certain types of magic. One cannot undo death, for example. Or an injury. That would practically mean turning back time, and there's no magic familiar to us that can do that."

The sapphire stopped glinting, and Tomislav picked the sceptre from the table, putting it back into his pocket.

"A mage doesn't necessarily need to hold the vessel — which is this sceptre in my case — to perform magic. It just needs to be very close to your person."

I stared at him, shocked. My mouth opened and closed.

"Lost for words?" Tomislav asked, his lips curling into a smile. He then leaned towards me, his expression serious. "Magic is real, and you have it. Can do a lot more than making it snow I daresay."

"Are you okay, dear? It is a lot to take in," Natasha asked, concerned. There was a long pause as I stared at them across the small table.

"Whatever this is, I don't have it," I managed, my head spinning with questions I wasn't ready to ask.

"Oh, but you do. In fact, you've already passed the test," Tomislav said, raising his glass at me and downing its contents.

Chapter 13
The Myth

"What is that supposed to mean? What test?" I asked, confused. I had no idea what to think any more. It has been easy until now, to believe that Tomislav and Natasha were just silly people or playing some weird joke on me. But now I've actually *seen* magic happening before my eyes.

"Please, just tell me what is going on. How did you just do all that? And what was... that shiny stick you had? The vessel?"

Now it was their turn to laugh at me. It was uncomfortable, sitting there, completely clueless, a subject of ridicule.

Natasha was the first one to get her wits back.

"Sorry, dear, but that was very funny. Shiny stick!" she chortled. "I know it is hard to believe, but magic is real. Only the people with the genetic predisposition can channel and control it — the mages. Both your parents were mages, so are you, too."

There was a long pause, as I sat there, staring at both of them. After a while, I said:

"Believe me, there is nothing magical about me."

She laughed again, and Tomislav snorted loudly, then said,

"You wouldn't have been able to walk through that door in Kairos Café if you weren't of magical lineage. Well, at least you wouldn't have been able to do it without someone else's guidance. See, nemages cannot see that door because it's magical, it's a portal. This is one of the consequences of Tanatos' Wipe; not only did he make the nemages forget that the mages exist, but he also made sure they remain oblivious to anything magical they might stumble upon. He is determined to keep the nemages in the dark of what is really going on."

"I'm sorry... *ne-mages*?" I asked, puzzled.

"Non-magicals. People without a trace of magic in their genes."

"But my grandparents aren't magicals. And from what you're saying, my dad was. And... I am."

"That can happen sometimes. Most likely, your grandparents' parents or siblings were mages. Then the gift skipped the generation," Natasha said and then added, as I opened my mouth to protest, "but it is possible for a person to have magical abilities without ever actually realising it. The magic doesn't always manifest. In any case, memories of any magical lineage would have been removed in the Wipe."

I sat there, thinking back. I did have this unusual ability I always explained as luck. Like when I survived a heavy beating from Davor, or yesterday, when that desk drawer in the City Hall's restricted section caught fire and opened against all odds. At school, I often achieved extraordinary results without doing any work at all. All I had to do was concentrate very hard on the end result I wanted, and it would work out somehow. I called it my inner luck, but perhaps it was something much more than that. Perhaps it was magic, I thought with a sudden surge of hope.

"And what about those tools you just used? The stick?" I asked them, not able to stop myself from believing what they were telling me. The dam was broken, the river surging through it, unstoppable and powerful. It was done.

"The 'shiny stick'," Natasha said with mock air quotations, "that you just saw Tom use is called the sceptre, and the stone on top is his birth gem. Birth gems are used to channel magic."

There was a short pause, and then she asked, "When's your birthday?"

"January the seventh. Why do you ask?"

"January... your birthstone must be garnet. Most mages work best with their respective birth gems. Tomislav was born in September, so he uses sapphire most of the time. My gemstone is emerald." She held her necklace out for me, the one she used to enter the hotel. A small, deep-green stone was glinting on it.

"A mage can master other gems too. Tomislav and I use three gemstones each, but we don't carry them all around as we don't need them very often. The more gemstones a mage masters, the more powerful he is. Since we spend most of the time in nemage Danubia nowadays, the shortage makes it impossible for us to exercise even the simplest of spells, especially with Tanatos watching our every move," Natasha explained.

"The shortage? But I thought Tayna was separated from the rest of Danubia... why would the supplies shortage mean there's... less magic?" I felt like I was missing something. I was right.

Tomislav pitched in, looking up at the ceiling and rolling his eyes. "Another half-information Tanatos served you. It is not a supplies shortage, not the way he presented it. It's a shortage of *magic*. You see, magic last only as long as many people exercise it. It works... sort of like muscles. The more you work out, the more muscular you get, right?"

I nodded in understanding, and he continued, "If a large number of mages suddenly stop using magic, the overall magical potency will weaken. It will take some time, but eventually, the magic will disappear from that location. This brings us back to Tanatos. Since he — stupidly, I might add — banned all the magic from Danubia, it is now nearly gone. I believe several people in his tight circle still use it, whose memories he spared. But that's not enough to keep up the levels. If he — and I suspect that much — uses magic to maintain the ludicrous totalitarian system in Danubia, then he's running on his last reserves. That might explain why there isn't enough food. He doesn't have enough magic to multiply it by magical means, and he doesn't do imports, because, well... he wants to shut the rest of the world out."

"The rest of the world?" I asked, surprised.

Tomislav raised his eyebrows. "You didn't think Danubia was all there is, did you? You must have known something was off. To be honest, I do not understand why people believe his nonsense."

He was right, I never believed it. But something he mentioned earlier didn't add up.

"But can't he just come here and take your magic?" Natasha shook her head.

"It doesn't work that way. You see, magical potency is very much... tied to location. We can create magical reserves here, in Tayna, but it won't work as well, or for as long, in Danubia. The best way to revive magic in Danubia is to exercise it there like we used to. Even though most mages lived in Tayna in the past, we travelled into Danubia for work, and there were a lot of mixed marriages across the two communities. Tanatos still allows us to travel into Danubia for work and even to live there, but unlike before, we're banned from using magic. I think he just prefers to have us under control, he's a paranoid man." There was a pause while Natasha sipped her wine.

Then she continued, leaning towards me and speaking in a hushed voice to not be overheard.

"But this also works in his favour because, with our numbers so low and the constant raids and arrests he's conducting, we cannot fight him. Even if we had enough people, we'd have to go to Danubia to overthrow him, and over there we're powerless. Unfortunately, the bastard will always find more soldiers to die for him, especially with this new personality cult he's got going. Whoever is helping him, they're good. We think he anticipated a moment like this when he'll run out of magic, which is why he's been working on his personal... *likeability* for all these years. He wants to keep the position no matter what."

Natasha finished with a deep sigh, looking over at Tomislav who just shrugged his shoulders.

"He's been doing it all these years. But Tanatos only became president last year." A picture of his pale pointed face and onyx eyes came to mind. The youngest President in Danubian history, the press called him.

"Maybe so, but his family was with the Biela caste from the very beginning... you know, from the Rift. Tanatos' father led the group of Turncoats who made a deal with the nemages just before the war ended in 1955. The nemages got the ways and means of defeating us... and the Turncoats got immunity and seats in the nemage government in exchange. Sweet deal, no?" Tomislav scoffed.

For a moment, I opened my mouth to ask about the "ways and means" to defeat the mages but thought better of it. Tomislav seemed wound up enough. This must be a difficult topic around here, I thought.

"Tanatos took his father's place in the Duma after the last Rebellion. Allegedly, the man resigned to make room for his son. But, as you know, Tanatos didn't become President until only recently. We think he just waited for the right moment to step into the light... didn't want to lose the people's trust, you see. He wants the people to like him, he's smart enough to understand the importance of an excellent public image. The idea of the Wipe came from him, of course."

I frowned, taking in the story. Something didn't add up.

"But if Tanatos' father were a mage, why would he do that to his own people? Why would these Turncoats choose to live in a world where magic isn't out in the open, where it might not even exist one day once the reserves run out?"

Natasha sighed and shrugged.

"Greed? Power hunger? We can only guess. All we know is that, because some of our own switched sides in the war, we lost. If they hadn't gone to the nemages, we might have had a fighting chance. Everything would have been different."

There was another pause while I tried to make sense of everything I've heard. I hated to admit it, but it all finally made sense. It was scary, but it made sense. I'd always hoped there was more to the world than the eye could see; that there was something more behind the mirage.

Now I'd found what I'd been looking for, only it was far more twisted and dangerous than I could possibly have imagined. The prospect of imminent danger didn't repel me, though. I was okay with that part, as long as I prepared for what was coming. Instead, all this time, I've been struggling to believe it all, to believe that magic was real. I, Sofija Filipov, the admin clerk, was somehow... valuable. After hearing all this, I realised for the first time my initial doubt was gone, and I somehow felt I knew Tayna was there all along. It made sense for this city to be here and for the magic to exist. It didn't feel out of place.

I suddenly remembered something else that made sense now.

"I've had these dreams ever since I was a small child, of walking into that Kairos Café we've just visited. I've been seeing... well, actually walking, the same narrow streets, and passing the little square in Agram old town. I've been entering the café and knocking on the back door with the two-faced man on the knocker. How is this possible?"

Tomislav and Natasha looked curiously at me, and there was a short pause. Then Tomislav said, "It could be a memory. Your memory. In the first year of life, our impressions are very strong as our magical abilities develop. This could have made your early experiences more... durable. That's why I asked you if the café was familiar, remember? I thought you might remember it."

He thought some more for a while and then asked, "You said you've been entering Kairos in your dream and then knocking on the back door? Was anyone else with you or were you alone?"

"I was alone, every time."

He glanced at Natasha, and she said, more to him than to me, "Well, her memory could be distorted. She was too young then, barely eight months old."

Seeing my puzzled look, she explained, "The day your parents died, Tomislav met your mother at Kairos Café. There is a portal, at the Kairos, that leads to Velesh. She gave you to him before joining your father. They took part in a diversion against Tanatos' army, you see. As you know, it didn't end well."

"That was the last time I saw Alina," Tomislav explained. Then, as if pushing the thought away, he added quickly, "Anyway, I waited at the Kairos with you until it was safe to go through into Velesh and hand you over to your grandparents. We weren't sure where they were at the time but managed to get hold of your grandfather soon enough. I then went through the portal and gave you to him. I'm sorry to say I haven't seen Marin since. He probably won't remember me now... not after the Wipe."

"My grandparents told me I was taken to the Velesh orphanage after my parents died. They weren't told who brought me there," I said, remembering suddenly.

"And what were you told about your parents' legacy? Did you inherit money or real estate?" Natasha asked.

I just took another sip of wine, almost spitting it all over the table at this.

"Um, no," I said, gulping the wine, "my grandparents provided for me my whole life. If my parents left me anything, I was never informed."

Tomislav and Natasha exchanged looks.

"Can't say I'm surprised," Tomislav said sympathetically. "Tanatos and his followers raided banks and houses of the League members immediately after the Rebellion and took everything they could get their hands on. Your parents lived here in Tayna of course, but their house was burned down after the Rebellion — it's Tanatos' trademark. For some reason, the bastard likes to burn things to the ground." Tomislav said in an angry voice, running both hands through his hair. "We did, however, anticipate this, and saved a little money for you should you ever return."

I looked up, surprised. Tomislav and Natasha smiled warmly at me.

"Each League member contributed money for food and gemstones in the years leading to the Rebellion. We stashed your parents' contributions at our home, here in Tayna. We'll show you later. What's left should last you about a year, I think." They smiled at my shocked expression.

Well, that solves my money worries, at least for a while, I thought. But there was something else that bothered me. I didn't get around to asking it yet, not with all these new pieces of information thrown at me.

"How did you know the government was looking for me last night? And why me of all people? If magic is real, then there must be more mages walking around, not just me. The two of you, for example." It felt weird referring to myself as 'a mage'.

"Oh, and how did you recognise me? I must have changed a lot since I was a baby," I pointed out, grinning.

"Well, the last part was easy. You look exactly like your mother. And Maya might have shown us your picture," Natasha answered, winking at me.

"Maya? But I only met her the other day!" I said, puzzled.

"Actually... you've known Maya for years now. She's one of us, just like her parents. You may know her as Martina."

I gaped at her. "Martina, the waitress? But how?"

"Maya is a shapeshifter. A rare, useful magical skill. She stopped changing as much due to the magical shortage in Danubia," Tomislav explained.

Sceptres with magical gemstones, shapeshifters, memory wipes; the world was upside down, but I felt at home. I grinned, feeling weirdly happy and took a sandwich from the tray in front of me. My stomach finally disentangled enough so that I could eat.

"As for the rest of your question, we were informed that Tanatos or one of his lackeys sent Armiya agents after you. We still have no idea who sent the message, but whoever it was, they're on our — and your — side. As for why they were looking for you specifically... well..."

Tomislav hesitated, eyeing his partner nervously. Chills went through me. What were they hiding, what was so terrible they couldn't spit out? They told me so much already, and I coped well, I thought to myself. How can this piece of information be so much worse than what I'd already heard today?

Natasha was the first to speak this time.

"There is an old... story. Actually, more like a myth, but some people believe it to be true. Allegedly, a child was born at the beginning of the Rebellion. This child is said to have extraordinary skills and unrivalled magic because it comes from an old royal family of Danubia. You won't know this as the Danubian history was rewritten to fit Tanatos' new reality, but Danubia was once ruled by the kings from magical dynasties. These dynasties were exceptionally powerful, keeping all the power among themselves for centuries. They rarely married outside the tight circle. The most magically powerful families came from the so-called Turquoise branch, the same one your mother — Alina — was born into."

I gaped at her.

"You can't seriously think me exceptionally powerful?" I emphasized the last part with mock air quotations. "I don't have unrivalled magic — in fact, I don't have *any* magic!" I heard my voice getting high with agitation but couldn't do much to control it.

Tomislav and Natasha smiled at me, both rolling their eyes.

"We'll see about that. Just because you haven't used magic yet, it doesn't mean you don't have it. As Tom said before, with two powerful mages for parents, you must be magical too," Natasha explained.

"Anyway, we think Tanatos is growing a little nervous. We believe he has been looking for this child, you see, because he's worried. He thinks that this so-called *promised* child — well, now an adult — will start the next rebellion. If you've noticed, many of your peers have been mysteriously disappearing lately. They would always reappear a few days later, not remembering where they were or what they were doing," said Tomislav.

And for the second time today, I started laughing, my shoulders shaking. They stared, puzzled, and I finally managed:

"And you think I'm this... powerful, *promised* child? That's the funniest thing I've heard so far!"

Tomislav and Natasha exhaled loudly, rolling their eyes at me again.

113

"Sofija, we told you — even though you have no magical experience, that doesn't diminish your potential powers. It's in your genes. *We* don't necessarily think you're this promised child... but Tanatos might. And we want to protect you, which is why you're here with us, and not in the rehabilitation centre."

I could see Tomislav wanted me to understand, and to start taking their words seriously. But I just couldn't bring myself to believe I was in any way powerful. Sure, I had a bit of luck getting things my way in the past, but to defeat Tanatos? Even without his magical powers, he was more experienced in fighting than me, not to mention he was physically stronger. And now that I learned he was a mage, how could I ever counter him? The very thought of myself going after him was ridiculous. I pictured myself, armed with a giant sword I could barely hold, running at Tanatos, his pale, handsome face twisting in a broad grin. As if getting rid of an annoying fly, he made a barely noticeable twitch with his index finger, throwing me off. The scene was beyond comical.

"Thank you," I said, now feeling guilty because of my laughing fit. I was utterly clueless, and the pair of them were just trying to help.

"You're welcome," Tomislav said and, as if eager to change the topic, he added, "Do you have your grandpa's medication with you? We'll arrange the delivery today."

"Yes, I do. How are you going to deliver it?" I asked, happy that one problem was solved at least.

"Maya will do it. As you know, she works at Nocturno in Velesh. You can give the medication to her tonight at the party, and she'll make sure it's delivered to your grandparents."

"Okay, that sounds simple enough. Thank you." And then, as an afterthought, I asked, "A party? What party?"

"Your magical Initiation party, of course," Natasha said, a broad smile stretching across her face. "We have to welcome you appropriately, into our society. Well, welcome you back, actually."

An image of some sort of high-society ritual came to mind, with long gowns and decorated face masks.

"I won't have to wear some ridiculous dress and a mask, will I?" I asked, half-joking.

Natasha chuckled. "No, no. No ridiculousness, don't worry. There will be lots of food and drink, some dancing and, of course, your gem ceremony."

My eyebrows flew up. "Gem ceremony? What is that? Can't I just go to the shop and purchase my gemstone?"

"Oh no," Tomislav said, grinning, "it needs to be done properly, not in such a pedestrian way. Your gemstone will, after all, be your weapon for the rest of your life."

"Look at the time!" Natasha exclaimed suddenly. "It's four already! Let's get you settled in your room and give you some time to rest. Big night tonight." She winked at me and stood up, motioning for me to follow her out of the lounge.

Chapter 14
The Initiation

Natasha led me out into the hallway and up the stairs to the first floor of the small hotel. Passing the reception desk, I noticed the hotel name was 'The Bayamonti'. It couldn't have more than ten rooms, I thought. The old building had only two floors and no lift.

As we arrived on the first floor, Natasha unlocked the closest door to the right, and we entered a spacious en-suite room with a small balcony looking out to the deserted street.

"I hope you'll be comfortable here. We'd host you in our house, but Tom and I are rarely there, and it's a bit neglected. At least here you'll have some company and cooked meals. The hotel bar is packed nearly all the time, members of the League visit frequently. Oh, and don't worry — your stay is free of charge," Natasha added as an afterthought.

Not knowing how else to express my gratitude, I gave her a brief hug.

"Thank you so much for everything. This is plenty."

She smiled awkwardly, apparently not sure how to respond to this sudden surge of emotion. As if trying to find something to do with herself, she opened the closet door and started taking out the contents.

"As soon as we learned we'd have to get you, I asked Vesna to stock your closet. It was lucky that I did since you have no luggage with you." She smiled slightly and took out a pretty, floaty dress of deep burgundy colour.

"I think this will do for tonight. Or if you don't like it, here's a pair of slacks... and a button-down shirt..." She seemed taken in by the contents of my closet.

"The dress is beautiful, Natasha. Thank you," I said, sitting down on the bed, "when should I be ready? Is there anything I should bring with me... like a tribute to the community? I have nothing but the stale crisps from the train," I babbled stupidly. I had no idea what lay ahead, but it didn't bother me too much. Instead, I was excited.

Natasha chuckled. "No — just get some rest and dress up for the party. That'll be more than enough."

I nodded. "Should I give you the medicine now... or should I wait to see Maya — I mean, Martina — tonight?"

"Best to give it to her directly. See you at seven, then? Tom and I will meet you downstairs."

After Natasha left, I tried to take a quick nap but couldn't fall asleep from agitation and excitement. Then I took out my phone, attempting to call Grandma, but there was no signal. Thinking it was just a temporary problem, I put the phone away and decided to try again later. Then, I took off my caste band, happy that I could part with it for a while. Hopefully, the horrible rash would heal, I could do without the constant itching. Gingerly, almost as if it were a hand grenade, I placed it in a round metal box I found in the desk drawer, along with keys to my grandparents' house and my bicycle lock key. Closing the drawer, I felt a rush of inexplicable relief at putting the caste band away. I might not need it for a while.

The large bed was comfortable, and the small bathroom was tidy, stocked with the usual bathroom necessities, fluffy towels, slippers and a bathrobe. The room even came with a little writing desk and a minifridge stocked with juice, water and snacks. I ate a chocolate bar and downed a small bottle of water in a few gulps. Curiously, both items reappeared in the fridge the next time I looked. *One of the many perks of being in a magical land is your fridge never gets empty,* I thought, amused.

Three hours later, I was standing by the reception desk, waiting for Natasha and Tomislav. Taking Natasha's advice, I was wearing the floaty burgundy dress that reached to my knees and a pair of elegant high-heeled shoes I found in the closet. Perhaps Maya could fetch some of my clothes while in Velesh, I thought. I should tell Grandma to pack some when I talked to her next. If I managed to reach her, that is. I had tried calling twice since this afternoon and had no luck. I started to think it had something to do with being in a magical province — perhaps phones just didn't work here. If that was the case, I'll just have to go back through the portal and into Danubia. *You are already in Danubia, Sofija. Just the mage one.*

I took the bag with Grandpa's medicine with me, a letter for my grandma inside. I explained I was safe, not going into details, and asked her to pack some extra clothes as I might be staying for a while. Until the travel ban ends at least, I said in the letter.

The entrance door opened and in came Tomislav and Natasha. They were both dressed up — Natasha had arranged her long, wavy blonde hair into a low ponytail and was wearing an ankle-length deep-green dress. Even though she was nearly fifty years old, her pretty face looked younger, only the creases around her eyes gave her away. Her emerald was shining on the necklace chain she wore around her long neck. Tomislav looked much smarter without the flat cap he was wearing the night before and earlier today. His hair was curly and light brown, with some greys here and there. He was wearing jeans and a button-down shirt.

They greeted Vesna at reception and gave me a warm smile.

"You look gorgeous, Sofija! Did you get some rest?" Natasha asked, eyeing my burgundy dress. "That colour suits you."

I blushed stupidly. "Thanks. Before we go, is there a way to check on my grandparents? I tried calling them, but no signal. Grandma will be worried."

Tomislav sighed, glancing up apologetically at me. "We must have forgotten to tell you. Phones don't work in Tayna, not since we'd implemented defensive domes around the whole city to keep us safe from attack. The spells block the network."

My face fell. "No phones? I guess no TVs either?"

Tomislav smiled. "No, but I'm sure you'll find something to do around here." He winked, and I had no idea what he meant.

"So, where are we going?" I asked.

"The party is in the back garden. I think the first guests are already there," Tomislav replied.

"Are you ready to become a mage?"

I thought for a while about the question. "I don't think anyone can ever be ready for that. But I'm looking forward to it, nevertheless," I said, grinning.

As with most things in life, I decided to put all my doubts aside and just jump. I was a champion when it came to throwing myself into new situations without thinking them through. Thinking led to overthinking and overthinking to giving up. I didn't like to give up, so I would usually just — jump.

I didn't notice until now there was a large garden behind the ancient hotel building. It was surrounded by stone walls of the neighbouring houses and beautifully lit for the party. Red and silver lights stretched above our heads, illuminating two rows of wooden tables with benches and a small stage at the back. Soft music was playing from somewhere, but I couldn't locate the band or the stereo. I'd never heard the music before, but it sounded old.

It reminded me of the folk songs I'd sometimes heard in the documentaries about the medieval Danubian kingdom.

We took a seat at one of the empty wooden tables. Tomislav disappeared soon after to fetch drinks from the bar set next to the small stage. While he was gone, more people came in, greeting Natasha and introducing themselves to me. All were mages, Natasha said. Most nemages left Tayna at the end of the First Danubian War over fifty years ago, right after the Rift between the mages and nemages of Danubia. Then, after the Wipe, the nemages forgot Tayna ever existed. Even before the Wipe, she said, Tayna was almost exclusively inhabited by the magical families, with only a small minority of nemages, mostly those who married here. Mixed marriages between mages and nemages were common in the past, but as the links between Tayna and the rest of Danubia grew fewer and fewer, so did the social interactions.

Tomislav returned with a bottle of white wine and three glasses on a tray. The three of us were in deep conversation when Maya and Ivan joined us, carrying more drinks. My stomach did a little jolt at the sight of Ivan, but I ignored it. This was not a great time for romantic endeavours, I told myself. I had enough on my plate without it. I convinced myself over the past few years that it was simply not my destiny to get a happy ending in a romantic sense. Even though I disliked this sort of thinking in other people, finding it cowardly, it was sometimes easier to blame everything on bad luck. At least that way, I wash my hands of any mistakes or lack of trying when the results aren't there — it's just not written in the stars for me. I knew this reasoning won't last long. I'm far from passive and too used to, even fond of, swimming against the tide.

Nevertheless, I told myself to at least try to believe it was not my destiny to be loved and to love, for now. Even two years on, the memory of Davor and everything that went down in our relationship was still fresh. Sometimes, I revisited the cold bench at Sopot Train Station in my dreams. I heard him yelling and saw him swinging at me. I ran, and I ran, but he somehow always caught up with me. And then I'd wake up. Between those dreams and repeatedly re-entering the familiar Kairos Café, it was a miracle I ever managed to get a restful night.

I gave Maya the bag with Grandpa's medication and a letter, thanking her for taking care of it.

"You have no idea how much this means. Grandpa needs those pills urgently." She just smiled and, with a casual wave of a hand, said, "It's nothing. I cross back and forth all the time."

"How come you can cross all the time, though? And how can Tomislav and Natasha work in Agram when all this" — I looked around, waving my hands in the general direction of other people in the garden — "is supposed to be a secret?"

She raised her eyebrows.

"We still have to earn money somehow. There isn't much going on here since most businesses are closed. Tanatos doesn't care if we cross into Danubia as long as we don't tell anyone what's going on or use magic. None of us dares try it, because he has a way of tracing magical activity across Danubia. If any of us attempted anything, Armiya agents would probably arrest us. We'd be playing right into his hands, he'd love a good excuse to put more of us behind bars," she said grimly.

I looked up, surprised. "Tanatos has a way of tracing magical activity in Danubia? But... How come he hasn't captured me by now? I used magic by accident many times."

Maya smiled, shaking her head. "It's not that simple. His system has a flaw... he can only pick up magic channelled through gemstones. What you did were random outbursts, uncontrollable and unpredictable, typical for untrained mages. Tanatos doesn't care much about those who have no clue how to use their powers... those without gemstones, or so to speak – weapons."

I nodded in understanding. So, our Supreme President was specifically searching for those who might be trained in battle. Who might pose a threat? A rush of dread washed over me, and I changed the subject.

"So how come you work in Velesh?" Of all places, I thought but decided to keep the comment for myself.

"My parents owned Nocturno, and I took over. It brings quite a lot of money. Besides, if we never crossed over, we'd have no idea what was going on. No television, or network, you figured that out already I think?"

I nodded in response. It was strange talking to Maya, now that I knew she was actually Martina. Or was it the other way around? I wasn't sure, the whole shapeshifter thing was confusing. I've been going to Nocturno for years and spent a lot of time talking to her. Instead of red-haired Martina, she was now dark-haired Maya, but other than that, she was the same person of course.

"You have no idea what a relief it is not to have to pretend anymore," Maya said, lighting a cigarette. "I've wanted to tell you about all this for years, but of course I couldn't. I promised Tomislav not to mention anything before he gets in touch with you, and he was waiting for the shortage crisis."

I raised my eyebrows at this, surprised. "Why the shortage crisis?"

"He thought it would give us a perfect chance to try another rebellion. Tanatos had to run out of magical reserves eventually, giving us the leverage – he's a very powerful mage, and he is not alone. Some of the Biela members are mages, too," Maya said pointedly. Then, lowering her voice, she continued: "See, if he's out of 'juice', that's only a bonus for us, provided we can use marbles."

When I gave her a questioning look, she explained hastily: "Oh, you know what those are. Tomislav told me he had to throw one at the Armiya guys when you escaped the train. We can store magic inside the marbles and transport it to Danubia, but they do have expiry date."

"Oh yes, I remember him throwing something at them." I commented, remembering suddenly. "But didn't Tanatos know the magic would run out eventually? Didn't he plan for it?" I asked.

Maya nodded, taking a sip and placing the wine glass back on the table in front of her. "That crazy system he's got going in Danubia was never going to last, only long enough for him to establish his rule. After that, magic or no magic — it wouldn't matter. He would've become a supreme ruler or whatever, and everyone would be too scared to say or try anything. Tomislav thought it would be best not to *wake you* — you know, tell you about the Wipe — before we're ready for action. That way, there was no risk of Tanatos capturing you before we're prepared to fight him. Besides... well, you were too young to face all this before now, I think. Tom believed you should get a chance at a relatively normal life and education before you're brought back to Tayna."

Maya was talking very fast. It seemed to me she relished the opportunity to finally have a conversation about something else other than menus, drinks and the boring social life of Velesh.

Before I could process all the new information, she went on:

"That day you came to Nocturno to ask for Goran and the travel permit, I should have known something was about to happen. But I didn't get a green light from Tomislav to clue you in just yet, so I kept my mouth shut." She shot an apologetic look at me across the table. "Then, when I saw the news about the travel ban, I crossed here straight away, but Tom and Natasha were already on their way to get you from the train. Someone informed them you were in danger, but you must already know that."

Almost without taking a break from talking, she quickly lit another cigarette. Inhaling impatiently, she continued:

"Tomislav may not admit it, but he thinks you're the *promised* child." She rolled her eyes at this, and I felt a rush of appreciation for her. "He flat-out refuses to attempt the next rebellion before you're fully trained and ready to join us. Assuming that you're willing to do it, of course." She gave me an insecure smile. "We won't force you, but we do hope that you'll... well, that you'll stay. Even if you're not *promised* or whatever... you must be a powerful mage, and we could use people like you. Not many of us are left, as you can see."

I didn't know what to say. I felt like a big fraud, afraid that these people would just end up being disappointed in me as I didn't have any magical powers. Desperate to change the topic, I asked quickly, "Are you planning to 'wake' all the other mages in Danubia? Are there any left?" Maya thought for a while, then said:

"Most remaining mages relocated here just before the Wipe, especially those connected to the League. Those who were stuck in Danubia were captured by Tanatos and imprisoned as war criminals or driven insane by his interrogation tactics. They wouldn't remember anything now, but I know Tomislav's been trying to reach out to them lately. I wonder if he's had any luck."

There was a short pause as we both sipped our drinks, taking in the injustice of it all. I felt the hatred toward Tanatos grow in me with every passing second. The more I knew, the more it was okay to absolutely loathe his pale face.

Maya was talking again, almost whispering:

"As I said, we didn't want to wake you because Tomislav prevented us. He felt it was vital that you stay where you were for a while. Not that I understand him much, he is a bit weird," — and she gave me a meaningful look at this — "but he's a good man and a great leader. He and Natasha fought in the last rebellion and managed to survive. If you ask me, they have a bit of survivor guilt because nearly all of their friends were killed and the two of them are still with us."

"Who wouldn't, though? They lost almost everyone they cared for," said a familiar male voice. Ivan joined us, sitting next to Maya and across from me. "But I think that's why they're trying to organise the next rebellion. To avenge those who died twenty-five years ago." He was speaking in a deep, seductive voice. I wondered if it only sounded seductive to me. He looked very handsome in a black button-down shirt and jeans. "Natasha and Tomislav are off to prepare the stage for Miss Filipov here, so I thought I'd join you." There was a small pause before he added, "If you don't mind."

"No, not at all," Maya said. She offered him a cigarette, but he declined.

"Trying to quit again?" Maya teased him.

"Just for the night," he said, grinning.

I sat in silence, frozen with the sudden fear. Natasha and Tomislav are preparing the stage for me? Why? Suddenly I was too aware of the curious looks directed at me. The turquoise strand was visible in my long brown hair, and the burgundy dress now seemed too short. Why didn't I just go for the slacks?

I did look forward to testing out my gemstone, though. Then a terrifying thought came to mind: what if I'm asked to use it on the stage, and it doesn't work? What if there's a test to see if I'm worthy of being here? What if they find out they've made a massive mistake?

Tomislav and Natasha's disappointed stares found me, and I shook my head, trying to get the disturbing image out of my mind.

Natasha was saying something, her voice oddly amplified over the loud chatter in the garden. Turning around, I saw her and Tomislav standing on the stage, smiling down at everyone present. The garden was swarming with people, I noticed with a jolt. The long wooden tables were full, and those who couldn't find a seat stood around, sipping their drinks and beaming curiously at Natasha. There must be at least fifty people here, I thought, my heart beating hard.

"… and now, would Miss Sofija Filipov please join us here on the stage. Let's encourage her with applause, everyone," Natasha said. She sounded like a television anchor. I stood there, staring at her, my body immobile. Faint applause followed her announcement, dying out quickly. Then silence ensued, and I could see several people crane their necks looking at me. I still sat on the wooden bench, unable to move.

"Sofija, they're calling for you. Go," I could hear Maya saying under her breath. I tried, but my legs wouldn't listen. I wanted to tell her that, but my lips were somehow sealed too.

Then, a warm hand reached for mine, and I reflexively withdrew. Ivan was looking at me, surprised by my reaction.

"That should have worked," I could hear him saying, more to Maya than to me. *What should have worked?*

Clenching my fists tight at my side, I forced myself to stand up finally. *Don't be a coward, Sofija. Since when are you uncomfortable with public exposures?* Sauntering towards the stage, I saw Tomislav and Natasha smiling broadly at me with palpable relief. I climbed the three steps and found myself standing next to Natasha, fifty-something pairs of eyes glued to my face.

Tomislav approached me with a large and heavy-looking

leatherbound book in his hands. Then he said in an amplified voice as if speaking into an invisible microphone, "On behalf of Tayna's citizens, I, Tomislav Antich, welcome you, Sofija Filipov, into our magical community. This, in my hands, is our Codex of Secrecy. The only rule we ask you to uphold is to keep the existence of magic a secret until such times when we've defeated our oppressors and become free again." He gave me a stern look, making sure I understood him. I nodded in response.

"If you agree, please put your right hand on the Codex and say, 'I accept the Rule'."

Awkwardly and feeling silly, I did as asked. The moment I finished the sentence, dark smoke-like wisps sprang from out of the book and wrapped themselves tightly around my wrist. Then, they stretched forward, entangling around my waist and, multiplying and moving swiftly, around Tomislav's waist too. It was as if we were bound together with a smoke-like rope emanating from the Codex. I glared at the wisps, wide-eyed, but no one else seemed surprised. It was as if they all expected it.

Then, Tomislav said, looking happily at me "You are now one of us, Sofija Filipov," and in an instant, the black wisps were gone. Placing the heavy book on the side table at the edge of the stage, he reached forward and embraced me in a warm hug. The applause broke out again.

Natasha approached me now, carrying something in her hands. It was a small wooden box.

"Here's your gemstone, Sofija. Remember: strive to do good, always." She looked at me, unusual severity in her voice.

I was taking part in an ancient ritual, I suddenly realised. This must be how the Tayna mages had been welcoming new members of their community for centuries. If I was nervous before, her words put additional weight on me. With trembling hands, I took the small box and opened it. Inside, on the bed of dark satin, sat a small, glittering blood-red stone. Natasha said earlier it was called a garnet. It was a gorgeous, dark-red colour.

Gingerly, I took it out and instantly jumped up, startled. The moment the small gemstone landed on my palm, it became warm, just on the verge of being unbearable to touch. At the same time, there was an explosion, so loud I thought it flattened the nearby houses. A thick cloud of crimson smoke covered the entire garden.

Chapter 15
Ivan

A shocked silence followed, and I wondered what went wrong. By the puzzled look on Natasha's face, I assumed this wasn't how the magical Initiation usually went. Then, as if it were never there, the crimson smoke disappeared. I looked down. The garnet stood, cold to the touch again, in my palm.

"Well, I'd say you came in with a bang," Tomislav commented in a low voice, chuckling. I stared at him, confused. *So... what just happened wasn't unusual after all? Did other mages cause explosions upon receiving their gems?*

"You're free to go, Sofija," Tomislav said under his breath and then added to the general audience: "And with this, the formal part of tonight's Initiation is over. Hope you'll all enjoy the wine and food — courtesy of the generous staff at The Bayamonti, as always — and have fun tonight!"

Waiters and waitresses came swarming in from the hotel, carrying plates crammed with food and drinks. They started dancing confidently between the tables, unbelievably fast. Vesna, the receptionist, was moving so quickly, she was a blur. The music, coming from nowhere, now became louder and its rhythm faster.

Still taken by what just happened, it took me a while to find Maya again. Ivan was still there, sipping his wine quietly and staring at me, just like everyone else in the vicinity.

"What is it?" I asked in a puzzled voice. It was getting old, always being stared at and not knowing why.

"That was quite a show," he said quietly, his eyebrows raised, full lips curling into a wide grin., "I guess congratulations are in order," and he raised his glass to me, smiling at my puzzled expression. That strange notion of familiarity washed over me once again, just like last night when I first saw him in front of the Rustica. It was the most peculiar sensation

– my mind was convinced that I knew this man, that I *felt* something for him. But there were no memories of us meeting before yesterday, no interaction of any kind. Somehow, it didn't matter at all, because we didn't need the beginning – we were starting from the middle. *I've been waiting for him,* I realised as inexplicable warmth swam through my body.

I looked from Ivan to Maya, who was watching me too.

"Would any of you mind explaining?"

"Your magical potential is greater than any we've seen since... well, I don't know when the last time was. But it didn't happen in my lifetime for sure." She turned to Ivan and said, smirking at him, "Ivan here might be able to fill in the blanks, though." There was something in the way she said the last sentence. It sounded as if she was referring to some underlying knowledge that was not familiar to me. I didn't want to dig and waited instead for his answer.

"I'll have to disappoint you. I've never seen anything like it before, not from what I can remember." Ivan looked up at me, his large emerald eyes serious and... impressed? "But I've heard stories of course. And the last person to put on a show like this was Alina Bayamonti."

I stared at him. Maya was looking from me to Ivan, sudden understanding on her face.

"Your mother! Of course!" She was now positively beaming at me as if seeing me in a completely new light. "No wonder Tomislav thinks you're the... *you know what,*" she said, noticing my expression. I didn't like to be referred to as their 'promised child'. It put additional weight on me, and I felt lost already, in a completely new world which should be familiar but isn't. With the gleaming gemstone now safely stowed in my purse, which is somehow supposed to allow me to do magic... and I had no idea how. All of this was becoming too much, even without this mythological nonsense Tomislav believed in.

And then there was him. Trying as I was, I couldn't help but feel my stomach quiver every time my eyes flickered to his, and my legs turn into sponges under his gaze. What was this odd pull I felt every time I saw him? Why is he so much different than any other man I'd known? My mind didn't seem to work right around him. Every rule I usually followed didn't seem to apply here; every argument I used to try and stop myself falling for him simply faded before even being formulated. Inside me, a battle brewed.

It's only been a day, Sofija, the inner voice cautioned me. *Have you gone completely insane?* Shaking my head, I dispelled the unwelcome voice. *I know him already, and he knows me. I've been waiting for this.* The inner voice gave up, as if blown away by the gentle summer breeze cooling off the night. It never stood a chance, anyway.

My eyes found Ivan again, taking in his beautiful features; the angular facial lines, the high cheekbones, the dark hair falling casually over his forehead. He came from this magnificent, magical land and no doubt was very skilful in everything he did, and who was I? I couldn't match him in any way, coming from an ordinary, boring world. I could tell him about my exciting days at the Velesh City Hall admin office, I thought with a scoff.

I had to get in touch with Helena as soon as possible. She would not believe a word I told her. And then a sudden realisation hit me, as I remembered the vow I just made, to the magical community of Tayna. I was supposed to keep the existence of magic a secret. That meant I would have to make up more lies to explain my absence, and I hated lying to my best friend.

Now was not the time to think about it, though. The night was warm and pleasant, and more and more people were getting up to dance. An unusual round formation was created in the middle of the garden. People were holding hands, dancing together in synchronised movements in the perfectly formed circle. It was a sort of… choreography. Everyone knew which way to go and what the steps were. I could see women using their gemstones to create beautiful magic at certain moments in between the dance steps. Wisps of red, green, blue, gold and violet filled the summer air. Everyone was laughing and singing along to the fast, traditional-sounding music. I wish I knew the steps, too, I thought to myself. I have always enjoyed dancing.

Suddenly, I heard the clattering of dishes, and the pleasant smell of the homemade food filled my nostrils. Large trays of pastries were brought to every table. I could see all types of mini *burek*: cheese, spinach, meat, mushroom and potato. My favourite small *kifli* sat next to large platters of Danubian goat cheese, prosciutto and *kulen*. Vesna, the receptionist, appeared from somewhere with a bottle of champagne and a piece of chocolate cake in her hands. I was surprised when she put both right in front of me.

"A little welcome gift from all of us at The Bayamonti. Congratulations!" she half-sang the last part, smiling widely at me. Then she produced a cake candle from her apron pocket, conjuring a tiny ball of fire out of nowhere and lighting the candle with it. I beamed at her, noticing a light-blue gem gleaming from a necklace she was wearing. "This is to celebrate your rebirth as a mage! Just a little joke we do around here at Initiations."

"Thank you!" was all I could manage without hugging her.

"Go on, Sofija, make a wish!" I turned around and saw Tomislav and Natasha approaching me. Maya and Ivan were also beaming at me from the other side of the table. I closed my eyes, and, thinking of nothing in particular, blew the candle.

There were soft whistles and claps from all sides of the wooden table, and I could hear shouts of welcome from all directions. Overwhelmed, I could feel my cheeks burning. For something to do, I drank some more wine and turned to Natasha who was now sitting next to me.

"Thank you once again for everything. I hope I don't disappoint as a… mage." It was strange to say the word, and even stranger to refer to myself as a mage.

We spent the next hour feasting on delicious food and wine. I found out from Maya that the Secrecy oath was added after the Wipe; Tanatos' condition for leaving Tayna and its citizens be, for a while at least. The bastard has his claws everywhere, I thought bitterly. The dancing crowd returned to their tables to eat, but the party was just getting started. Savoury food was now replaced with all kinds of tiny bite-sized cakes, from coconut balls to chocolate cubes. Vesna and other waiters from her team were moving between the tables, as quickly as before, offering refreshments. Ivan motioned for her to stop at our table and ordered five shots of rakija. Clinking our glasses together, Tomislav, Natasha, Maya, Ivan and I downed the contents in one gulp. The strong plum spirit burned my inner organs but felt good.

"We've got you something," Tomislav said, glancing pointedly at

Natasha who rummaged through her handbag. She produced a small, shiny package.

"A welcome gift from the two of us. Every adult mage gets a guardian upon their Initiation; someone to guide and protect them, other than their parents. It's like a magical godfather, only for young adults," he winked, "of course, magical Initiations usually occur on a person's eighteenth birthday, so you might not need as much guarding since you're older now... but anyway, we thought I could be your guardian. If you agree, of course," He said in a half-apologetic, half-hopeful voice. I beamed again.

"No one better," I managed and gave him a brief hug.

Tomislav released me after a few seconds, smiling fondly at me. "Well, as your guardian, this is mine — and Natasha's — gift to you. Hope you like it." They were beaming at me, expectantly. Ivan and Maya stopped their conversation too, watching us from across the table.

I opened the small packet and inside was a tiny jewellery box. Gingerly, I took the lid off and found a silver ring inside. It came with a large square mounting in the middle, and I knew why immediately.

"Should I put my garnet in here?" I asked, looking up at Natasha.

She gave me a soft smile and nodded. "Yes, we'll get it fixed for you. There is a spell, it modifies the size of your gemstone and fits it into your chosen magical vessel. If you like the ring, it can be your vessel."

"I love it!" I said, trying the shiny ring on. It fitted perfectly.

I was hoping to ask so many questions that night but decided to wait until the next day. Most of all, I wanted to know about the explosion that happened on the stage, and about my mother, Alina Bayamonti. Wasn't the hotel called The Bayamonti? Was it a coincidence or did the building belong to her (and my, I realised) family?

But I was in such a good mood, feeling unburdened for the first time in forever, that I decided the questions could wait. I caught myself stealing glances at Ivan more often than before.

He was, I noticed with a jolt of excitement, glancing in my direction more often than before, too. Or perhaps I only imagined it? Maya was gone somewhere, probably to talk to other people in the garden, and he was suddenly sitting on her spot, opposite me.

"More champagne?" he asked, reaching for the bottle.

I tried to say no. I should have said no. But...

"Yes, why not. Thanks."

He poured the sparkling golden liquid, his movements as swift as Vesna's. If I'd tried to do it the same way, I'd spilt the wine and probably dropped the bottle halfway through. I realised I was staring, and he explained:

"One of the many perks of using magic daily is extraordinary speed, strength and agility. You'll realise soon enough."

I couldn't believe how seductive his voice was and how elegantly he moved. Everything he did, even the simple things, he did seductively. Or perhaps I was just losing my mind, I thought. His large eyes gleamed against the bright moonlight, giving my heart a start.

"So, Sofija, do you miss home yet? Anyone in Velesh to get back to, a boyfriend perhaps?" Ivan asked in a casual voice, gazing up at me underneath his dark eyebrows. This, alone, sent my heartrate through the roof.

I blushed immediately, avoiding his gaze. "No, not really. My latest relationship didn't go well, so I got used to the single life."

He looked up, suddenly curious. "What happened? I'm a good listener; you can tell me."

I was surprised at his interest in my personal life. It did not bother me as much as it should have, seeing as we didn't know each other well. Instead, I was compelled to tell him more.

"We lived together for a while. He was a bit troubled, to say the least. Could get a bit aggressive at times."

Ivan was searching my face for any sign of emotion, probably expecting me to have a public meltdown. His eyes bore into mine, and I looked away, blushing. "Don't worry, I won't burst into tears. It was a long time ago."

His eyebrows raised. "What? Oh, that is not what I was thinking. Sorry if I'm making you uncomfortable."

We sat in silence for a while, enjoying the atmosphere.

"Do you think anyone will ever be up to the task? To restore your faith in happy endings?" Ivan asked, a slight edge in his deep voice.

Looking up at him across the table, I held his gaze for a moment, pondering the strange question. The warm garden around us was swarming with people, all ready to welcome me into their ranks.

"Yes, I do. I know exactly who'll restore my faith in happy endings."

He didn't speak but raised his eyebrows and cocked his head to one side slightly, a cue for me to continue.

Surprised he didn't guess my answer, I replied, half-amused: "The only person who has the power to do it. Myself."

He beamed at me for a few seconds, silent. Then a wide grin stretched across his face.

"You're quite a fighter, aren't you?"

"Only while awake," I answered simply, smiling back at the magnificent man across from me. To keep my hands occupied, I took another sip of wine.

"What is your gemstone?" I heard myself asking suddenly, desperate to change the topic. He produced a small metal stick, like the one Tomislav was using earlier. I remembered Natasha said it was called a sceptre. Instead of Tomislav's blue stone, Ivan's sceptre had a deep-golden gem on top of it.

"Topaz," he said simply, showing the sceptre to me. "I was born in November."

"Which year?" I asked without thinking and regretted it immediately, seeing his gaze drop to the ground, his brow furrowing.

"None of my business, I guess," I concluded quickly.

"Perhaps we should get to know each other a little better before discussing such serious matters?" he suggested, his lips curling into a smile. I felt a rush of relief and smiled in turn.

"What do you have in mind?" I asked, attempting to imitate his seductive voice. I did not think it worked, but miraculously, he asked:

"Care to dance?" My cheeks felt hot under his gaze; I nodded and got up, a little too eager. The caution has left the stage, obviously, taking what was left of my dignity with it.

His right hand was outstretched, and I took it, allowing him to lead me towards the clearing in the middle of the garden. Several other couples were dancing to a soft song, and we joined them.

He pulled me closer, placing his left hand on my waist, his right hand steering us in slow whirls to the rhythm of the music. My heart rate accelerated on his touch, that inexplicable warmth running through my

133

every cell. He could dance, I thought. He even had a stance of a dancer, something I rarely saw in men I knew in Velesh.

I hadn't, until now, paid attention to just how tall Ivan was. Being close to him, I noticed he wasn't as skinny as I thought, muscles silhouetted through his shirt. His eyes were dark emerald and wide, gazing intently at me — *an emerald sea, unending, unwavering.*

"You dance well," he said, smiling.

"You're not bad either," I answered quietly, trying to gaze back but his eyes were too intense. I looked away, my cheeks reddening.

The song ended, and another one started. Then another one after that. We didn't pay attention to the world around us, swirling slowly, enjoying each other's presence. I could have been anywhere in the world at that moment, it didn't matter. All my defence mechanisms started tumbling down, I could almost see the walls around me tearing and dissolving into the warm night. No one ever accused me of being cautious anyway, I thought with a grin. It was time to jump again, and I was all too willing.

Chapter 16
No Turning Back

Suddenly, Ivan stopped moving and let go of me, breaking the magic. I looked up in surprise and saw the worry on his face. Turning around, I followed his gaze across the garden; a large group of people was gathered around our table. Something was up. He gazed into my eyes, his expression unreadable.

"We had better return to our table. Come." Taking my hand, Ivan led me through the crowd.

Natasha was the first one to approach us, her eyes wary and sad. *What happened?* My heart started racing again, this time from fear instead of excitement. All the ease I felt just a minute ago was gone as if it was never there.

"Sofija... please, sit. We have just received the news from a League member stationed in Velesh tonight. Terrible news." Tomislav was standing behind me, his arm on my shoulder. Ivan sat to my right, my hand still in his. It seemed like he was trying to concentrate very hard on something, but I couldn't understand what it was. On the other side of the table, I could see Maya eyeing me.

"Just tell me. What is it?" Fear rose in me like a raging fire, and I tried not to think the worst. Not my grandpa, please, I pleaded with some invisible being. Not Grandpa.

Natasha started, careful, "Tanatos and his followers found out that you've reached Tayna. Or they might only be assuming as much, we cannot be sure. In any case, they visited your grandparents yesterday, just after we escaped them on the train. They were probably asking about your whereabouts, and your grandparents must have declined to cooperate because..." Her voice broke.

No. NO! My mind was protesting, begging me to turn away, to clasp my ears shut, to not listen. I did not obey — I had to know.

"Because... what?" I heard myself asking, my voice trembling.

Tomislav let go of my shoulder and came around, crouching in front of me, his worried eyes locked on mine. Before speaking, he took a deep breath and ran both hands through his brown curls. Cupping my free hand in his, he said, "Because we've just received intelligence that they've paid Irma and Marin another visit. They're both dead".

No. No. No!

No, it can't be true. I must have misunderstood what Tomislav had said just now. Maya was about to take the medication to Grandpa tomorrow, and I was going to ask for my clothes. I even wrote them a letter, explaining where I was. They cannot be dead, Tomislav and Natasha must have misunderstood. Grandma and I had a deal; we agreed to help Grandpa recover. I got the permit, I managed to come to Agram, I did my part... they can't be gone *now*. She had promised she will be waiting when I got back! She always waited for me in the cosy kitchen. Who will be there now? Who will make the coffee in the morning?

"No," I finally said out loud after what seemed like hours, "no, it cannot be."

I could feel at least fifty pairs of eyes on me, but I did not care. They were all wrong. My grandparents are not dead. They survived so much, they were probably... hiding or... or pretending somehow, to escape Tanatos. I looked down at my hands and noticed I was trembling, head to foot.

"We're so sorry, Sofija," I could hear someone saying. "You're with us now. We'll help you through this."

Nonsense, all this was utter nonsense. Was this part of their initiation too? Welcome to the magical world, here's a sick joke to scare you to death? Well, I didn't think much of it. I took out my phone and dialled Grandma. No signal. I tried again, and again. I kept on trying until someone snatched the phone from me, patting me on the shoulder and saying something in a comforting voice.

I pressed both hands to my ears and started rocking back and forth. There was a silence, even the soft music stopped playing. Someone in the vicinity was still speaking to me, but I didn't hear them. I couldn't hear them because I was in the other place entirely now. Somewhere where there's water, I thought, for suddenly, I felt like I was drowning as my lungs yearned for air.

A pair of strong hands lifted me off the bench, leading me away. I tried to resist, but the hands were too strong, keeping me in place and steering me away from the crowd. My head was spinning, and I could not breathe, still submerged underwater. Trying to inhale, I must have alarmed my carrier as he stopped in his tracks, picking me off the ground.

"Try to breathe deeply. It'll be okay," I heard a deep voice and knew it was Ivan who held me.

As we entered the hotel and went up the stairs, I noticed my awareness getting weaker and weaker with every step Ivan took. I felt dizzy and unusually sleepy as if I had been given a sleeping pill. By the time his strong hands placed me gently on the bed, my eyelids were too heavy and my tired mind too weak to fight the sleepiness. In a matter of seconds, I fell into a dreamless sleep.

My eyes opened, and the thick darkness found me. I blinked twice, trying to regain vision. For a split second, I didn't know where I was, my eyes searching the room frantically.

"Good morning," said a deep, familiar voice.

Startled, I looked around and saw Ivan sitting in the armchair next to my bed in a hotel room.

"Did you sleep well? Natasha is downstairs, fetching some breakfast for you. You slept for a while."

His gaze was worried, careful. As the memories of the last night came rushing back, my heart started filling up with immense, soul-tearing pain again. It was now harder to deny it, more challenging to think it was just a bad joke. Ivan had, by the looks of things, spent the night with me there. Natasha was downstairs, fetching breakfast for me. They are worried. Worried because of me, because now I had... nobody.

A massive weight was pressing on my chest, making it difficult to breathe. The reality hit me yet again, fresh and devastating. *My grandparents are dead. Gone... and I didn't even get to say goodbye.*

Ivan stood up and, approaching the tall windows, pulled the heavy curtains open. The sun swam into the room, blinding me for a moment.

"I'm sorry, that wasn't very subtle. How are you feeling?" He cocked his head, waiting for my answer.

"Miserable." It was the truth, and I had nothing else to add.

"It'll be okay. You are not alone," said Ivan. There was a short pause before he went on, his voice careful, "Would you like me to leave? I only stayed in case you woke up in the middle of the night. We didn't think it a good idea for you to be alone."

"No," I said firmly, realising suddenly that I was still holding it together precisely because he was here. If he left now, I'd fall apart into a million pieces.

He seemed pleased. "Okay. I'll stay then."

The rest of the day went by in a haze. In between constant crying fits, I dressed without paying much attention to anything. I then dragged myself into the lounge, where Natasha force-fed me. By midday, I had no more strength left in me to talk or walk around. Not now when the world was broken.

The throbbing pain in my chest remained ever-present as I followed Natasha and Tomislav into a small graveyard just outside the ancient walls of Tayna old town. Two large, oak coffins laid open at the edge of the sombre cemetery, a crowd of people standing quietly around them in a circle. There, as still as human-sized wax dolls, lay my grandparents. One glance at their white, unmoving bodies brought endless fits of desperate cries and sobs. The service followed, but I couldn't remember much of it. All that remained in my tortured mind were Natasha's hugs and Ivan's warm hand in mine. When he held me, the burning fire in my chest was a little easier to bear. It did not go away completely, but it felt a little subdued, the large, wild flames gone. When he was close, it was a little easier to breathe.

The next several days, or it could have been weeks, became a never-ending blur. Pain, now rarely followed by crying fits as I didn't have any tears left, was the only constant. I spent hour after hour lying on the bed in my hotel room, curled in a ball. I was utterly unaware of what I did earlier or when last I ate. When I closed my eyes, sometimes dreams came, and I was trapped again on that small graveyard, staring down at the white faces of the two people I loved most in the world. Sometimes they remained still, while tears kept pouring down my face and onto the grass next to their coffins. At other times, they stood up, miraculously, regaining colour in their cheeks as they came back to life. Every time, I woke up in tears, my pillow soaking wet. Grandpa's favourite song kept on playing in my head, each verse flooding my entire being in pain that kept on pulsing through me. Almost like a living organism, it spread and contracted in rhythmical sequences, tearing me apart as images of my only family lingered in front of my eyes. *"If I could be reborn, I'd spend the entire life by the Dunav once more, watching the white boats passing by..."*

Sometimes I noticed other people around me. Natasha and Tomislav kept on coming in and out with trays full of food and coffee, feeding me, talking to me. But I wasn't really there with them, my mind floating helplessly somewhere between waking and dream, part of it trapped in that graveyard, still mourning my grandparents.

At other times, I felt Ivan's warm touch, and the fire was subdued for a moment. But this only allowed me to sleep; sleeping meant dreaming, and dreams were agonising, bringing all the horrors back to the surface.

As time passed, it slowly became easier to resurface for extended periods, and I noticed a pattern in my friends' behaviour. Natasha and Tomislav were with me in the mornings, Maya usually taking over during the day. On the bedside armchair, Ivan was there every night, holding my hand until sleep finally came.

When the terrifying fire in my heart subdued a little, I made myself stand up and get dressed, paying attention to what I was doing for the first time in weeks. The throbbing pain in my chest was now more bearable to live with; it was always there but under the surface, allowing me to continue living. Instead of sadness, waves of burning anger consumed me now — anger at Tanatos and his agents who killed my grandparents. The intense feeling of hatred ignited in me, and I let it wash over my body and mind. I wanted it to enter my every pore, block any other emotion and intoxicate my heart. I lay curled up on the bed, imagining my hatred for Tanatos engulfing me, twisting itself around my body just like those black wisps on Initiation night.

I had to do something about it, I kept telling myself. If I stayed in my room forever, Tanatos would do this to someone else. My grandparents and parents deserved to be avenged. He took too much from me, and even though I'd lived the past twenty-five years stupidly unaware of his evil deeds, I could make up for it. I owed it to my family, those I did know and those I never had a chance to meet.

"We need to be careful. I understand you're eager to act, but we're not ready yet." Tomislav was trying to reason with me after hearing my demands for immediate action.

"I'm ready," I blurted out without thinking. I could see Tomislav's mouth twist into a small smile. He would mock me openly if I were in my right mind, I knew. But, given the circumstances, he mercifully toned down on teasing. I was surprised to learn three weeks had passed while I was stuck in my room, and it was already July. I couldn't waste any more time.

"You will be once we've trained you. We had tried to bring the government down before and know our mistakes now — it is crucial that you listen to us. Don't act on your own." There was no trace of humour in his voice now, as he was trying to pass some unspoken, serious message to me, to make me understand.

"When do we start?" I asked eagerly.

"As soon as we find a place to practise. You channelled a surprising amount of energy upon Collision, so we want to make sure it's somewhere safe."

I nodded. The magical Collison, I was told, is the first contact between a mage and their gemstone. It manifests the person's magical potential, and mine was... well, substantial. I couldn't help but smirk a little. At least we knew now I wouldn't be a total failure.

We were sitting out in the garden at one of the wooden tables, finishing up our lunch. It was quiet in the hotel nowadays, more quiet than usual. Tomislav, who was the de-facto leader of the League, advised an extra caution as they expected further attacks by Tanatos any time soon. The murder of my grandparents, he said, was a warning. Tanatos wanted to demonstrate what he was capable of and hoped to scare me into submission. Unlucky for him, I wasn't that easy to scare away and too angry to give in. My grandparents' lives weren't taken away so that I would bow my head down.

I wanted to cross back into nemage Danubia, but it was impossible now. All the portals were under surveillance; perhaps Tanatos hoped I'd try to cross back and get myself caught.

Maya and several other mages who frequently travelled into the nemage territory still managed to get through, but only after they were thoroughly searched. It was a miracle Tomislav, and several others managed to retrieve my grandparents' bodies when they did.

Tomislav said that Tanatos was worried about public opinion; on the surface, he maintained a carefully looked-after image of a concerned, approachable leader who did all necessary to keep the peace. Now that I thought about it, I never heard of him killing anybody. But I knew that did not mean that he never did it. Instead, it meant that he hid it well, and this skill at concealing his true nature and the ability to gain people's trust was the greatest threat of all. We had to expose him for who he was — a dark mage and a monster. And we only had one shot at it.

I was brought back from my reverie by the sound of Natasha's voice. "Here, this belongs to you." She set a heavy metal box at the table in front of me. Looking up at her questioningly, I opened the box. Under the heavy lid was a large stack of Danubian money — enough to probably last me for a year.

"When we moved to Danubia, all our funds were stored at The Bayamonti, in a safe. Since the hotel cannot be entered by anyone whose gemstone hasn't previously been registered and approved, it's the safest place there is. Perhaps you should do the same," Tomislav advised.

I thanked him and asked that he puts my money into The Bayamonti safe too. I didn't fancy carrying all that cash around, and in any case, I didn't need much while in Tayna.

Chapter 17
Vilenak

I spent my days at the hotel, which had once belonged to my mother's family, as I discovered soon after the Initiation night. This was not so unusual, I soon found out, as all the property in Tayna was in the hands of the five wealthiest, most powerful families. Now that most of them had either gone into hiding or joined Turncoats, who infiltrated the nemage government, the houses just stood there, abandoned. The Bayamonti Hotel was one of them.

"Those are the Turquoise dynasties, descendants of old royal families that used to rule Danubia centuries ago. Back when it was united, and the mages and nemages still lived together, you know. It must be very confusing for you, reconciling these two intertwining histories."

Ivan and I were on one of our evening walks. This had become our little habit ever since I left the bedroom and started moving and eating again. The promenade was off-limits. Tanatos' agents patrolled the area, keeping the mages in check, collecting taxes, conducting raids and arresting anyone who spoke back to them. The mages were forbidden from lingering by the seafront to avoid being sighted by occasional visitors from the Outer Lands that came on trade ships. The government did not want to close the harbour as the maritime trade brought lots of money into their Treasury. In any case, it was safer to stay within the old town. So, the League created a sort of sanctuary at the hotel, and the area around it was relatively safe to roam. Visitors rarely went into the old town. Not that many of them ever came; due to the Wipe, no one in Danubia knew Tayna existed. As for the rest of the world, apart from trade ships, there were no transportation links to Tayna. Those who sneaked a rare peek from the seaside at Tayna probably thought it was an abandoned city or a tiny, uninteresting village. Tanatos did fine, meticulous work at concealing the entire province.

"What happened to the royal families?" I asked Ivan.

"After the Rebellion, most of them fled, unwilling to spill any more royal blood for our cause. Cowards, if you ask me. I bet they'll come running back when we defeat Tanatos. Hope the League will be clever enough to tell them to crawl back into their hole."

As we entered the small park leading to the graveyard, Ivan stopped in his tracks suddenly and took my hand. "Actually, I should call you my queen," he said with a small smile, but his eyes remained impenetrable. "How rude of me."

This stirred something in my memory. "What did you say?"

"You come from the Turquoise dynasty. You are the Blue Queen. Or would've been if we didn't destroy the Monarchy."

I stared at him for a few seconds, and then it came to me. "The beggar! In the old town, in Agram! He called me his queen, but I thought he was just talking rubbish."

Ivan did not seem surprised at this. "The Siva member probably. I guess he noticed your hair?" He reached forward and tucked the turquoise strand behind my ear. I shivered at his touch.

"Um... yes, I think so. Does it mean all these... *turquoise* people have the same hair as I do?"

"Some of them do. It's some sort of genetic anomaly that runs in your dynasty. No one really knows why, but it is interesting. It certainly makes you stand out," Ivan said, winking at me.

We reached my grandparents' grave. There was a small bench in front of it, and Ivan sat down while I rummaged through my bag, searching for a candle I had brought with me. The oak coffins were now in the ground, covered by an elegant, rectangular tomb made of marble. The tombstone had my grandparents' names, birth and death dates and a short verse Natasha chose. It read, *"You live on, forever, in the souls of your loved ones."* I could feel the tears coming and, struggling to stop them, quickly placed a small candle on the grave. I lit it with a lighter as I still hadn't learnt how to use magic, then joined Ivan on the bench.

"How come that beggar knew about the Turquoise dynasty? I mean, wasn't all the mutual history lost in the Wipe?" I asked, desperate to occupy my mind with something other than the thought of my two favourite people lying lifelessly underneath the marble tomb.

"The Wipe didn't work equally on everyone. The stronger the mage, the harder it is to take away the memory. Or to alter it, which was what Tanatos had done," Ivan explained, looking out into the night, towards the ancient walls of Tayna. "The minds of powerful mages come with a sort of protection. A shield, for lack of a better word. So, they never forgot, and they know exactly what's going on."

I looked up at him, surprised. "Then why don't they say something, if they remember?"

Ivan raised his eyebrows. "Would you? Do you really think the nemages would believe them?"

I thought about it for a while. He had a point... when Natasha and Tomislav first told me about Tayna, I did not believe them. And then, when they said that magic was real, I thought they were downright insane. I only started to believe when I *saw* it, I thought with a smile, remembering the incredible elemental magic Tomislav demonstrated on my first day in Tayna.

"No, I don't think they'd believe it, not unless they saw it with their own eyes. That's what did the trick for me." I smiled a little, more to myself than to Ivan. Stubbornness can be a virtue; that's what I've always thought. Even though my mind usually kicks and screams before letting anything new in, it does an excellent job at shielding me.

Then another detail came to me. "There's something else... that beggar was looking for his gems. *Gems,* as in more of them, not just one."

"Powerful mages can use more than just one gem. You must know that Tomislav and Natasha both use three."

I nodded, remembering Natasha mentioned something about it at The Bayamonti on my first day here.

"Anyway", Ivan continued, "that's as far as anyone goes, I think... I've never heard of anyone using more than three. Tanatos confiscated all gems, stole them from their owners... well, at least from those he managed to imprison. Needless to say, it is impossible to purchase a gemstone anywhere in Danubia. The bastard saw to that. Those who still remember can't actually prove what they're saying is true, not without their gemstones," Ivan said, his voice unusually bitter.

"I see. Is that why Tanatos put the mages in the Siva caste? So that no one would believe them even if they tried something? It's as low as you can go in Danubia."

"Yes, he wanted to discredit and humiliate them. I also heard that, right after the war, he did some nasty experiments on them in Kalemgrad. He probably hoped insanity would drive sense and any lingering memories out of their minds. You know, since the original master plan failed, and the Wipe didn't do its job on them."

There was a long pause as we sat, hand in hand, looking out into the darkness.

"We tried to help them; you know. The League knew a lot of mages were stuck in Agram and, just before the Rebellion was crushed, we ran a diversion in an attempt to release them from the prison near today's Kalemgrad. Before Tanatos built his headquarters there, the location was notorious for the most dreadful underground prison in Danubia."

"We? As in… you, too? But how?" I stared, doing quick calculations in my head. Ivan could only be five or six years older than me, and the Rebellion happened twenty-five years ago. "Don't tell me children are recruited here because that's a deal-breaker", I said, half-joking.

He sighed.

"Well… I guess I cannot hide it forever. I'm surprised Maya didn't tell you already; she's such a blabbermouth."

I shifted in my seat to face Ivan, looking up at him expectantly.

"My mother is a vila, that makes me a part-vilenak. My kind age slower and live twice as long as humans. So, technically, I am sixty-two… but physically, I'm thirty-one. I was born in 1948, here in Tayna."

He said all this very quickly as if trying to get the words out before I could understand the meaning. His gaze was glued to the ground.

I gaped, unable to put my thoughts into words. The seconds passed, and Ivan looked up, concerned.

"Please say something." He let go of my hand, leaning away slightly.

"Well… that is yet another amazing thing about you. Not only are you a mage and know all these things I don't, but now you will also… live longer? Great. Just great."

My reaction surprised us both, and I could feel the frustration rising in me. Ivan was so special, and I'm a nobody. How do I ever make up for my… ordinariness?

Ivan studied my face carefully, baffled by my reaction. *I cannot*

145

really blame him, I thought to myself. Irritated, I stood up and walked away from him, unable to sit there next to his ageless perfection.

"Wait, you are... jealous of me?"

That did it. I turned around, staring at his handsome face.

"Of course, I am! You get a *free* year for every human year... and you get all these magical powers, and you can say you've done something with your life! When I'm just... I'm floating through it all, letting things happen to me!"

He started laughing, shaking his head in disbelief.

"What?" I asked, some of my irritation going away, now mixed with confusion.

"It's just... you're so *funny*. It doesn't worry you that I fought in Rebellion with *your parents*, nor that I've actually been around for twice as long as you did. It doesn't bother you that I'm only partly human. No, you worry about the knowledge gap between us!"

I looked down, embarrassed.

"I wouldn't care if you were completely inhuman. But there's just so much for me to make up for now! Argh," I blurted out, frustrated again. Now all the magic in the world will not make me good enough for this... this amazing *creature*. I did not shudder at the word, and I wasn't scared. I was fascinated.

"You must tell me more about your family. Aren't *vilas* similar to fairies?" I asked, sitting back on the bench next to him. He stretched his arm around my neck, and I leaned in, my head resting on his shoulder.

"Sort of, but not quite. Fairies are more... fictional. We are not, as you can see," Ivan said shortly, pointing his index finger at his chest. "Enough about me for the night. If you really want to learn more about us, I'll introduce you to my mother and show you around our house some time."

I nodded briefly and decided to drop the topic for now. What Ivan had told me was plenty to keep me thinking for days, and I'd be sure to ask Maya for details anyway. I had an inkling she'd be happy to share more information with me.

"Anyway, I mentioned the diversion to free the captured mages from the prison near today's Kalemgrad. We tried it just before the Rebellion was over. I was there, too, freshly recruited to the League. That is when your parents died." He eyed me, his gaze full of compassion.

I shrugged, unsure how to react.

"At least you tried something. It's not like I remember my parents anyway. I'm sure they were nice people and all, but I have no memory of them," I said quickly, trying not to think of the only parents I *did* remember. They were dead too, and it was all Tanatos' fault. I dropped my gaze to the ground, staring at the carefully maintained lawn.

"Hey, look at me." Ivan's long fingers lifted my chin up, and his eyes locked on mine. Green to brown.

"It'll be okay. We'll make you the most powerful mage the world has ever known, and you'll defeat the bastard."

"Yeah, right. I can make my gemstone explode at Tanatos, not sure if that'll scare him away," I scoffed, remembering what happened the first — and the last — time I tried using the garnet. For some reason, I did not dare take it out of the box ever since the Initiation. Not willing to leave it lying around, I carried it with me in the messenger bag, where it was safely stored. I acted as if it was a bomb, not a magical tool. On some level, I was even scared of it a little... of the fact that I couldn't control it. And causing another explosion wasn't on my list of priorities right now — or ever.

"We'll see," Ivan said, winking at me, "I bet you can kick my ass once you're fully trained."

I laughed.

"You'd better watch out for yourself then".

"I'd better, yes. You're scary in so many ways, you know." He was gazing down at me, his eyes intense.

"How so?" I asked, ignoring the loud thudding in my chest.

"Let's just say I've never met anyone like you."

I beamed, unsure of what to say. Ivan pulled back his arm and straightened up on the bench, suddenly serious. It was like he was trying to make up his mind about something.

"I have this... ability. Please don't freak out!" he prompted as I started frowning. *More abilities? What is it now, he can fly?*

Ivan went on before I could say anything. "I can make anyone do anything only by my touch. I make them obey. It usually works on everyone; one brief touch on a hand is enough to make people fall asleep if I want them to, for example. But it doesn't work on you." He paused, gazing up at me, waiting for a reaction.

"Why do you think that is?" I asked, confused.

"I don't know. It never happened before."

I thought for a while about this new piece of information and realised something.

"At my Initiation. When I couldn't get up, you reached for my hand." It was a statement, not a question.

He nodded. "Yes, and you should've gotten up and walked to the stage immediately. Instead, you resisted, somehow. Then, when your grandparents… had gone, I tried to be as close to you as possible and to make you fall asleep, to take away the pain. I don't think it worked at all. Anyone else wouldn't have been in such pain had I used my ability on them. They would be hurting, of course, but not as much. They would be able to get up and eat had I made them. And I really tried to make you, but you would not *hear* me. It's like you're deaf to my ability."

His eyes scrutinised mine as if trying to reach under the surface to find answers. "The only time I think it worked slightly was when I carried you to bed after you've… heard the news. But that's probably because of the shock you've been through that I managed to breach your defences, or whatever it is keeping me out. It didn't last long, though."

I still didn't understand what he was talking about, remembering how it was only his presence in my room that kept me from falling into pieces. I didn't want him to ever leave, and the moment he was gone, the pain would grow the size of a mountain.

"I don't understand. You did help me. I… felt better when you were around." I could feel my cheeks turn red, grateful it was dark, so he couldn't notice.

He looked at me seriously, his emerald eyes glittering.

"I feel better when you're around too. That doesn't mean you have superpowers… other than the fact that I'm falling in love with you."

I froze, beaming back at him, knowing it was too late to turn back now. "I… feel the same about you."

His full lips stretched into a warm smile as he cupped my face with his hands, reaching forward to kiss my lips lightly.

"Thank the heavens that you do."

Chapter 18
First Comrade

We walked back, hand in hand, away from the graveyard and towards the hotel.

"What is this?" Ivan demanded, coming to a sudden halt. His eyes were glued to my right hand. I knew that, even in the dark, he could clearly see how red the small patch of skin on my wrist was.

"Oh... it's nothing. Just a rash from my caste band. It's healing slowly." The itching was less annoying ever since I stopped wearing the satin band, but the skin was still raw on touch.

"The caste band. Like those Natasha and Tomislav wear?" Ivan asked, his eyebrows rising in surprise.

"Yes, everyone has to wear them in the nemage Danubia, at least when in public and at work. Easier to recognise our caste that way," I replied briefly, hoping for a change of subject as I didn't like to discuss the nemages, the ridiculous caste system or anything else that might remind me of my hometown. Mercifully, Ivan didn't press the topic any further.

As always, we stopped at my parents' graves situated near the exit. I came here almost every day, just to lay down a flower and a candle to the two people I had never met yet loved dearly. Their tomb was larger and shinier than most I saw in the graveyard, with a massive tombstone enumerating their achievements for the League. As the final sacrifice, Luka and Alina Filipov had laid down their own lives.

I could never stay for more than ten minutes, for that was when tears would usually start swimming in my eyes. So, after a while, I felt Ivan's hand tugging on mine, towing me back towards the hotel.

Replaying our recent conversation in my head as we walked back, I couldn't believe how happy I felt, despite everything. My feet didn't seem to touch the ground; it was almost like floating. My eyes kept darting to Ivan as I was scared he'd disappear if I turn away.

149

"What are you thinking about right now?" I heard him asking.

"Just how quickly my life changed. It will take some getting used to," I replied without thinking, then added, worried that he'd take my words the wrong way, "But I like the changes, most of them. I wish my grandparents didn't have to... pay the price."

We walked for another minute in silence, now getting closer to the walls of Tayna old town and the hotel.

"All you need is time. And action. I think training to fight will help a lot," he said, winking at me, "I can't wait to see you use magic. You'll be extraordinary. I remember your parents; they were fantastic mages, even for humans."

I looked up, surprised at the comment. "For humans? Does that mean vila magic is... stronger?"

"Kind of. Our genes are more magical, or at least magical in a different way. It is a slightly different brand of magic. We also use gemstones, but unlike humans, we don't necessarily *need* them to channel magic. It is just easier and more convenient to use gems... I don't personally fancy explaining my family tree every time I cast a spell." He flashed his most beautiful smile at me.

"Do vilas and humans get along? I mean, you seemed guarded when you told me. Like it's a secret or something."

"You are very observant," he said with a chuckle. "There is a history between our two species. We are used to... cohabitation."

He looked ahead, fixated on the ancient walls of Tayna in front of us, and I knew he didn't want to get any further into it. We walked some more, entering the old town and arriving at the familiar ancient square one street away from the hotel.

Just as I took the garnet out of my messenger bag, knowing I'd need it to enter The Bayamonti, Ivan pulled me to his side. Pressing his index finger against his lips, signalling for me to be quiet, he towed me across the small square, and we crouched behind the stone sphinx statue.

"She's not here; your visit is pointless." Tomislav's voice was loud and clear, coming to us from somewhere behind the square.

"You're lying," a male voice answered, sounding almost bored. "Tell us where the girl is, and we'll be on our way. We don't want any trouble either, Tom."

"I already told you, Atanasov. She is not here. You may leave now, you're making an unnecessary scene, and it is late."

Someone started pacing, their heeled shoes echoing against the cobbled street.

Then the voice spoke, high and cold. Or perhaps it was only cold because of the malice that was coming out of it? I did not know, but it wasn't a voice I wanted to hear ever again.

"Stop toying with us, Tomislav. Give me Sofija, and we shall leave you be." There was a pause before someone said:

"Why don't you get her yourselves if you're so tough?"

Ivan's hold on me tightened, and I could hear him draw a short breath. My heart wanted to leap out of my chest from fear as I leaned closer to him.

"You never had much sense, did you, Novak?" said the malicious female voice. "I'm tired of our little exchange; it leads us nowhere. Perhaps this…"

A long, horrifying shriek ensued, followed by screams and shouts from all sides. Something, or someone, I thought in horror, hit the stone ground with a loud thud.

"… will inspire you to help us. Am I correct?"

"Not her again, you bitch!" Someone shouted, and loud cries filled the air, terrifying as they resounded against the stone walls. I heard screams of agony as spells reached their targets, but I had no idea who was getting hit. The night sky was suddenly illuminated in celeste, deep blue and white light bouncing off the surrounding houses.

People moved around hastily, their clothes rustling. But no one spoke for a while.

Then I heard Tomislav's voice, barely recognisable from the amount of coldness in it.

"Losing your touch? Or has it been too long since you've last used magic without rationing?" I could hear him laugh a humourless laugh, and my veins froze at the sound. "You'd have to kill us all before getting to her. And your boss wouldn't like that, would he now, *Comrade*? The precious magical blood would be no more if we were all slaughtered by his favourite *pet*." He spat out the last word, his tone ice-cold.

Another long silence ensued. Someone was sobbing quietly in the background.

"Have it your way, Tomislav. Just this time," I heard the malicious female voice say, "but tell her that we're waiting. Tell her she has three days to reach out to the President, or she'll lose more than just Irma and Marin."

I started getting up, but Ivan stopped me. His hand was now clenching my mouth shut so that I would not give us away. I wanted to go. I wanted to see who is making all those horrible threats! My whole being yearned to fight, and I didn't care if it had to be done with my bare fists, even though I had no idea how to punch.

"Please, Sofija, there's nothing to be gained by jumping the gun", he whispered in my ear. His steely grip tightened, and I slowly gave in, my body frozen in place, crouching behind the sphinx statue.

"Have a good evening, gentlemen… ladies. Hope we won't see each other again", I heard the malicious voice say. Then, their footsteps receded away from the square, towards the promenade.

Ivan let go of me, warning me with a gesture to stay quiet.

"You heard all that? How?" Ivan asked, half-whispering, as we left our hiding place and rushed to the hotel.

I looked up at him, confused. "What do you mean? Didn't you hear it, too?"

"I did, but I'm part-vilenak. We are different. A human mage wouldn't be able to hear so far away."

"I don't know. I just heard it." It didn't matter at that moment, I thought to myself.

About a dozen people were standing, some sitting on the ground in front of the hotel entrance. Some were conversing quietly, most of them gathered around a figure lying by the hotel door, her head propped up on someone's jacket serving as a pillow.

"What was that?" I heard myself asking, my voice panicked. "What happened?"

Surprised gasps came from all sides, and then Natasha was there, hugging me tightly. Maya was standing right next to her, her hand on my shoulder. I noticed a small violet stone glinting on her bracelet, clearly visible against the dim lamplight. Amethyst.

"Thank the heavens you weren't here." Then Natasha stepped away, her worried eyes scrutinising my face. "Did you see all that? Where were you?"

"Natasha, let's take this inside before they return," Tomislav said, unlocking the hotel door with his gem and ushering everyone in. I could see Vesna, the short-haired waitress, standing next to him. A tall, grey-haired man wearing square-rimmed spectacles was helping a young girl up off the floor, picking up the jacket she was lying on just a moment ago. I recognised him instantly, my eyes bulging in surprise. It was David Novak, a member of the Velesh Local Assembly, who I thought was in prison. That would make the woman on his right, his wife, Sandra. And a girl between them, the injured figure, must be their daughter. It was Mila Novak, whose classified file bought me a travel permit to Agram what seemed like a lifetime go.

"What was that?" I repeated my question a few minutes later. We were sitting in the hotel lounge, chairs pulled up around a coffee table in the back to accommodate everyone. The place was bathed in golden lampshade coming from the sides of the spacious room.

"That, Sofija," Tomislav started in a strained voice, "was the Danubian government. The *real* one. I don't know who the woman was. She only visited once before, right after the Rebellion was crushed." He sighed deeply, looking around at others in agitation. The silence was complete; no one seemed to feel like talking. "Her official title is First Comrade. Whoever she is, she's a nightmare to deal with. No heart, no soul, just a war machine trapped in a human form, she is. She outranks the others from what we know... the rest of them are simply called agents."

"And they were looking for me?" I could hear my voice trembling, either from fear or anger; I wasn't able to tell any more. Ivan, who was sitting next to me, took my hand and squeezed it gently.

"Yes... they were. We anticipa—" Tomislav started.

"You *didn't* anticipate it, obviously, Tom! Otherwise, Mila wouldn't have been hurt — again!" an angry voice interrupted. David Novak was staring at Tomislav, his eyes wild over a pair of square-rimmed spectacles. He was pointing to his daughter and wife at the back of the room. Mila was struggling to get up, and Sandra was sitting next to her,

153

caressing her hair. Maya stood over Mila with her gem-adorned hand outstretched, the amethyst gleaming with violet light. The faint rays caressed Mila's body gently, concentrating on the back of her head and her shoulders. She must have fallen hard on her back.

Tomislav turned to David, his face composed. "What I meant is we knew they might attempt this. It was inevitable; they are looking for Sofija, you know that. I am sorry Mila got hurt, but that's why we're going to fight back — because they can't keep on getting away with this, not anymore." The calmness of his voice seemed to have some effect on David, who simply nodded and went back to his coffee.

"What happened to Mila? Is she going to be all right?" I asked when I saw Maya returning to the table, somehow feeling partly responsible for her injury. After all, it was me the horrible woman was looking for.

"She was hit with a kicking curse. I don't think that woman meant to hit her specifically; Mila just happened to be in the way. Hit her head a little, but she'll be fine," she replied, looking exhausted. "Physical injuries are a sort of a speciality of mine, and I did my best. She'll heal quickly." Maya sat down next to me, taking a cup of coffee from the tray.

"It shouldn't have happened. Why are we risking this much, risking all we've accomplished… for *her*? I've been in the RC, Tom, you don't want to experience that!" David started again; his gaze fixed on Tomislav.

"What have we accomplished exactly, David? The right to keep hidden? The luxury of walking among the nemages, unharmed, as long as we pretend to be something we're not and hide our true nature? Or were you talking about the raids and disappearances that keep on happening? I don't understand what you're referring to, my friend, as it all looks rotten to me!" Tomislav challenged him, agitation seeping into his voice now.

David sighed.

"At least they agreed to leave us be. Yes, we paid the price… a heavy price, but at least there are no more killings," he answered in a calm, resigned voice.

I looked down, my heart pounding hard in my chest. David was right. I knew he was. They were risking their lives for someone they didn't even know, someone who wasn't even worth it — for *me*. It didn't escape my notice that David kept on talking about me as if I weren't in the room. He wouldn't even look my way as if trying to ignore the fact that I existed.

"What are we supposed to do, Novak? Just let Tanatos do Sofija in? Because that's what he'll do! I'd never peg you for a murderer". Ivan spoke this time, his voice low but nevertheless audible as all the quiet chatter suddenly died down. I still couldn't look up from the floor, even though his hand kept on squeezing mine, trying to comfort me.

"I'm not a murderer, *vilenak*," he spat out the last word with furious dislike, "but I am trying to be realistic. She might not even be important; the whole story might just be made up! I say we train her, and then we stop shielding her. She's an adult, isn't she?"

I looked up slowly, pride rising in me. They kept on talking as if I weren't in the room. If these people didn't want me here, then I'd go, but there was no reason to treat me as if I were invisible.

"I'm right here, you know," I managed, my voice strained. "If I'm the real problem here, then don't worry, I'll go away. But Tanatos and his First Comrade are still out there, and my leaving won't change the fact that he has you on your knees."

There was a pause as everyone stared at me. I wasn't going to look down again, I thought to myself. Squeezing Ivan's hand to let him know I was okay, I looked up, straight into David's eyes. Turning to Tomislav, I asked, my voice high with agitation, "Will you train me, please? The sooner I can use my gemstone, the sooner I will be out of your way."

Tomislav rolled his eyes at me.

"Don't be ridiculous, Sofija. You're not going anywhere; this is where you belong. Besides, I think Ivan would rip my head off if I sent you away," he said, grinning.

"You know me so well, Tom," I could hear Ivan saying from next to me. Others agreed, some of them patting me on the back.

I looked around at all of them with gratitude, even David, who still seemed unconvinced. I was relieved though I didn't want to admit it to myself. I abhorred my need to belong somewhere. I was never good at being alone and positively terrified of being lonely. Tayna was starting to feel like a real home, not so much like the one I had with my grandparents in Velesh, but close enough. I didn't know where I'd go or what I'd do if I had to leave now. My old job wouldn't be available to me any more since I haven't shown up for work or talked to anybody in a month. My grandparents' house was empty now, and the President of Danubia was looking for me. From what I'd seen tonight, he very much wanted to find me. So, where would I go? Try to cross the border? No one I knew ever did so, and I finally understood why. From what I had been told, Armiya officers patrolled all borders, letting no one out unless instructed explicitly by Tanatos.

Perhaps I could head for the mountains in Inner Danubia, I thought to myself. The Pirum kanton is a possibility; that was remote enough. There must be at least one abandoned cabin out there, a place for me to hide and live, in peace. *For the rest of my life, alone.* The thought made my veins freeze, and I quietly hoped I'd never have to leave Tayna.

Someone screamed. There were unintelligible shouts from the street side as David and Tomislav ran for the door. Others followed suit, and I went with them.

"No! She didn't!" Someone was shouting and swearing from the hotel entrance. Running towards the door, I saw massive flames rising up into the night sky, growing larger by the second.

The blonde, bearded man whose name I thought was Marko rushed to the hotel entrance, pointing at something behind him as he did so. "I was by the promenade when I saw it; I couldn't stop her!"

"Tom, that isn't... could it be...?" Natasha started, her eyes widening in shock. But Tomislav was already out of sight, Marko and David at his tracks. We waited a few minutes before the fire died down, no doubt magically extinguished by the three of them. Natasha sat down on stone steps in front of the hotel, her head in her hands.

"Did that woman set the fire? What did she burn down?" I asked in a careful voice.

"No one else would be that vile. By the looks of it, the First Comrade burned down our house as a farewell gift," Natasha replied quietly, staring up in the sky, now devoid of flames. The pungent smell of burnt wood filled the air, chilling my body to the bone.

Chapter 19
The Plenum

The next morning, we were all up early, having breakfast in the back garden. It was sunny again, and I felt optimistic, despite the dread I felt inside ever since the attack last night. I kept on thinking how close I had come to getting caught; it was only luck that made Ivan and I stay on that graveyard for as long as we did. Had we returned ten minutes earlier... I shuddered at the thought. Tomislav's and Natasha's house was completely burned down, beyond magical reparation. They said it didn't matter much as they didn't use the house anyway, but I knew they were lying. It was their home for so long and losing it in such a barbaric way must have been hard on them.

"I think they were hoping you were inside, Sofija, hiding. Though I don't know why they'd burn it down, I think the orders were to bring you to Tanatos alive," Tomislav explained.

Finished with breakfast, I pulled my hair up in a high ponytail, exposing the back of my neck as my head rested on the wooden table, soaking up the sun. It was comforting and warm. I lay there, listening to the sound of footsteps moving around the garden. Church bells were ringing faintly from somewhere nearby. So, it was a Sunday, I thought in surprise, realising I had completely lost track of time. The sound of bells brought me back to childhood, back to when I'd attend Sunday masses with my grandparents. We sometimes went to a church just around the corner from our house. My grandparents were never the most devoted churchgoers, and I doubted they were even believers, but they took me, nevertheless.

I never developed an ability to believe in God. I asked too many questions, Grandma once told me, to be able to believe in something without seeing the proof. But I liked churches; I always thought them to be beautiful, especially the tall, white spires that adorned the highest of the cathedrals. Unable to travel, I visited them all in my imagination, through pictures and films that were sometimes shown on Danubian television.

"One coffee with milk for the Blue Queen," I heard Ivan's voice from somewhere above me. I looked up, sunglasses askew on my nose. Pulling them up on top of my head, I squinted against the bright sunlight, looking around the garden.

Almost all remaining League members were present at The Bayamonti today, and the anticipation levels were high, nearly visible in the morning air. Today, we were going to decide — vote on — whether we fight or give in.

"Don't call me that," I grunted. Ivan flashed one of those beautiful, seductive smiles at me, and I rolled my eyes.

"That will get old, you know. Won't work every time," I warned him.

"I'm happy to test my luck," he retorted. Then he turned around, motioning for someone in the back to join us.

"This gentleman tells me he knows you. Thought you'd want to say hi."

I followed Ivan's gaze and noticed a bulky, tall figure approaching us, carrying a pint. His dark beard was bushier than the last time I saw him.

"Goran! What are you doing here?" I stood up, shaking hands with Goran Novak, the supplier of my illegal travel permit.

The newcomer greeted me enthusiastically, looking genuinely pleased to see me.

"Got Tomislav's invite to come and join the fight. Wouldn't miss it for the world. Glad to see you've made it out here okay," he said. Then, he leaned in closer to me, adding in a low voice:

"Listen, I'm sorry I've given you such a hard time with the permit and all. I had to be sure you can be trusted... no matter who you are," he explained, taking a swig before continuing.

"See, I set up my little *business* — for lack of a better word — to help Tomislav get in touch with the remaining mages in Danubia after Tanatos came into power. We figured if there are any left, and we knew some of them were still hiding among the Siva, they'd want to travel to Agram to reach the portal to Tayna. You must know travel was made nearly impossible under Tanatos, so that's where I helped. Tom and I developed a thorough screening process to make sure our clients aren't just Armiya agents in disguise."

I nodded in understanding, seeing as Goran was visibly uncomfortable.

"Hope you can understand, now that you've been clued in?" He asked in a half-apologetic, half-defensive tone. "Of course, I realised who you might be when I saw your surname, but I treat all my clients the same way." It seemed to me he wanted to apologise for making me jump through hoops but somehow couldn't muster the energy to do it.

"Don't worry, I understand. I wouldn't expect you to treat me any differently. Especially when I didn't know back then what was going on, or that we might come from the same... place," I said, giving him a reassuring smile.

Then, remembering suddenly, I asked, "But there is another portal in Nocturno, in Velesh. Couldn't the Siva members just use that one?" It seemed easier than to seek an illegal travel permit for Agram, I thought.

Goran sighed. "Not as far as they know. The Nocturno portal is a secret, exclusively used by the former members of the League. Since Tomislav wants to attract the bigger crowd this time, we hope others might want to join, too."

I frowned. "Why didn't they join you the last time? Why would they not fight with their own?"

"Some of them thought it wiser to hide or flee to the Outer Lands. Some laid low in Danubia, trying not to pick sides. It was a real pity because most of the Siva members are very powerful mages, too," Goran explained.

This piece of information surprised me. I assumed that all mages were connected to the League one way or another. It didn't cross my mind that some of them might have chosen to stay away from the fight. But now I finally understood Goran's reaction when I first visited, and his strict rules made a lot more sense. He had to make sure I could be trusted.

I noticed David, Sandra and Mila watching us from across the garden. Mila looked much better today; the fact that she left her room and was sitting up was telling enough. But David still seemed untrusting, and I wondered if I'd have to leave Tayna after all before the League falls apart. I wouldn't want for that to happen, not because of me.

"Did that file I got for you help, at least? I can see you found Mila." I asked, realising I never found out what exactly happened to her.

"Yes, it did; it helped a lot. Gave us the location where she was being kept. But by the time we got to her, she was already released. Tanatos is locking all these young women up in a research facility in Kalemgrad. Mila couldn't tell us much as she lost the memories of those few days while she was missing — Tanatos' doing, no doubt. That man could specialise in messing with other people's heads," Goran said bitterly. "But she's back and unharmed; that's what matters most. We had her examined by the best doctors, and nothing's missing or altered. Whoever he's looking for, it isn't Mila."

Lost in thought, I glanced towards the Novak's again, wondering if Tanatos was, in fact, looking for me. Tomislav was convinced that he was, but I was still doubtful. Or maybe hopeful, I didn't know. Perhaps the disappearances will stop now he knows that I was in Tayna? Chills went through me at the very idea, and I felt a surge of guilt.

Goran followed my gaze, noticing his brother's suspicious glare. He shrugged and said:

"Don't worry about him. He'll get on board. David has always been the stubborn one."

"I know a thing or two about stubbornness," I said, smiling. "I'm not worried; I just wish I weren't causing discord in the League. Everyone I met had been around here for a long time, knew each other. I've just appeared from nowhere. It doesn't seem right for the League to be ripped apart because of some stranger."

Ivan stood nearby while we talked, not commenting though I knew he could hear us. But then, with an annoyed expression, he moved closer to speak to me.

"You're not a stranger. Your parents lived here, fought here. Fought with us. The least *some* people can do is help protect you from that bastard Tanatos." Ivan glanced towards David, making it perfectly clear who he was referring to. "No offence, Goran. I know you two are not very much alike."

"None taken, Angelov. If you two will excuse me, I'm going to talk to my dear big brother." He shook my hand again, raised his pint to Ivan and walked away.

I turned to Ivan; my eyebrows raised. "Angelov? Your full name is Ivan *Angelov*? You didn't think to mention that before?"

He chuckled. "Does it matter?"

"Yes, it does since the Angelovs are only the most powerful family in Danubia! After Tanatos, that is, but I don't think he has a family."

He sighed and took a long swig before answering.

"The Angelov you're referring to is my father's brother. I suppose you've heard of him since he owns half of Danubia?"

I nodded in understanding, and Ivan went on:

"They've been estranged for a long time. Fought on opposing sides in the Rebellion. My father married a vila, so he naturally sided with the mages. His brother didn't have much understanding for that, called him a traitor. Then my father died, and they never had a chance to bury the axe. So, I don't have much in common with him... apart from the famous surname."

It took me a few moments to process this.

"Why would Angelov — the one from Danubia, I think his name is Borna, he's one of the Taykuni — why would he choose to fight against his own brother?" An image of an older, tall man with greying hair in a red blazer denoting the privileged Cherwona caste came to mind. He looked nothing like Ivan.

"Yes, Borna Angelov — my nemage uncle. He went pretty high in the Taykuni ranks, from what I know. I honestly have no idea what made him turn on my father, on our family... well, his family. But he always hated that my father had magic, and he didn't. Could be a simple matter of human jealousy," he suggested with a shrug.

"Maybe you're right. Humans are led by such raw emotions sometimes, it's astounding... and weirdly unexpected," I said, lost in thought. "Wouldn't you expect us to act differently, not in such a *basic* way?"

Ivan shook his head, chuckling. "Just because you don't push people aside for something as irrational as jealousy doesn't mean others wouldn't do it. There are many different kinds of humans."

Then he hugged me around the waist, placing a light peck on my cheek. My heart rate accelerated at once, and I felt butterflies fluttering in my stomach, yearning to burst out.

"But enough about my complicated family. I think the Plenum is about to start. Come."

Ivan took my hand, towing me towards the centre of the garden, and we sat at the table with Maya and some other people I didn't know. She smiled widely at me; her dark curls pulled into a bun at the top of her head. She sipped her coffee, an inescapable cigarette between her fingers.

"You all right?" She asked, leaning in so I can hear her over the surrounding chatter.

"Yeah. Getting there," I answered, knowing Maya was referring to all those weeks I spent shut in my bedroom, refusing to eat, talk or function in any way. The hole was still there, still huge, but somehow more bearable to carry around. That must be what they call 'living with the pain', I thought to myself. Shaking my head to dispel the unwelcome thoughts, I directed my attention to the crowd around me.

I saw Marko, the blonde man who alerted us about the fire last night, sitting at our table a few seats away. I waved at him, and he waved in turn, smiling. Ivan got off his seat and walked away to talk to him.

"So," Maya started as soon as he left, speaking in a low voice, "I see you and Ivan are an item now." I peered at her for a second, then grinned widely but said nothing.

"Oh, *come on,* you need to give me something more than that. The good news of any kind is welcome in these troubled times, you know." She winked.

I rolled my eyes. "I don't want to jinx it. It's still new."

Maya chuckled, taking a sip of her coffee. "Oh, please. That man is so intense about you; nothing about it seems new. He looks at you like you're his own, personal sun." I blushed at her words, my eyes travelling to Ivan, who talked to Marko a few seats down. I knew he could hear us perfectly, and so did Maya probably, but she didn't seem to care.

"Did he tell you yet, about his ability? And who he really is?" She asked matter-of-factly.

"Yes, I know he's a vilenak. And I know about his ability," I replied, deciding I wouldn't tell anyone that Ivan's powers didn't exactly work on me. Somehow it felt like betraying his trust by sharing this with other people.

Maya rolled her eyes again. "He is so annoying with the controlling thing. That's why I try and stay away, don't like being influenced that way. But" — she leant in closer, almost whispering now — "there is a trick. I think nicotine dampens his mind-controlling powers. When he smokes, he can't do it." She gave me a knowing look as if suggesting I should use that piece of information to incapacitate Ivan.

"Interesting," was all that I could comment because the subject of our conversation just approached us, sitting next to me. Maya winked at me and went back to her coffee. I felt Ivan's gaze on my face but didn't return it. Instead, I smiled widely and nodded towards the centre of the garden, where Tomislav and Natasha were ready to open the meeting.

Natasha's necklace was alight with her gemstones glinting against the morning light, as she used both her hands to direct the magic radiating from them. Apart from the usual deep-green glare coming from her emerald, the necklace emanated a deep blue and golden light. Sapphire and topaz were her additional gems. I looked from her to Tomislav, who was holding his sceptre low on his right side, directing the emanating beams of light with his left hand, outstretched in front of him. His sapphire stood over a bright, hot-white gemstone that could only be a diamond. Beams of light coming from the diamond changed their colour with every twist and turn. All the colours of a rainbow were showcased before my eyes, I realised. Right underneath it, imbued into the sceptre, was a deep-red stone, just like the one I had in my messenger bag – a garnet.

Other people followed suit and soon, the garden was bathing in colourful light floating and swirling across the sky above and around us. Wisps of all colours joined in, directed above us, creating an opaque sheet stretched over our heads and covering the whole garden. The moment the colourful wisps reached their destination, they'd become translucent, blending into the massive barrier in the sky. A shield of some sort, I realised, barely visible to an untrained eye. It was a magnificent sight — the mages' gemstones were putting on the most beautiful light show. I was so taken in that I didn't notice at first that everyone around me — including Maya and Ivan — did the same with their gemstones. Ivan's topaz emitted a glorious golden light, somehow more pronounced and of a deeper shade of gold than Natasha's. I wondered if that was because Natasha only used topaz as her additional stone, while Ivan was born in the month of topaz.

I kept on watching, noticing Maya's amethyst joining the symphony of colours, generating the familiar violet light, just like last night when she cured Mila. Glancing towards the Novak's, I saw all three of them joining in, helping whatever this was. David and Goran were using metal sceptres, identical to those Tomislav and Ivan had. Sandra and Mila had matching bracelets. Goran used a peculiar stone of olive-green colour I hadn't seen before, and David's gem was a diamond, by the looks of it. Both of them had two additional stones, like Tomislav and Natasha. Sandra was directing rose-coloured wisps towards the sky, her wrist adorned with a most beautiful stone attached to a thin bracelet — a ruby. My gaze travelled to Mila, who was also on her feet like everyone else, A familiar deep-red light emanated from it, and I recognised my own birthstone once again.

Looking around the garden, I noticed an unfamiliar group of people dressed in grey clothes. They were the Siva members, I realised; the mages who managed to get to Tayna through Goran. They were all using magic, too.

Finally, the light faded as everyone drew back their gemstones. There was a lot of commotion as everyone but Tomislav retook their seats. Then, complete silence fell.

"That ought to make us invisible for a few hours. Thank you, everyone, for helping with the shield." Tomislav took the central position in the garden, beaming around at everybody.

"To those coming from Danubia — welcome! Our little magical community is happy to see you all again. Some of you we haven't had a chance to host since the last Initiation, I think."

Some people turned around, craning their necks to look at me. My gaze fell to the floor automatically. Even mages sometimes lacked basic human decency, I thought bitterly. It is not polite to stare.

"And some of you only joined us recently, a very warm welcome to you. It's good to have you back," said Tomislav, beaming at the Siva people I'd noticed before. The newly arrived men and women looked very much out of place but relieved to be here. They've probably been woken up recently, I thought. All of them looked like they've only recently gotten out of the RC; there was that empty look in their eyes, paired with weak appearance, courtesy of beatings and malnutrition no doubt. Curiously, all of them still wore the caste bands. *They're probably unaware just yet that Tanatos' hand cannot get them here so easily,* I thought to myself. They must be scared.

"I'll cut straight to the point if you don't mind. Don't like beating around the bush, as some of you might already know." There was a round of faint laughter at this, but it died down quickly as Tomislav's expression became severe.

"We have another chance — a real chance — at Rebellion. That is why I called this Plenum today, the first one since we lost all those years ago. This time, we could succeed and turn the tables for good. I asked you all here today to lay out our plan for you and ask for your support and participation. Now, it won't be easy, and it won't happen quickly. A lot of thought, time and planning will go into this, but we have real leverage on our side this time."

Again, countless heads turned around to look — no, stare — at me, and I felt my cheeks go red. Damn it, Tomislav, I cursed inaudibly.

"Needless to remind you, we've been through this before, so the next time around, we should — and we will — be better prepared. I believe, and I think I speak for Natasha when I say this, that we owe this not only to ourselves but to our friends and family who we lost twenty-five years ago."

There was a round of approval and "Hear-hears" before Tomislav continued, determined to finish his speech without interruptions.

"Last night, we had a less-than-pleasant visit from First Comrade and several agents, looking for Sofija. Tanatos seems to be getting nervous; we think he is looking for the promised child, the threat to his rule. You all know the story, some of you even believe it, so I won't go into details." Tomislav flashed an apologetic smile my way, knowing how much I hated being referred to as 'the promised child'. Directing his attention to other attendees at the meeting, he continued in a confident voice, "Luckily, Sofija wasn't on the premises at the time, and we managed to get rid of the agents without casualties." He glanced towards Mila, his expression apologetic.

"Although they *tried* to harm us. The agents will be coming back; they made that much clear. Our house was burnt down in the process, but we'll live; First Comrade had to leave an impression after all!"

There was a round of shocked gasps at this, but Tomislav went on.

"Now, it isn't unusual for the agents to drop by; they're here almost all the time, as those of you who live in Tayna must know. Someone's got to keep us in check and hidden. But this was the first time since the end of the Rebellion that Tanatos' First Comrade herself — I don't know her real name; if any of you do, please enlighten me — it was the first time *she* came here. She said Sofija has three days to turn herself in, or Tanatos will go after everyone connected to her. Just so there are no delusions about his intentions — he *is* going to torture and kill Sofija's friends if she doesn't comply."

Grave, shocked silence ensued, and the stares intensified as I wished for the ground below me to open so that I could slide in and never come out again. I hated being on the spot like this, and I should mention that to Tomislav once the show is over, I thought bitterly. Ivan's warm hand found mine underneath the table, and I felt my body relaxing instantly. I looked up at Tomislav, determined to keep my gaze steadily fixated on him.

And then I heard someone speak in a most gentle voice. It was odd to hear such a tender voice, coloured with the anger that emanated from it so clearly it travelled across the garden.

"But that is unacceptable. We must help the girl. Her parents would have done the same for anyone of us!"

My head snapped up, and I saw a tiny, grey-haired woman dressed in a yellow blazer designating the Zolta caste. She was standing up, her eyes bulging at Tomislav, her hands curled into fists. One was outstretched in front of her, towards Tomislav as she spoke, proving the point.

Then other people joined in, agreeing with her and nodding vigorously.

"I couldn't agree more, Professor," Tomislav said, his face gleaming. He was obviously pleased by this turn of events. I realised then that he couldn't have known how this would go. Last night we saw that even the closest, most dedicated people may not go with the plan of shielding me from Tanatos. David's words still echoed clearly in my mind: *Why are we risking this much, risking all we've accomplished... for her?*

Today, Tomislav took a leap of faith. He trusted these people with his cause, with his and Natasha's life... with *my* life. Any one of these people could go back to Danubia and report to Tanatos what they'd heard here today. Then he would know what we were planning, and the Rebellion would be crushed before it even started. But, for some reason, Tomislav trusted all of them — he trusted the League of Tayna's Defenders, I realised as I scanned the full garden.

"The first stage is to make sure Sofija doesn't have to turn herself in. I say we protect her friends; anyone Tanatos could harm or take hostage. That would mean constant surveillance, at least for a while. I'll start Sofija's training as soon as we're sure none of her friends are in danger. Some of you may not know, but Sofija was awoken just recently, and she is yet to be trained to use her gemstone. Her grandparents fell as the first victims of this new Rebellion. Tanatos ordered their murders when they wouldn't give away information about their granddaughter's whereabouts."

This time, there was no reaction, nothing but stunned silence. It was the most dreadful silence I'd ever heard, one that echoes loudly in your ears. Tomislav continued.

"The second stage is waking up the nemages. We need to go prudently about this, as we don't want them to turn on us. It is best to have as many of them on our side before the Rebellion starts as we cannot fight Tanatos *and* the people of Danubia. Given our history with the nemages, their reaction is bound to be hostile once they learn about us – or, more accurately, once they *remember* us. We need to show them who the real enemy is, otherwise, they'll join Tanatos and we'll lose again."

Tomislav paused at this, letting the truth of his words sink in. Then, someone spoke, and I recognised Goran's voice:

"How do we plan on convincing the nemages? Waking them up won't be exactly easy."

Tomislav nodded, starting to pace with both hands in his pockets.

"That's correct, it certainly won't be easy. We'll need as much help as possible with this, and we might have to use marbles to demonstrate what we're telling them is true. As you know, most of them are determined to keep their mind shut to magic… or any possibility of that which they hadn't experienced themselves."

There was nodding and even some faint chuckles at this, but Tomislav went on.

"The third stage is the actual attack. We'll have to either bring the fight on our terrain, which means here, in Tayna… or revive the magical supplies in Danubia. We cannot rely on marbles alone; they are too weak and don't last long. Besides, we believe Tanatos has a way of preserving magic, but the reserves are limited to his headquarters at Kalemgrad. So, unless we can get all the way to him or revive the supplies in Agram, there is no way we can fight on his turf. This is something to be discussed in the future, but we'll find a way, I'm sure."

There was a short pause as everyone stared at Tomislav.

"So, any questions? Comments? I'd also like a show of hands to see who'd like to participate. Please, do not hesitate to walk away if you'd rather stay out of this. But I do ask you not to report anything to Tanatos if you choose to leave. We need a fighting chance, at least."

He finished with a reassuring smile, beaming at everyone with a hopeful expression.

"I'm in," I heard Maya say as she stood up, followed by Ivan, Natasha, Vesna and Goran. Soon, others followed suit, and I noticed not one person was sitting any more — apart from me. Everyone was ready to follow Tomislav's plan and to help me. I looked around the sunny garden, taking in the faces of my new-found family.

Chapter 20
The Gemstone

"That's... great, truly great. Thank you all!" Tomislav beamed, surprised at everyone's readiness to join the fight, to follow his plan. "We have a real chance this time. I know it!" He was so exhilarated it was contagious.

The rest of the day was spent in a more relaxed atmosphere. We all agreed on the course we'd take together. From now on, it was just careful planning and execution. The newcomers from Siva members were all housed either at The Bayamonti or adjacent abandoned houses. Regular Plenum meetings were scheduled a week in advance, allowing everyone who still had to travel back to Danubia for work to attend.

The League agreed they'd guard Helena and her family, as they were most likely to be attacked. There was no one else in Velesh I was very close to, I thought in sudden realisation. Perhaps Anton... but we weren't that close, and I still believed that he'd turned me in, though I didn't understand why. By telling the Armiya about my illegal travel permit, he was probably given immunity by Tanatos. That's how it worked, Tomislav said.

"The bastard did this twenty-five years ago, too. To turn people against their relatives and friends, he promised they'd be protected no matter what comes after. The one sure thing about him is that he always kept his word... I'll give him that. So, you see, if you think Anton turned you in, then he'd be well-protected by that little act of cooperation with the Armiya."

Vesna, the receptionist, offered her help in looking after Helena and her family. She was a skilled mage and had a lot of experience with the nemages. She also used to work in Agram before taking over at The Bayamonti from her parents years ago.

"Don't worry, your friend and her family will be safe with me. I'll introduce myself to her, maybe even get a job at Velesh City Hall. They must be looking for someone to replace you," she said, looking at me thoughtfully, "and I'm sure I can blend in. That way, Helena would know me, and it wouldn't be strange to her that I'm around. For the time being, I'll have to move there to be close to her if anything happens. I'll just say I moved back from Sopot or somewhere close enough to avoid suspicion."

I nodded, surprised at the speed at which Tomislav's plan progressed. Vesna was getting ready to leave in two days. Since magic was non-existent in Danubia, the League devised a plan to deliver marbles to Vesna. The marbles didn't last long in a non-magical environment, Natasha explained, which is why Vesna would need a new batch every day. The magic within them loses its potency in magic-free Danubia. Every evening, one of the League members would deliver new marbles, carrying small amounts of magic, to Vesna through the portal by the Promenade.

"Maya's parents created the portal to Velesh just before the Rebellion. They needed a way to be connected to Tayna if things got ugly as they did. Kairos Café had always been a sort of magical crossroads for us; no one gets in or out of Tayna without going through there. It used to be a mere student café before the Rift, you know," Natasha explained as we sat down at The Bayamonti Café to go over the plan for an umpteenth time. "That's how you were brought to your grandparents, don't you remember? Tomislav took you through the portal in Kairos and straight to Velesh."

I nodded, remembering the story she and Tomislav told me when we first met and everything Goran said about the less-known portal in Velesh.

But then something else came to mind as I looked around the hotel bar, noticing it was more crowded than ever before. The mages were returning from their posts in Danubia, preparing for the fight.

"But if you go, who'll take care of the hotel and the bar?" I asked, turning to Vesna, who was munching on a piece of chocolate cake and sipping her coffee.

"Natasha here offered to take over while I'm on guard duty," Vesna replied matter-of-factly.

"It is no problem at all, Sofija, don't you worry. Tomislav and I will move back into Tayna anyway now that the fight is finally happening.

And, with our house burnt-down, we'll just stay at the hotel from now on, so it's convenient for us to run the place too." Natasha spoke in a reassuring voice, although it didn't escape my notice how she twitched at the mention of the house they'd lost.

"Are you sure there is nothing I can do to help? Perhaps I can deliver the marbles—"

"No, you can't. We've been through this," Natasha reminded me. "Tanatos should have made a move by now, and for some reason, he didn't. That is very worrying and could only mean he's planning something, waiting for the right moment. We cannot take any chances; you are not to leave Tayna under any circumstances."

None of the League members seemed upset at the prospect of another war or even scared of the imminent death or imprisonment. In fact, it was as if the long-anticipated event they'd all been preparing for was finally scheduled. They were all more than ready. The only one who wasn't ready was me.

A whole week passed in preparations for the first stage Tomislav outlined. Vesna was already stationed in Velesh, working at the City Hall and taking care of Helena. Every night, a different League member would take the next days' worth of marbles to her to avoid suspicion. Armiya checks were more frequent now. Tomislav believed they'd sometimes enter cafés incognito to observe the crowd. Vesna would normally wait at Nocturno in Velesh, using after-work drinks as an excuse for frequent visits there.

Helena had no clue she was under constant surveillance nor where Vesna came from, of course, but that was for the best. I didn't hear from Vesna, although I was yearning to know how my best friend was doing. She was probably worried about me and possibly annoyed because we hadn't spoken in a month. Every time that issue came to mind, I just pushed it away. There was nothing I could do; crossing into Velesh was out of the question. Tomislav said they'd now be watching every portal, and I'd be captured within seconds. When I asked why the rest of the League weren't in danger, Tomislav explained that Tanatos didn't have proof the League was planning anything. And, worried about the public opinion as he was, he didn't want to alert Danubians by arresting innocent people. So, he waited for us to make a mistake.

Phones, computers, and the network didn't work in Tayna. The only thing I could do is write a letter to Helena for Vesna to deliver it. She couldn't say where she got it from or even that she knew me, of course. So, she left it at Helena's post box, or at least she promised she'd do that.

The letter explained that I was well and safe and that she needn't worry. To keep the tone light, I mentioned Ivan briefly. I hoped Helena would believe that I was okay if she knew I was in love. It was one of the most challenging letters I'd ever written, next to that which I wrote to my grandparents, the one that they'd never had a chance to read.

I couldn't reveal anything else to Helena due to the vow I'd made to Tayna's magical community. Not being able to put it any other way, I just asked her to trust me again. And to not ask around about me, as I was sure she'd been doing. I hoped with all my heart that she'd listen.

Today was my first lesson with Tomislav. He'd found a place safe enough for me to practice, and we were headed there after breakfast.

"So, where is it?" I asked as we left The Bayamonti, heading further into the Tayna old town. I couldn't suppress my curiosity; Tomislav was annoyingly mysterious.

"You'll see. We're nearly there." He chuckled, seeing my annoyed expression. "Patience is not your strong suit?"

"No," I retorted.

"Neither was it your father's. He was my best friend, you know."

I looked up, surprised. "You never said."

"Yes, well... he was. We were more like brothers. Your mother was also a friend, but not like Luka. We met at university here in Tayna."

"What did you study?" I asked, wondering why I hadn't posed the question before. I had no idea what my parents' professions were.

"Politics for nemage degree, Defensive Magic for the magical degree. We were going to teach in Akademia." I could see him smiling, no doubt amused by some memory he'd conjured up in his mind. "Your mother was on the same course."

"You've got two degrees?" I asked, impressed.

"Yes, that's how it was back before the Wipe when the nemages knew about us. Most mages would choose two degrees, to be able to compete in both… for the lack of a better word, markets."

I nodded, working up the courage to ask a question that bothered me ever since First Comrade's unpleasant visit.

"Tom… can I ask you something?" I kept my eyes glued to the ground beneath my feet.

He glanced down at me, slowing down a little. "Of course. What is it?"

"You believe I'm the promised child", I muttered, "For some reason. But now, ever since that night, the night of the attack… I think Tanatos might believe it too."

Tomislav's voice was careful but pleased when he replied. "Yes. Yes, I'd say he believes it too."

"How come he didn't come find me earlier? I lived in Velesh, at the same house, for the past twenty-five years. If he thought I was a threat of any kind, he could have just had me arrested," I asked.

He shrugged and said: "Good question. I'm still trying to understand that part myself. If he believed you to be the promised child, he could have tested you much sooner, captured you, murdered you." He glanced at me apologetically. "But he didn't. He waited all this time, and only when you decided to leave Velesh, he finally acted. I have no idea why."

There was a pause as he mulled the question over.

"Perhaps Tanatos waited for his power to be consolidated before making a move, or for you to reach full magical potency, which actually *is* just about now. Still, it doesn't explain why he simply didn't imprison you earlier, keep an eye on you. I certainly waited until you were old enough to face all this, and at your full magical potency. I was very reluctant to wake you until the League was ready for the next rebellion. Perhaps it wasn't the best decision on my part, but I wanted you to live a relatively peaceful life for as long as possible".

He smiled down at me, and I read a smidgeon of remorse in his brown eyes. He blamed himself for not getting to me sooner. I nodded, deciding not to press the issue any further. Yes, I had a peaceful life in Velesh, with my grandparents. But I was also utterly blind the whole time. *At least my family was there with me.* Now they're gone, and I'm wide awake.

Tomislav came to a halt as we reached a small, iron gate leading into what looked like an abandoned tunnel. The lock was rusty and covered in rainwater from the thunderstorm last night. Tomislav lit up his gem, and the lock came off, hitting the ground with a thud.

"This is not where we're practising, don't worry," Tomislav said reassuringly, noticing my puzzled expression, "but we do have to go through it. Come."

I followed him into the tunnel, a strong scent of damp earth filling my nostrils and deep darkness embracing me immediately. The tunnel was unusually low, more like a bunker, bathed in dim lamplight coming from both sides, illuminating the narrow path. The further we went, the dimmer the light became, ominous darkness growing denser. I wasn't afraid of the dark or closed spaces, but after a few minutes, my heart was in my throat.

"How much longer?" I managed, hoping not to sound scared.

"Any minute now," Tomislav said, his voice relaxed, almost entertained.

I followed him in silence for what seemed like an eternity, minding my steps as the earth below my feet became less level, the muddy ground now covered in gravel.

Tomislav stopped in his tracks suddenly, scraping the ground below his feet as if searching for something.

"It must be somewhere around here... perhaps a bit more to the right..." he mumbled under his breath, moving his feet back and forth, looking for something in the ground. A trapdoor, perhaps? The thought of going down the dark, narrow opening sent shivers down my spine, but I didn't say anything.

"Ah! Found it!" I heard Tomislav exclaim as his sapphire suddenly lit up, filling the tunnel in blue light. There, right in front of us, a narrow stairwell led downwards. Tomislav was standing at the top of the topmost stair, beaming at me expectantly.

"Shall we?" he asked, grinning. I nodded briefly, wondering where the stairs will take us.

The staircase was narrow, also covered in damp earth and gravel. I wondered quietly when last another human being was here. About a dozen stairs down, the staircase winded sharply to the right. A moment later, I stepped into a massive room, more like a dancing hall than anything else.

The room had dark, wooden floors surrounded by warm, mahogany walls, like those in the Kairos Café. A large, embroidered rug sat in the centre, making the room cosy and inviting, giving it a sense of style. As we approached the central part, I could see a couple of coffee tables placed in the middle, paired with cosy-looking sofas. A large fireplace dominated the room, now unlit as it was the middle of July. I wondered if this room was inspired by the Kairos Café design... or perhaps the other way around?

But it wasn't the tables that caught my attention. Walking to the side of the room, I realised what I was looking at were gemstones. Dozens and dozens of them... perhaps even hundreds? Glinting in all shapes and colours, they were mounted to the wall, taking up the room's whole right side. I stood there, beaming at the beautiful stones. I've never seen so many in one place, and some I didn't recognise. The opaque, green-blue gemstones I've never seen before but thought I knew what they were. That must be the turquoise, my family's home stone, according to what Tomislav told me. My hair strand was of precisely the same colour, I realised suddenly.

"This is our gemstone collection. Few are left after Tanatos' raids at the end of the Rebellion. Still, it's enough to cover our small community." I didn't even notice Tomislav approaching me before he spoke.

"Is this where my garnet came from?" I asked, eyeing the tiny blood-red stones at the top of the wall. It seemed to me all the different gemstones were sorted somehow... perhaps by birth months?

Tomislav glanced at me, nodding. "Yes. Natasha and I came here to get the garnet for you just before the Initiation. We call this room the Vestibule, for it used to be an antechamber to the Akademia of Magic we ran in the past. The place wasn't safe for training straight away, so we spent the past month securing it with protective spells. This is where we get everyone's gemstones nowadays because they've disappeared from the market after the Wipe."

"What happened to Akademia?" I asked, glancing sideways at Tomislav. He took a deep sigh before answering.

"Tanatos happened, of course. The bastard demolished the whole thing, and this is all that is left. I don't think he knows the place still exists... well, at least *some* of it does. We keep the entrance unpleasant on purpose just in case unwelcome visitors come sniffing around."

It was unpleasant, all right, I thought to myself. That tunnel would discourage even the most determined visitors from entering.

"Why would he destroy the Akademia? I mean, he's a mage himself, isn't he?" I asked.

"Yes, he is a mage, but he's also a traitor. Probably doesn't want any competition around if you know what I mean. He doesn't fancy young mages being trained to fight. He's scared."

I looked up at him.

"But... you do train young mages, don't you? I mean, you're about to teach me, for starters." I could see him smiling now.

"Of course, we do. Don't need Akademia to pass on our magical knowledge. It is a bit challenging, but we generally use this room. Some parents choose to do the home training, although that does occasionally end up in accidents... young mages cannot control their powers at first."

We stood there, staring at the beautiful gemstones for a few minutes. I imagined young children being taught to use magic in their own home, blowing things up. Who would have cleaned it up after them? Was there a way to undo magical disasters with a simple spell? Too bad I couldn't see the Akademia when it was still active. It must have been a fascinating place, the underground school of magic.

"Should we start then?" Tomislav asked eagerly, his voice excited. I didn't much like it, as I was pretty certain where his excitement was coming from. He expected a lot from me. I was, after all, the promised child he so strongly believed in. Yet there I was, standing in the beautiful Vestibule, surrounded by magical objects I didn't know how to use.

"Yes, sure," I managed, attempting to sound brave.

"You have the garnet with you?" Tomislav asked expectantly.

A few seconds later, I produced a small box from my messenger bag. Inside was a shiny blood-red stone, resting next to a silver ring I was gifted the same night. Gingerly, I handed it to Tomislav. *It's not a bomb, Sofija. As far as you know, the sarcastic voice jeered.*

"Ah, we should merge them first. Come."

I followed him to the nearest coffee table. Placing the silver ring and the garnet down in front of him, Tomislav produced the metal sceptre from his pocket. He then tapped the garnet twice with the top of his sceptre where the sapphire stood. The moment the two gemstones touched, they both gleamed in their respective lights: deep blue on blood-red. I watched as the garnet rose into the air, levitating above the tiny box where it had been resting for the past month. Leaning the sceptre slightly to the side, Tomislav directed the garnet towards the silver ring. He held the ring up with his free hand, holding it steady as the garnet stopped in mid-air, only a few centimetres from the silver ring resting in Tomislav's outstretched hand. The dent in the ring grew slightly larger, adjusting itself. I could see the creases moving this way and that to match the garnet's shape. Simultaneously, while still levitating in the air, garnet was self-adjusting too, twisting and turning in the air, its form changing so that it matched the dent in the silver ring. Finally, Tomislav directed the garnet towards the ring, and they moulded together, perfect as if they'd never been separated.

I gaped.

"Pretty neat, huh?" Tomislav grinned at my expression. "Let's do some magic."

He handed me the ring, now no longer gem-less. The small garnet glittered beautifully on top of it, and I put it on my right hand without thinking. I was no longer scared of it, I suddenly realised. It was too lovely to only be looked at, too precious to sit in a box. The moment I put the ring on, a surge of unexpected excitement went through me, making me energised and trouble-free. Anything was possible from that moment on; I knew it. I couldn't remember why I ever backed away from this beautiful object before.

"Feeling the pull already?" I could hear Tomislav asking as I examined the ring, now resting on my middle finger.

My head snapped up. "What do you mean?"

"The pull, from the gemstone. There is a strong connection between the owner and his gem. It only manifests when the mage has chosen the vessel like you have now. The ring is your vessel. You should feel... optimistic. Energised."

He clearly enjoyed it; I could see from the way he was smiling at me. He loved the role of a mentor and couldn't wait to test me.

"Yes, I can feel it. Let's start. I'm ready."

Chapter 21
The Panmage

"The way a mage channels magic through the gem is simple. You communicate with the gemstone; you feel it. That way, you can show it exactly what you want to do. Of course, your hands need to be free for the channelling to work. The gemstone only facilitates magic, brings it to the surface, but you need to direct it otherwise it'll have nowhere to go."

We were standing in the middle of the Vestibule. Tomislav's sceptre was outstretched in front of him as he was getting ready to cast a spell.

"For example, if I want to produce a ball of fire..." He held his sceptre outstretched for a second, and the sapphire lit up. A moment later, a tiny fireball was levitating a centimetre above Tomislav's sceptre. "I don't require all three of my gems for simple spells. They do come in handy in a fight, though. If they're not lit up, that means I'm not using them," Tomislav explained. I noticed his secondary gems resting, unlit, underneath the gleaming sapphire.

"Now, let's light something..." He looked around, the tiny fireball still hovering over the metal sceptre, as his gaze concentrated upon a candle sitting at one of the coffee tables. His free hand lay outstretched mid-air, and his index finger moved as if motioning for the candle to come to him. The candle flew in the air, levitating towards him and a few seconds later, he caught it with his free hand. In one swift movement, Tomislav placed the tiny fireball on top of the candle, and it started burning.

"How'd you do that? You just *tell* it what to do?" I asked puzzled. It sounded too easy; I must be missing something for sure.

"Not quite. You need to have a clear visual representation of what it is you want to happen. And another thing. Mages use communication through *sensations*, rather than words, to establish an initial connection to their gemstone, to get it to light up and respond. Once the connection

179

is established, it is easy to do magic, as easy as speaking to an old friend." He paused, looking up at me to make sure I understood. I nodded and motioned for him to continue.

Tomislav started pacing around the spacious room, speaking as he went.

"Every gemstone is ruled by one prevailing sensation; we call it the gem *flavour*. You need to understand which sensation it is and, when conjuring a spell, you must reach to it to communicate with your gemstone. You'll notice your own gem has a special flavour to it. For example, amethysts are very calming, make you feel safe. My sapphire gives me a boost of self-confidence like there's nothing I cannot do. And garnet... well, it should make you feel energised. Strong. Even more so for you than for me because garnet is your primary gem. Use this notion emanating from your gem to communicate with it, to work with it. This is its language, and you should adjust to it to reach through to the stone."

He started pacing again, twisting the sceptre between his fingers as he went.

"There's more. Simultaneously, you need to concentrate on your own *anchor* emotion; that is what we call it. Your anchor helps you light the gemstone, get it to work. The easiest way to understand this process is by picturing a sort of tunnel where your mind connects with the gemstone; on one end is your anchor emotion; on the other, the gem flavour awaits. The communication is established once these two meet. Your anchor can be anger, or happiness, or hope. There is no firm rule. The important thing is that it's overwhelming and that it leaves no space for any other sensation. Your mind must be filled with it."

He glanced up, turning on his heel to face me. "If you've ever accidentally used magic before, you might remember that it was always under huge emotional strain, wasn't it? Fear, or frustration, perhaps? Maybe even exhilaration?"

I stopped to think for a moment. Tomislav was right. The last time I used magic was in the Classified Files section when the drawer would not open. I was scared and frustrated, more like terrified because I was about to get caught... and so it worked. The drawer *magically* opened, I remembered.

"Yes, you're right... it was mostly fear or frustration. Does that mean I always have to be terrified to perform magic?" I did not like the idea one bit.

Tomislav stopped pacing, grinning at me.

"Of course not. Any strong emotion, strong enough to drive everything else out of your mind and leave it a blank slate, will do. Still following?"

"Yes, I think so. Anchor emotion lights up the gemstone; reaching out to gem flavour helps me communicate with it", I replied, eager to hear more. I'll worry about the details later once I've tried using magic. Tomislav nodded, satisfied.

"The other way is to just clear your mind completely, but some people find it difficult, as we're always thinking about something or the other. Even when you're not aware of it, you think, mulling things over, remembering or daydreaming. We are, after all, creatures of the mind. So, choose one thing and let it consume you. Understand? Why don't you give it a go?"

I looked down to the floor, remembering my anger with Davor, my fear from him, my pain from losing Grandpa and Grandma. My happiness when I am with Ivan. *Yes,* I thought to myself, *I think I can understand. Strong emotions are something I felt way too often... more often bad than good emotions, though, but Tomislav said any would do.*

Here goes nothing. I closed my eyes, concentrating, searching for my anchor.

My mind was suddenly overtaken with still-fresh pain at the loss of my grandparents. I let the memory of their white faces come to me, their frozen bodies lying in the ground. Then, the infuriating feeling of anger came as I recalled what happened after the last time I visited their graves. The First Comrade and Tanatos' agents came here, to Tayna, to look for me. They made threats, they hurt Mila, they burnt down Tomislav and Natasha's home. I grunted in frustration and heard faint chuckling.

Looking up, I saw Tomislav's happy face. He was looking at something, and then I noticed what made him so pleased: the garnet on my ring was lit up, gleaming in the most beautiful crimson light. It wasn't as wild as the first time I used it. The light was subdued and denser, concentrated around the ring. It gave me a feeling of comforting warmth and... energy? I felt as if I could run a marathon or lift heavy objects.

Perhaps I should try with some of the statues in the old town? The sphynx might do, I thought with a grin.

"Whoa, this is great," I said, surprised. This must be the gem flavour Tomislav just talked about, I thought. Immense energy.

"It worked. And so quickly! Well done, Sofija," Tomislav exclaimed, clapping his hands in excitement. "Now, try to do something — perhaps extinguish the candle. Remember, anchor emotion plus gem flavour equal successful casting."

I peered down at the garnet, still gleaming with beautiful red light. The little stone did not feel like an inanimate object to me anymore. Suddenly, it was like I was talking to a person, a person with this colossal positiveness emanating from it, a person who was making me more powerful by the second. My own anger with Tanatos, my pain at the loss of grandparents, allowed my mind to concentrate on the gem only, to drive every other preoccupation out of my head. The moment the garnet lit, my anger, my anchor emotion, took a back seat, remaining steady in the back of my mind. Now, the prevailing feeling, almost radiating through me, was overwhelming energy. I could do anything, be anything, as long as I don't let my anchor go and as long as the gemstone still *talks* to me.

It was so natural, so... expected — nothing about this seemed novel to me. I wondered why I ever feared the gemstone when it was clearly the most beautiful thing in the world, my most prized possession, my counterpart.

Slowly, I moved my gem-adorned hand a little to the right. Concentrating on the candle now burning at one of the coffee tables, I closed my eyes and commanded the garnet to fetch it. It did. The red light gleamed more intensively, and the candle was suddenly in the air, levitating into my free hand. I took it eagerly, and a moment later, asked my garnet to extinguish the flame. Unsure of how to do it, I hesitated for a moment, realising the gemstone's light was getting weaker. I had to develop a method soon, I knew; otherwise, the gem's light would fade completely. I concentrated hard and, making up my mind, decided to put out the candle with droplets of water. At the very same moment that the thought came into my mind, several large drops of water appeared out of thin air and I directed them with a gentle motion of my gem-adorned hand towards the candle. Obedient, the droplets rained over the lit candle, and the flame was extinguished.

"Extraordinary!" I could hear Tomislav exclaim. "I've never seen anything like this before. Are you *sure* you haven't practised magic already at some point?"

I could only nod stupidly. Still exhilarated from the extraordinary feeling of strength and energised to the breaking point, I couldn't find the words to describe how happy I felt. I could do it! I could do magic. It wasn't difficult; if anything, it felt very… familiar.

"I want you to try something." Tomislav was now standing next to me, visibly excited. Looking up at him, I grinned happily.

"Sure. What is it?"

"Let's find out if you collide with any other gemstones."

Still grinning widely, he turned towards the gem-adorned wall we examined earlier.

"A simple spell will tell us if you can use any other gems apart from the garnet. What you need to do is have your garnet collide with every type of gemstone here. Those you can control will light up instantly. Those you can't, won't."

I nodded in understanding. Once again, I didn't need to ask how to do it. I knew, somehow, what I had to do.

This time I chose a happier memory for an anchor. Thinking of Ivan and his lips on mine, I willed the garnet to light up once again. Then, I stood in front of the gem-adorned wall, concentrating on every single gemstone in there, having them all clearly in my mind. The garnet's burst of energy was already flowing through me, my body almost vibrating with the intensity of it. In my mind, I told the garnet what to do. *I need to find out if I collide with any other gemstone… I need to know if I can control more of you.*

The next thing I remember was a burst of blinding light coming from all sides, the heat from the ring where the gemstone was perched, and Tomislav's shouts from somewhere far away. Then, my body hit the wooden floor, and everything went dark.

Voices woke me — terrified, urgent. One voice stood out from all the others.

"Is she all right? What happened, Tom? How long has she been out?"

Ivan. What was he doing here? Tomislav said this would be a one-on-one lesson. I tried to look up, but my eyes wouldn't open. *Was I dreaming? Did I just fall asleep halfway through my training session?*

My arms moved, and I felt something soft and smooth beneath me. Surprised, I forced my eyes to open and realised I was lying on the sofa at the Vestibule. Standing up, I noticed the mahogany room around me was in complete disarray; half the furniture was misplaced, tables were overturned, and the gemstones…

"No!" I bellowed, staring at the mess in front of the gem-adorned wall. Half the gemstones had fallen off somehow and were now scattered all around the wooden floor.

Someone was helping me up, and there were gasps of relief.

"Don't worry about it, for now, Sofija. We'll fix it. How are you feeling?" Ivan's strong hands led me to the nearest chair, and I sat down, looking up at his concerned face. He was crouching in front of me, levelling his gaze with mine. Searching for something. *Why was he so worried? And what were all these other people doing here?*

Now I noticed that half the League was down at the Vestibule. Natasha and Maya were smiling at me from the centre of the room, but they too seemed worried.

"Oh no, what did I do now? I'm so sorry!" I sighed, exasperated, angry with myself. "I should have warned you I'm a walking disaster!" I scanned all the faces in the room, giving them my most apologetic look. They'd worked for who knows how long to put together the gem collection, and then I show up and wreck it all!

"You didn't do anything, sweetheart. And don't worry about the wall; I said we'll fix it," Ivan said, his voice calm.

"What do you mean I didn't do anything? Then *who* blew those things up?"

Tomislav walked over now, smiling widely at me.

"*You* did, but only because all the gemstones collided with you, Sofija. We've never seen anything like it. I certainly didn't expect it; I didn't even think you'd get the Collision spell right the first time! The moment you willed your garnet to collide with other gemstones, they *all* responded. It was phenomenal. Of course, the surge of energy was so strong you passed out for a while. We were worried you wouldn't wake up anytime soon," he said carefully. *Well, that explains why everyone had such worried expressions,* I thought.

"The explosion knocked some of the gems down too. It's nothing unusual; you need to get used to every gemstone and its own flavour. Even experienced mages wouldn't do much better in that situation. Only I never met anyone who had to deal with the energy outburst from all the twelve gemstones." He was smiling so widely the grin would go all over his head if it weren't for his ears. I still didn't get it; it didn't make sense.

"All gemstones collided with me. But that's impossible! Ivan told me no one controls more than three—" I protested.

"No one we know of. I suppose history is about to be rewritten," Natasha interrupted. She, too, was beaming at me happily. "All twelve gemstones! There is a term for it... a Panmage. I always thought that was just a myth, but here you are... in flesh and blood. Only you're supposed to have silver eyes. Guess that's the mythical part."

There were chuckles from all sides.

"Yeah, I always thought silver eyes were a bit over the top," Tomislav commented, grinning.

They all beamed at me so warmly and intensely that my cheeks were about to explode from the heat.

"How did you all get here?" I asked, aware that we were underground and that phones don't work in Tayna.

"Tom called me, and I brought the others. We have our own ways of communication," Natasha replied but didn't say anything further.

They were all looking at me with such devotion it was sickening. Maya was sitting next to me, her amethyst gleaming. "Just checking for any serious injuries," she answered my unspoken question. "Looks like you're okay."

"All right, you all need to calm down. I can't be this Panmage; that just doesn't make any sense! I probably did something wrong or... or somehow broke my garnet," I managed, glancing nervously at my ring, which was still in one piece.

Ivan laughed, still crouching in front of me, his hand in mine.

"No, I'm afraid there's no way to explain this away. You *are* a

185

Panmage. Remember I told you you'd be extraordinary? Too bad we didn't make a bet; I'd have won." He winked at me, smiling fondly.

I stood up, walking over to Tomislav.

"Please tell me what's going on. And don't mess with me; I'm not in the mood," I demanded.

"I just did," said Tomislav, rolling his eyes at me. "It was the truth, Sofija. Panmages, people who control or collide with all gemstones are rare, but they do occur sometimes."

"How often do they occur? Are there any others in Tayna?" I asked, half-annoyed for some reason.

"Not exactly. The last one lived some five hundred years ago, and… well, everyone thought the Panmage was part of a myth. It was so long ago it became a sort of fairy tale."

I gaped.

"Now you think I'm some fairy-tale character?" I asked in a strained voice.

"Not if the fairy tale is, in fact, real," Tomislav answered simply.

My eyes narrowed as I scrutinised his face for hints of humour. It seemed he was serious; there was no trace of irony in his ageing features.

"So, what now then? We continue the training?" I urged, attempting at a lighter tone though I didn't think it worked.

"Wait a second. Tom, you will let her rest, won't you? The training can wait; she could have hit herself severely." I heard Ivan protest.

Tomislav sighed. "You forget she's probably stronger than both of us. Could you imagine what that amount of magical potency does to a human body? Now that she's found her vessel, and once she learns to control all gems, she'll be invincible. She certainly won't have to worry about such pedestrian occurrences like injuries," he explained, smirking.

"You should let her have a break, still," Ivan insisted.

I looked up at him, smiling. "I'm fine, really. We can continue." Suddenly, I was eager to learn more. Tomislav's optimism was somehow seeping into me.

"No, Ivan is right. Take the rest of the day off; we'll clean up here, lock the entrance again and continue tomorrow. I believe you two had plans for the afternoon anyway?" He was looking at Ivan, his eyebrows raised.

I looked from one to the other. "We did?"

Ivan grinned, his straight white teeth gleaming. "Yeah. I'm taking you to meet my mother."

Chapter 22
The Purge

"What? Are you serious?" I asked, surprised. My stomach quivered nervously at the thought of meeting Ivan's mother, the vila.

"I never joke about bringing human girls' home," he said, leaning in to plant a light kiss on my lips.

I frowned. "How many were there?"

"You're the first one, of course," he retorted, smirking.

We went back to the hotel so that I could freshen up and change into something more presentable. I didn't think meeting a vila in a pair of jeans and a t-shirt would be such a great idea, so I went for the burgundy dress I wore at my Initiation.

Ivan waited patiently while I went through my rituals, showering and then attempting to disentangle my long, chestnut hair. Once done, I replaced the garnet ring on my right hand. I started noticing its absence; I felt somehow emptier without it, like a canvas in black-and-white. The moment the garnet ring was back on, all colours sprang back to life.

"How do I look?" I asked, standing at the bathroom doorway.

He cocked his pretty head to one side, examining me. "Perfect as always. The dress looks familiar," he added as his lips curved into a crooked smile.

Still sitting on the edge of the bed, he extended his hand to me, and I took it. The moment we touched, the familiar wave of warmth I already associated with him washed over me. If he couldn't control my feelings, then why do I always feel this way? *Stop trying to rationalise it, Sofija,* I said to myself. *Reason doesn't apply here. You've been waiting for this.*

"I have something to tell you, Sofija," Ivan said slowly. He put his arms around my waist and kissed me lightly on the neck. I shivered.

"Yes?" I managed, kissing him on the lips and gasping for air when we resurfaced half a minute later.

Gently, he cupped my face with his hands and stared deep into my eyes.

"I love you. You are the most important being to me now." .

My heart wanted to jump out of my chest from happiness. I knew I felt the same way; I had known it for a while now. And now this beautiful man, this amazing creature, loves me back. Grinning like an idiot, I hugged him tighter, kissing him fiercely again.

"Care to comment?" he asked in between kisses.

"You should already know that I love you too. I have probably loved you from the moment we met. Which, by the way, wasn't that long time ago." I leaned back, peering at him, trying to keep my expression serious. "Did you bewitch me? Gave me a love potion?"

His smile grew wider, and he buried his head in my chest, listening to the insane rhythm of my heart.

"No, no bewitchment, no tricks. Just my sheer charm", he teased, "you amazing woman." Another peck on my forehead, both my cheeks, then lips, then neck. Just when I was starting to lose my breath again, he said:

"We better leave, or we'll be late. I think my mum is preparing dinner. We don't want to keep her waiting."

Ivan led me outside the Tayna old town, toward the hills I didn't even notice until now. Ever since I arrived in Tayna, I'd been staying within the confines of the ancient centre, only visiting the graveyard just outside the city walls every now and then. He led me up the hill, and we hiked for a while.

"Don't worry, it isn't far away," Ivan said, noticing my expression as we started hiking, "and not very steep either. We have a small cabin just behind the first slope."

"How come you live in the hills?" I asked, wondering if the remote location has anything to do with animosities between the vila kind and humans.

"Our kind traditionally lived in the mountains to stay away from humans, to remain hidden," he explained. "This house has been in the family for generations. It was built by my great-grandfather, so my mum and I stayed. Other vila families also live around this area. This part of Tayna is known as Feyar."

I nodded, looking around the pretty landscape. The footpath in front of us was covered in tiny pebbles, and tall cypress trees lined either side. The Adriatic Sea was visible in the distance, growing larger as we climbed.

"Actually, a very long time ago, when Danubia was but a province in the Eastern Empire, Feyar stretched into what we today know as Tayna, too. The province of Tayna was only created later, during the dark period."

I glanced at him in surprise. "Dark period? Like in the Middle Ages?"

"Yes, that's the nemage term, I think. History is not my strong suit, but I know there were strong animosities between mages and nemages. Most mages served at the Eastern Court at the time. Some nemages saw this as working with the enemy, with the oppressors. So, there were lots of armed clashes between the two groups. The vila kind that traditionally lived in these parts offered the old town as a sanctuary to their mage friends; we often helped each other due to shared abilities and, for some, hatred towards nemages. Hatred is a strong unifier". There was a pause before Ivan continued, towing me further into the hills.

"The mages could regroup here, plan attacks and hide effectively; nemages rarely ventured into Feyar, for they were always wary of the vila. Over time, as mages took over the old town and the vila fled to the hills, the name changed. That's how Tayna was created."

I frowned, lost in thought.

"What you're telling me, in fact, is that Tayna is Feyar, just stolen from the vila by the mages a very long time ago?"

"No, not stolen. At least not technically. But over time, as more of the mages moved there, they sort of took over. It happened a very long time ago," Ivan added sympathetically.

A small, wooden cabin came into view. It looked old but well-maintained, positioned in the clearing between the trees. The footpath leading to the cabin entrance was lined with flower beds of all colours and kinds. This truly is a vila home, I thought to myself. It was as if I'd walked straight into one of the fairy tales Grandma used to read to me when I was a child.

We were just about to turn onto the cabin footpath when a strong surge of energy hit me, and I had to fight to stay upright and not fall down.

"Whoa! What was *that*?" I asked, balancing on still-unsteady feet.

"I forgot to mention the house is protected by a defensive spell. Should have thrown you off your feet, but then I guess it's one of the perks of being a Panmage." Ivan smiled down at me, his emerald eyes full of pride. I looked away, embarrassed.

"Or maybe I'm just not as clumsy as I thought," I murmured under my breath. Ivan heard me, of course.

"Just embrace who you are. Being a Panmage must be such a great thing once you get used to it and learn how to control your powers." He beamed at me excitedly. Then, frowning slightly, he added, "But I guess it *does* take some getting used to."

I wasn't in the mood to discuss my newly found skills, so I changed the topic.

"So... your house? Should we go in now that we're past the defensive spell?" I asked, motioning towards the cabin entrance just a few steps away.

He didn't have the time to answer as a tall woman, probably one of the most beautiful women I'd ever seen in my life, opened the door.

Even from a distance, I could see her eyes were shaped exactly like Ivan's, glimmering like emeralds in the afternoon sun. Her long hair was of deep ebony colour, and her cheekbones high and pronounced. There were no signs of ageing on her beautiful face; only the creases in her neck gave her away.

"Are you two going to spend the whole afternoon here, or do you plan on coming in?" She asked, her lips twisting in a broad smile as she looked from Ivan to me. "Welcome to Feyar, dear," she added kindly, eyeing me.

Ivan took my hand and led me to his mother.

"Hello, mother. Meet Sofija Filipov, my... partner," he said. I wondered why he chose to call me his 'partner' instead of his 'girlfriend'.

The woman shook my hand vigorously and then leaned in to kiss both my cheeks.

"Nice to meet you, finally. Ivan talks about you so much," she commented, chuckling at her son apologetically. "My name is Eva

Angelov."

"Nice to meet you, too. Thank you for inviting me," I managed nervously. I've never met my *boyfriend's* parents before and hoped not to embarrass myself. As the word 'boyfriend' came to mind, I suddenly understood why Ivan chose to use 'partner' instead. It didn't fit somehow; it sounded too simplistic, too... ordinary.

We followed her into the cabin. The interior did not surprise me at all; it was precisely where I'd picture a vila to live. A small hallway led into the spacious living room, looking out to the mountains through wide windows. The walls were cream-coloured, with wooden pillars placed along the room's sides, supporting the low ceiling. A spacious seating area dominated the centre of the living room, and I noticed the entire wall behind it was covered in floor-to-ceiling bookshelves. I approached the nearest one and saw the books were old, almost ancient — probably first editions. I recognised some of the titles, but most were unfamiliar.

"Our little collection, covering thousands of years of the vila history and heritage. You're welcome to peruse them if you'd like," I heard Ivan's mother speaking behind me. Startled, I turned around to face her.

"Oh no, thank you, I was just admiring the books," I said, "you have a beautiful home, Mrs Angelov."

"It isn't much, but it's ours. And please, call me Eva, I want none of that 'Mrs Angelov' nonsense," she said, smiling. She then turned to Ivan, asking, "Will you show her the rest? Dinner will be ready soon, but you still have some time if you'd like to take her downstairs." Ivan nodded and led me to the adjacent room.

There, right next to the living room, was a staircase leading downwards. Another underground room, I thought to myself, unpleasant memories of going into the Vestibule with Tomislav that morning coming to mind.

"I'd like to show you something. It isn't exactly... pretty, but it might interest you anyway," Ivan said as he led me down the staircase into the mysterious room.

We descended into a circular, compact space. Every inch of circular wall was covered in black-and-white photographs and newspaper articles, giving the place a gloomy appearance.

"What is this?" I asked, walking around the small room, reading the newspaper headlines.

Hundreds of vila children lost in the Purge... The League stays firmly with the vila despite the increased threats... Nemages of Danubia gather steam. Is the Rift inevitable?

"This is a memorial museum for all the vilas and vilenaks lost in and after the war. My mother's idea... she's a sort of collector and a vila historian. You've seen her books," he explained, unsmiling.

I kept on scanning the newspaper titles, noticing that one term kept on reappearing. "What is the Purge?"

Ivan sat down on a two-seater sofa set next to the staircase and motioned for me to join him.

"The Purge is a very ugly part of our history and a reason so many of us cannot live peacefully with humans, even today, after all this time." I sat down as instructed, waiting for him to continue.

"I already mentioned that the vila magic is different from human magic. I didn't explain that the difference is considerable and comes in handy in a war. You see, our brand of magic is more potent and much more powerful. But what matters more is that we can feed it into the overall magical potency of a specific location. In this case, in Tayna. My kind accumulates magical supplies faster than humans, and that was our main occupation in the past. We supplied magic for Tayna's mages. In turn, humans left us be here, in Feyar, paying us good money meaning my kind never had to cross into Danubia and deal with nemages. Vilas find it harder to cohabitate with the nemages than humans. If you ask me, that's just prejudice, but that's what it is. My kind prefers to be left alone; it's always been like that." He stopped for a moment, staring ahead of him at gruesome newspaper articles stretched across the round walls.

"The nemages knew this, of course. Their leaders hoped to find our hiding place and destroy the magical supplies that we kept on creating. The trouble was, they didn't know our location; Feyar was well hidden. We were safe until one day, a group that later became known as Turncoats switched sides. You might have heard of them; they were led by Daniel Obrenovich, father of one Boyan Obrenovich, or as you might know him... President Tanatos."

I beamed at Ivan in surprise. "Tanatos is just a name he acquired later. Mother told me it means 'the one that brings death' in old languages. Perhaps he wanted to be theatrical or intimidating," he explained.

"Anyway, the Turncoats went to nemages, giving away Feyar's location and the means to defeat the Vila. There is a weapon... a very old, almost forgotten weapon. It can immobilise us and strip us of our powers. The effects of it don't hold for long, but long enough to kill us. Enough for the nemages to win. So, Daniel Obrenovich came to Feyar with the weapon in question and a battalion of nemages he'd just sided with. They raided Feyar, burning it to the ground. Hundreds and hundreds of the vila, male and female, were killed on the spot. Immobile, devoid of speech... all they could do was watch their homes burn, watch their families die and wait for their own demise. It is a horrible way to die. Imagine, to be trapped in your own body, unable to do so much as run. This event is called the Purge in the vila history. Of course, you won't find it in Tanatos' new, rewritten history, which took place after the Wipe, but we still remember."

Both my hands leapt to my mouth as I stifled a small scream. Ivan was still staring at that same spot on the opposite wall, his eyes unmoving.

"Those who weren't at home that day saved themselves. So, our kind lives. The Akademia was still operating at the time, serving more like a bomb shelter than a school in the war. Most children were there when the attack happened. They came home that day, only to find their homes burnt down and their parents dead."

Ivan stood up suddenly, walking over to the wall. He pointed to a newspaper headline reading, *"An orphanage in Tayna to house five hundred vila children."*

"So, the League built a home for them by the Promenade, and at least the poor children were safe. They had shelter, food and someone to take care of them; not a huge consolation after losing a home and a family all at once, but at least they had something. That all ended when the war was lost."

There was a pause as Ivan started pacing the round room, clenching his fists.

"The League had struck a deal with the nemages already. The mages gave in, vowed to stop all the fighting. But Daniel Obrenovich wouldn't stop. He suggested that the nemages come into Tayna one last time. Respecting as they were of the peace treaty they just struck, the League let the nemages in. The nemages said they'd come to discuss the Rift, which was about to occur between our two communities. As the nemages kept the League occupied at the negotiating table, Daniel Obrenovich paid a visit to the orphanage."

I realised I was clenching my fists too, knowing what was coming. I imagined an evil mage, looking just like Tanatos, striding along the promenade to a house full of children. Children who lost everything and whose only consolation was a warm bed at night and a full stomach. But this wasn't enough to keep the nightmares away, I knew.

"He took them all out of their beds. Killed the caretakers on the spot. But the children... a swift death by magical means would be merciful, you see. Daniel Obrenovich wasn't a merciful man. He loathed our kind because we're a threat; we're more powerful. So, he drowned them instead. He threw the children into the Adriatic Sea, and they were all dead within minutes. The bodies found later had bricks tied around their abdomens to keep them below the surface."

Chapter 23
The Grudge

I felt something warm and wet fall in my lap. Instinctively, I touched my cheeks only to discover I was crying. Hoping Ivan hasn't noticed, I wiped the escaped tears quickly. But he was lost in thought, standing frozen in front of one of the photographs on the round wall. I stood up and joined him, curious to see what got his attention.

"Unfortunately, that's not all," he explained, pointing at the black-and-white photograph. In it was a sort of hospital for small children. There were dozens of baby cots in the sturdy-looking room. There was no explanation or description, only the year scribbled in the right bottom corner, reading '1948'.

"Vila babies, even partial vilenaks like myself, are born with a pair of wings," he explained, smiling a little at my surprised expression. "I guess we are similar to the mythical fairies in some ways. Though, unlike them, we can hide our wings from sight if we're not actually using them." I nodded and took his hand, encouraging him to continue.

"Three years after the war started, the Duma passed a new law. It was decided that all new-born vila babies born in federal hospitals should have their wings cut off right after birth. The nemages were hoping to weaken us by taking them away. Luckily, it didn't work, for our magic is in our genes, not in our body parts or wings for that matter."

I stared at him, unable to find the words for how I felt at that moment. Terrified? Angry? Saddened? Probably all of the above.

"Wait, 1948... were your—" I started.

"Yes, my wings were cut off too. My parents tried to hide me after birth but to no avail. I was already registered in their system when the law in question was passed."

We stood there in silence, holding hands and staring at the black-and-white photograph of the hospital. Waves of anger, burning, horrifying, kept on washing over my body as I attempted to remain calm.

My garnet lit up, responding to the amplified emotion emanating from me, but I ignored it. Magic cannot help to change the past or make me feel better about what Ivan just told me.

"So now you see why the vila kind has issues with humans. Most of us understand that not all humans are the same but still prefer to keep the distance. It is, to put it mildly, a very complicated relationship," I heard Ivan saying.

I nodded briefly, suddenly wishing to leave the gloomy round room, to be away from all the bad memories accumulated in it.

Ivan must have assumed what I was thinking or feeling the same way because we were climbing back up soon. The living room was empty, and we found Ivan's mother in the back garden, setting the table ready for dinner. The garden boasted a magnificent view of the valley, encircled by tall, jade-green trees creating a comfortable shade. The blue Adriatic was visible in the distance. I could see two neighbouring houses just on the other side of the hill, rising up among the green slopes and peeking out from between the trees.

"Do you have many neighbours?" I asked Ivan as we stood in the shade of the nearest tree, watching his mother getting the table ready. I was eager to change the subject, to drive the unpleasant history I'd just learned about out of my head.

"Only two other vila families live on this side of the hill. The rest live further away; Feyar is quite vast," he explained.

I'd never seen vila magic in its original form before. Ivan used his gemstone around humans, probably to attract less attention, but he did mention vilas and vilenaks didn't need gems. Eva's hands were outstretched before her as she directed the dishes out into the garden through one of the cabin windows. I saw a casserole dish levitating in mid-air, landing neatly in the middle of the table. It was followed by plates and cutlery, all arranged so neatly a human hand wouldn't have done it better. Eva wasn't using a gemstone, not from what I could see. As she turned our way to direct a few candles towards the table, I noticed her usually emerald eyes were gleaming in bright violet light. It was an intense and protruding gleam, almost fluorescent.

"We don't need gemstones; our magic is channelled from inside of us. It comes *from* us; that's why we don't need external aid, so to speak.

Our bodies act as vessels. Hence our eyes change colour when we do magic, in place of a gemstone," Ivan commented from next to me, his lips curling into a small smile as he watched his mother.

We sat down to have dinner as the table was set. I was starving at this point, and Eva's cooking was extraordinary. A plateful of casserole and a piece of Dobosh cake later, I sat back, relaxed, sipping sweet white wine. It was getting close to sunset, the view over the valley becoming even more glorious than before.

"The mages have a thing for emerald roses, I see," I commented, pointing at a vase with three emerald roses set at one end of the dinner table. "Any particular reason for that?" I asked, looking from Ivan to Eva.

"They're traditional around here, especially in Feyar. Back when we used to live with nemages, small amounts of magic were trafficked inside these roses. I don't exactly know why the emerald roses in particular, but they worked best," Ivan explained.

"Trafficked? To where, Danubia?" I asked, puzzled. Eva answered first.

"Yes. The nemages were all too eager to get their hands on magic, even if it came in such small amounts. They don't have magic themselves; of course, it's either in a person's genes or not. But these roses carried enough for small spells, nothing dangerous. It was a lucrative business for a while. Then, of course, the Wipe happened, and emerald roses weren't as useful any more. Except for decoration, of course."

Rearranging the roses in the vase, she added as an afterthought, "Tanatos banned the emerald roses from nemage Danubia, afraid that we might smuggle tiny bits of magic to the nemages. Perhaps he thought seeing magic happen before their eyes might stir something in their memory and wake them up."

"The ways nemages used the magic stored in the roses were hilarious sometimes," Ivan said, suddenly laughing and looking at his mother. "You remember that woman who tried to change her looks, ending up with massive boils all over her face and body instead?"

Eva nodded, smiling at the memory. "Yes, and the mages had to jump in to undo the spell. We'd always warn the nemages to use these roses for simple enchantments only — you know, fireworks at birthdays, simple cleaning spells to keep the home tidy or get lunch done faster. Major improvements in one's appearance don't exactly come under simple magic. But some of them never listened, the poor fools," Eva said, still chuckling. "Of course, we had a team of amethyst mages who'd step in and help."

"Mages with amethysts as their primary gems have a higher affinity for healing spells," Ivan added for my benefit.

I remembered Maya healing Mila on that horrible night when the First Comrade came to Tayna and hurt her. Maya's gemstone was amethyst, too.

"Emerald roses all over Kairos cafe are Lydia's idea of a silent protest, I think. You might have met her, she works there," Ivan said. I nodded, remembering the plump blonde waitress who served me when I visited Kairos what now seemed like aeons ago.

"How so?"

"Well, Kairos is in Agram, so technically part of the nemage Danubia. Those roses were banned by Tanatos himself. It is brave and a little foolish at the same time to have them on display all the time. A very subtle reminder to the President that we're still out there and haven't given up," Ivan explained, a hint of pride in his voice.

I realised that, without even noticing, I'd learned plenty about the mages and their ways of life. Little by little, I'd grown to love all the small things about Tayna, its ancient streets, and the long walks through the park with Ivan. Breakfasts at The Bayamonti with Tomislav and Natasha, coffees in the afternoon with other League members to discuss the fight plan. A comfortable routine was created, and I felt useful, probably now more than ever before. Sure, I used to help my grandparents in Velesh and worked at the City Hall for a decent salary, but it didn't compare to the role I had here in Tayna. Tomislav's convictions and beliefs aside, with a little bit of practice, I could help save lives in the coming fight. As much as I wasn't comfortable with the idea of being the promised child, I embraced the Panmage in me almost immediately. However, I wasn't in a rush to voice it just yet. That, at least, I could use to help others in real, practical ways. The promised child was part of a story, nothing more, and I didn't believe it to be true. Not that I would express my opinion on this in front of Tomislav; I knew that battle was lost.

"Looks like our neighbours are about to join us," said Eva, looking towards the hills on the opposite side from where we were sitting. "We'll need more wine." Her eyes turned fluorescent violet again, and she made a swift, swooping motion with her right hand. A couple of wine glasses and a fresh bottle flew out through the nearest window, landing soundlessly on the table in front of us.

"Good evening, Sven," Ivan said to the young man who had just entered the garden. A girl, seemingly my own age, was clutching his hand. Only a few seconds ago, they were no more than a tiny dot on the horizon, yet now they were standing right in front of us. Their eyes were still gleaming in protruding silver light, not violet, like Eva's, I noticed. The gleam faded away as they reached their destination. I noticed how their skin looked smoother, ageless and how their eyes had a more pronounced brightness in them, even when they weren't using magic. Those were the same features I saw and loved in Ivan and now his mother, too. The newcomers had that alluring glow that clearly gave away their true nature. They were vila and vilenak; that much was obvious. Their movements were swift and elegant, just like Ivan's.

"Good evening, Ivan, Eva. Care if we joined you for a drink. We saw you out here and thought we'd say hello." The man spoke in a deep, authoritative voice. Not at all typical of someone so young-looking. Then I remembered Ivan told me that the vila kind age twice as slow as humans, which means this man was at least sixty in human years.

"Sure, come sit," Eva said, pouring two glasses of wine for the newcomers. Just as they were about to sit down, the man's eyes met mine. He eyed my face, then his gaze paused at the turquoise strand, which was clearly visible in the sunset, combed down in my chestnut hair. Sometimes I thought it became more pronounced, almost neon, in the darkness.

His features changed, and he froze on the spot. He glanced from me to Ivan, struggling against something he obviously wanted to say.

"Is there a problem?" Ivan asked, putting his hand on mine in a protective gesture.

The vilenak hesitated for a moment. "The Angelovs consorting with *her* kind? The Turquoise dynasty? I wouldn't have believed it if I hadn't seen it with my own eyes!" The words came out in a cold, low series of hisses. Sven's eyes narrowed as he scrutinised me with such hatred, I had the need to defend myself. As if reading my mind, the garnet on my ring lit up immediately. The girl standing next to him was quiet, but her expression was downright angry.

"There is no need for such hostile reaction, Sven. Sofija is Ivan's partner and a friend," Eva said, her voice calm.

"Have you lost your mind? You took *her* as a partner? She's an enemy!" The man was now positively shaking with rage, pointing his index finger at Ivan, who stood up from his seat, pulling me behind him to shield me with his body.

"You're out of line, Sven. She's not like the rest of them," he retorted in an icy voice.

"I think we'll skip the drinks. Excuse us; we no longer feel welcome here." The couple stepped back from the table, looking livid. Their eyes lit up with the silver light for a brief moment, and they were gone from sight.

Ivan pulled me in a tight embrace, caressing my hair. Remembering we were not alone, we parted a few seconds later, retaking our seats at the table.

"I'm so sorry you had to witness that. Some of us can't let go of the past," Ivan said bitterly, pulling me down on the bench next to him.

"Are you all right, dear?" Eva asked as she poured more wine into my glass. "Don't worry, he's just a frustrated soul. We won't let him talk to you like that again."

We sat in silence for a while, mulling over what just happened. *So, the dynasty my mother came from was not very welcome around here. Will an incident like this one happen again? Will I have to start concealing the unusual hair strand I'd grown to love?*

"Why was he so upset that I'm from the Turquoise dynasty?" I asked after a while. Eva and Ivan eyed each other for a moment, then Eva answered, her tone careful.

"The vila have long memories, and some of us are no strangers to holding grudges. The Turquoise dynasty was very powerful in the past, and some were prone to doing bad things. Unspeakable things, even. You've seen my memorial below; perhaps you understand now why vilas

201

and humans don't get along."

I nodded in understanding, waiting for Eva to continue.

"As bad as you think the vila-human relationship is, it is nothing compared to how the vila kind was treated by the powerful magical dynasties. You see, some of them — not all, of course — would capture young vilas and vilenaks, locking them up for months, even years. The young ones create more magic than adults simply because their bodies are more active, more able. The Turquoise dynasty was notorious for capturing our young ones, forcing them to create magical supplies. They'd take the magic for themselves, of course, and when the children grew too exhausted to be useful, they'd beat and torture them. Some were found by their families or managed to escape. But most of the time, it would end tragically."

Eva's gaze dropped to the floor as she finished speaking. I found myself staring at her, wide-eyed. Suddenly, the pretty turquoise strand in my hair started to bother me. I didn't want to be associated with such horrible crimes, no matter how long ago they'd occurred.

"It has nothing to do with Sofija, though. She didn't choose her family!" Ivan said in an agitated voice.

"Of course not, but she needs to understand Sven's reaction. There is nothing in this world that should ever make you embarrassed of where you come from, dear," Eva replied calmly, beaming at me across the table, "you are welcome here anytime. You are family now, as far as I'm concerned," she added, smiling widely.

Chapter 24
The Soulmate

The night fell soon, and Ivan and I were on our way back to The Bayamonti.

"I take it you'll stay with Sofija now?" Eva asked Ivan, her tone amused, almost mocking.

He raised his eyebrows. "Yes, I will. At least until the danger has passed."

"Sure, son," Eva said, her voice slightly sarcastic, "because that's why you're spending nearly every waking moment with her. Protection, nothing else." She winked at me, and I felt my cheeks burn.

We thanked Eva for the dinner and company, promising we'd visit again soon.

"Does your mother always tease you like that?" I asked Ivan as we waved Eva goodbye and headed down the pebbly pathway towards the old town.

"Yes, she enjoys it immensely. I don't mind; it's our thing."

I followed him in silence for a while, taking in the warm summer night and the sound of crickets coming from all sides. It was so peaceful, so beautiful, like the calm before the storm. The storm that was coming won't be easy to surpass, I thought to myself and shivered from the sudden dread.

About ten minutes later, I noticed we weren't heading for the old town.

"Have we taken the wrong turn somewhere?" I asked Ivan, surprised that he'd get lost in his own neighbourhood.

"Of course not. I'm taking you somewhere special; it's not that late yet," he replied, smiling down at me, his brilliant eyes gleaming against the moonlight.

My stomach quivered with nervousness and excitement, but I remained quiet and let Ivan lead me into the night. Soon my nostrils were filled with the smell of the sea. We were by the coast, I realised suddenly. Ever since I'd arrived in Tayna, I hadn't had a chance to go to the beach, not while the Promenade was dangerous with Tanatos' men patrolling the area.

Ivan took my hand, leading me through the narrow passage between dense trees, moving the branches to clear the path for me. A moment later, I felt sand underneath my feet.

"Give me a moment," I said and, stopping in my tracks, I took off the heeled shoes I was wearing, carrying them in my free hand. "That's better." He just smiled at me, towing me further onto the beach, stretching endlessly underneath the calm, starry night.

We were utterly alone; there was not a soul in sight. The water was like glass, still and unmoving in the warm night, glittering under the bright moonlight. We walked all the way down to the water but didn't stop there. Ivan kept on going until we reached a secluded bay, surrounded by high rocks covered in moss on one side. There, in the middle of the beach, a large blanket was stretched over the sand. Two wine glasses and a single bottle, along with a pair of unlit candles, waited, set sideways on the blanket.

"I thought it was about time we had a proper date," Ivan said, glancing nervously at me.

"Would you like to join me?"

I couldn't suppress my happiness, grinning like an idiot.

"I'll take that as a yes," he said, his features relaxing. We sat down on the blanket opposite each other, the dark sea on our left side, high rocks surrounding us from the right. Ivan's eyes suddenly lit up just like his mother's, only his had a familiar deep-golden colour. The colour of topaz, his gemstone, I realised. He didn't hold out his sceptre, so he was practising gem-less magic. In one swift movement, Ivan turned the bottle of wine and the two glasses upright, bringing the candles in between us, holding them steady. In a matter of seconds, the candles lit up, and the wine glasses were filled with ice cubes.

"The wine has been sitting out here all afternoon; I thought we'd need some ice," he explained. He poured the wine, handing a glass to me. I took it without speaking but had no intention of drinking the wine, too preoccupied with the intensity of his gaze. His wide eyes were back to emerald-green. The way he was looking at me was so fierce, I wouldn't be surprised if he could see right through my skin at that very moment. I reached out and took his hand, our fingers intertwining.

His thumb moved down, caressing my wrist gently, and I responded in turn. Our fingers kept on swirling, twisting like vines, hungry for contact, sending fire through my body - a kind of fire that soothed, leaving me craving for more. I closed my eyes, revelling in the incredible feeling of his touch on my skin, taking in the scent of salty air. After what seemed like centuries, his fingers stopped moving, and his hand let go of mine. I opened my eyes in alarm, unwilling to stop.

With his free hand, Ivan swiped the candles away, digging them into the sand next to the blanket we were sitting on and removed the glasses. Not taking his gaze off me, he pulled me to him gently, kissing my forehead first, his lips travelling across my eyelids, nose and cheeks, landing finally on my lips. And suddenly, I was drowning, drowning... drowning in his sweet scent, hoping to never emerge to the surface. This is where I'm supposed to be; this is where I finally belong; a wandering ship finding its haven. Minutes passed, perhaps even hours, but I didn't bother learning to swim, for I knew he'd keep me from harm. He'll pull me with him... when it's time. We kissed for what seemed like an eternity, listening to nothing but the sound of summer breeze shaking the nearest trees and the insane rhythm of our hearts beating in unison.

I pulled away after a while, cupping his perfect face with both my hands, staring deeply into his eyes. I felt braver now. Slowly, I climbed onto his lap, hugging him tightly and kissing his lips again. He responded immediately, running his hands down my spine, my waist, my thighs.

Then he stopped, pulling away, and my heart sank.

"Trust me, I want to. But there's something you need to know first."

I climbed off his lap, my heart beating fast. *Too good to be true, the sarcastic voice mocked. Told you already — dream simpler dreams.*

"Okay. I'm listening," I said, attempting to put on a brave face.

"The vila kind are not made to have multiple partners. You see, we mate... pretty much for life. The need to bond with just one person became even stronger after the war when our numbers were decimated. It's a sort of survival instinct, I think. So, a person we... make love to becomes our soulmate. Not just in a romantic sense. Soulmates can always look after one another, always find each other. I've never experienced it before; of course, there is only one soulmate for our kind. From what I know, it is like having a sixth sense about where your partner is and how they're feeling at all times. The bond grows stronger with time; at least, that's what I'd been told." He stopped then, waiting for my reaction.

"And you... don't think I should become your soulmate? Is it because I'm not a vila?" I asked, unable to control the crushing disappointment in my voice. How could he tell this to me now, after all this time? Shouldn't he have made up his mind earlier, before he introduced me to his mother?

He started laughing, his white teeth gleaming against the moonlight.

"I should have known you'd react that way!" he chuckled as I stared at him, clueless. "Of course, that's not it! You are my soulmate; I know it. I've never felt the same way about anyone before. Perhaps it has something to do with the fact that my powers don't work on you the same way they work on others. You know, the way I can control people with my touch only, and it doesn't impact you. You're a sort of mystery to me." He winked. "No, this is about you. See, the way to 'seal the deal' with your soulmate is to make love to the person. After that, the bond is formed, and it cannot be broken, not ever, only in death. That means you get no say in this. I want to be sure that you wish this to happen as much as I do. I'd hate to be in your head forever, knowing where you are and what you're doing, and you knowing the same thing about me if... if this is not what you truly want." He looked down at his hands, falling silent.

It was my turn to laugh this time. Ivan looked up; his eyebrows raised in confusion.

"It's silly that you should even *think* I'd have second thoughts about you. It was a done deal from the moment we met, you know," I replied, blushing. Somehow, I couldn't meet his eyes. The blanket we sat on became increasingly interesting with every passing moment.

Ivan lifted my chin up with his long fingers, meeting my gaze. A wide grin stretched across his magnificent face.

"Still glad I asked. You should know what you're getting yourself into." He took both my hands, kissing them quietly. "Even without the strange soulmate thing, I'd still want you for good. I don't do things halfway. When I'm in, I'm in for life." He wasn't smiling now. Instead, his eyes bore into mine, searching for something. A smidgeon of doubt, or fear perhaps? Whatever it was, he wouldn't find it, I knew.

"That doesn't scare me. I'm a serial monogamist myself. You better watch out," I said, winking at him.

"Let's see if I survive tonight, then," he replied, pulling me back onto his lap.

The next morning, memories of the previous night were hazy at best. I remembered Ivan carrying me back to the hotel room, so effortlessly as if I were a rag doll and not a full-grown human being. I didn't remember falling asleep, which must have happened quickly because I was utterly exhausted. All I remembered was that I was beyond happy. Happier than I've ever been before in my life, so ecstatic I wanted to jump around and scream about it.

My hand went instinctively to my neck, bringing memories of Ivan's kisses from the night before. Then my lips and cheeks. There was no centimetre of my skin his lips did not touch, I recalled with a shudder. And his smile, his magnificent smile that made his emerald eyes turn to slits, gazing at me through the strands of dark hair that kept on falling on his forehead. He kept on cupping my face with both hands so delicately as if I were a fragile doll made of glass. Kisses planted on my eyelids, the tip of my nose, my chin — they still burned as if fresh. All that time, he smiled, grinned like a child, gazing at me with unmistakable adoration. This is how I will always remember him; I knew. Every look upon that face sent me drowning in the sea of emerald; never-ending, shimmering, soothing. *Mine.*

When I opened my eyes, I found Ivan there, propped on his elbow, watching me quietly.

"Morning, princess," he said cheerfully, his lips curling into a smile. "Did you sleep well?"

"I slept great," I answered in a sleepy voice. The hotel room, which was now my home, was bathed in morning sunlight coming through the wide windows. Must have been past nine at least, by the looks of it.

"Shouldn't we be downstairs at the Plenum? Are we late?" I asked, suddenly alarmed. I didn't want to miss a League meeting and was looking forward to another training session with Tomislav.

"We have another half an hour, don't worry. I just wanted to give you something before we head out," Ivan said. Then, he climbed out of bed and walked over to the writing desk. Taking something small from the desk drawer, he turned to face me.

"I want you to have something." Sitting back on the bed next to me, he put a silver bracelet in my hand. A single, golden gemstone was hanging from it, glittering in the early morning light.

"Topaz? It's beautiful!" The little stone was enchanting, gleaming in deep-golden colour, just like Ivan's eyes when he was doing vila magic.

"It is customary for a vilenak, or a vila, to gift their soulmate with something they hold most dear. This is a small piece of my own topaz. I know that, as vilenak, I don't necessarily need my gemstone to practice magic, but it is still the most treasured possession I have. I've had it ever since I was a child. Now, a small piece of it is yours," he said, winking at me playfully. "Hope you'll take good care of it."

Chapter 25
Defensive Magic

The next few weeks went by quickly, as I spent almost every hour of every day in training sessions with Tomislav. Both he and Natasha took some time off work so that they wouldn't have to cross into Danubia every now and then. They planned to leave their jobs altogether eventually.

"Once Tanatos figures out what we're planning to do, every mage will be under death sentence in Danubia. Best to get out while we can," Natasha explained.

Sometimes others helped with my training too. Maya showed me her brand of healing magic. She taught me how to mend small injuries, stop the bleeding from the wound or freeze the patient's condition until someone more experienced could help them.

Even David chipped in, which was a surprise. He had a slight change of heart since the argument at The Bayamonti, and I suspected Tomislav, and his persuasion skills had something to do with it.

"I used to teach at the Akademia, you know. I very much enjoyed my job and was good at it, I think," he said to me one morning as we were getting ready to practise defensive spells.

"This was once a great place, with at least twenty classrooms, each designed for a different brand of magic. The halls were always packed with children going in and out of classes. Now all that is left is this place," he said as he looked around Vestibule where we were standing, "Tanatos made sure of it." The longing in his voice was all too audible, and I could tell he missed his old job.

"How come the school was placed underground?" I asked, wondering at the unusual choice of location.

"It wasn't, not originally. The League sunk it, so to speak, just after the Rift. They hoped to preserve what was left of the school, hide it." David answered.

"The League sunk the school? How?"

"It's a complicated bit of magic. Tom's old man was an expert at it. Connected to elemental magic, but you also need to know a bit of architecture to do it right. Interesting combination if you ask me."

I nodded in understanding before asking: "Do mages normally combine their... um... nemage skills with magic?"

David peered at me over his square-rimmed spectacles, mildly surprised. "Of course. We all share the same knowledge of science, arts, and humanities. We learn same skills as children and young adults. Some of us only go one skill further", he said in a lecturing voice, nodding towards his sceptre, outstretched at the table in front of us.

"I take it you preferred being a teacher to working at the Local Assembly in Velesh?" I asked, though I already knew the answer.

"Oh, yes. Unfortunately, that was the only choice I had after the Wipe. The Akademia was gone, and most parents chose to train their children at home. With Tanatos checking the place constantly to make sure no new generations were trained in combat, I had to find another income source. You might have noticed most League members ended up in the Zolta, doing research or political work. I guess it could be worse, so perhaps I shouldn't complain." He shrugged. "I did have some problems with the Biela, as you already know. There is only so much nonsense I can take from them. The one time I didn't go with the party line and vote the way they wanted me to, I ended up behind bars. I'm sure Mila's disappearance was somehow connected to it too." He paused, his gaze dropping to the floor. "I'll never forgive myself for exposing my family like that. It was foolish to think my protest vote could change anything while Tanatos is in power," he added in a sad voice.

I'd never heard David talk so much, not around me, and I was glad we were finally on good terms. The League didn't need more internal tensions, not with all the preparations for the new rebellion.

"For what it's worth, I'd have done the same thing. It was courageous of you to stand up to the Biela like that. Not everyone can just bury their heads in the sand; some of us have to show some backbone," I commented, looking up at David's ageing face. He had a look of a true intellectual, with the pair of glasses over his slightly crooked nose and greying hair. He has always dressed the part too, wearing smart shirts even in the middle of summer.

"Thank you. Not everyone understood, though, but that didn't matter anyway," David said, picking up his sceptre from the table, "now, let's start with some basic spells. Firstly, how are your new senses coming along? Do you feel any different?"

"I'm not sure that I do," I said truthfully.

"Yes, she does," I heard Tomislav saying from somewhere behind us. He'd just entered the room, walking over to where David and I were standing. "She heard us from across the square that night when First Comrade paid us a visit. That wouldn't be possible with normal human hearing," he explained, smirking. "It's just a matter of time before other skills kick in."

David looked from Tomislav to me, thinking. "It could be that she has them already but just hasn't tried using them yet. Just because she hasn't attempted to lift something heavy and throw it across the room, it doesn't mean she can't. To a normal human being, or someone who's used to being one, that's a ludicrous thing to do." Suddenly excited, David walked back a few steps, putting more distance between us, then said, "Let's try your speed."

"Okay," I said, eager to test my new skills. "How?"

"I'll hit you with a curse; you avoid it," David said simply. It was as if he was commenting on the weather outside, not announcing an attack on me.

"David, I don't think—," Tomislav started.

"This is how she learns, Tom. It has to be under pressure. Don't worry; if you're right about her hearing, then her reflexes should be through the roof right now. She should dodge my every attempt easily."

I wasn't sure what to do. Was there a defensive or fighting pose I should assume? Or do I just wait for David to hit me with something? I got reasonably good at throwing fighting spells by now but didn't think fighting back was the point of this exercise.

"Just listen to what your body tells you, Sofija," David said, his diamond gleaming on top of the metal sceptre he was holding. Just before he cast a curse, I noticed two secondary gemstones lined underneath it.

The diamond gleamed in hot-white light, and a blast came rushing towards me. Instinctively, I stepped to the right, thinking I didn't move far enough; that I was still in the range of the blast. But when I looked around, I saw David and Tomislav standing at least ten metres away from me. In just one move, I'd crossed half the room.

"Well done!" Tomislav exclaimed, visibly relieved. "I wouldn't want to deal with the curse damage later. Though I don't think David hit you with anything serious".

"Of course not; it was just a freezing curse," David said, looking content, "but you acted exactly how I expected you to. Well done. Do you know how you did it?"

"I'm... not sure." I spoke at my normal volume, knowing they can hear me even though I was standing on the far end of the room. "I just knew I had to get out of the range. Can we try again?"

The next hour went by quickly, as David kept on hitting me with the freezing curse, unsuccessfully. I dodged every single attack, ending up further and further from my starting point. My speed increased every time I avoided the blast coming from David's sceptre. After an hour, I was able to do it even without being threatened by a curse; I could move incredibly fast at will. It was fun and exciting, almost like dancing, but my feet didn't seem to touch the ground very often. I thought back at my first day in Tayna, when I saw Vesna moving incredibly fast between the tables in the hotel garden. *Now I can do it, too.*

Tomislav was sprawled across the sofa in the corner of the room, watching David and I practise. He'd comment or help here and there, mostly staying out of the way. I thought he rather enjoyed watching me learn. I was, in a way, his project, and he wanted to make sure to be there for every step of the way — sort of like a caring parent watching his child take the first steps.

"I think you've got that down now," David said, smiling at me, "now, your speed will help at defending yourself. Defensive magic I'm about to show you, combined with your reflexes and speed, give excellent results. You should be able to avoid almost every curse thrown at you. Unless, of course, you find yourself surrounded by enemies and hit from several sides at once." He spoke in a relaxed voice, almost amused at the thought of a full-on attack, as it presented an intellectual challenge for a tactician like himself.

Then he glanced at Tomislav. "Tom, care to assist?"

"Happy to be of service," Tomislav said brightly, jumping off the sofa eagerly and joining us in the centre of the room. His sceptre was ready, the sapphire already gleaming in startling blue light. The other two gemstones were inactive, as usual. I wondered what kind of magic required all three gemstones to be performed. The only time I saw Tomislav using his secondary gems was to put up the shield around The Bayamonti just before the first Plenum was in session.

Tomislav faced David with his sceptre outstretched. "No need to be nervous, David," he teased.

"Not even a little, Tom. Do your best," David replied.

Blue light left Tomislav's sceptre, directed at David's chest, but it was stopped halfway through, suspended in mid-air. David was standing in what I assumed was a fighting position, one leg in front of the other, his hands level with his chest. He cast a shield which prevented Tomislav's curse from reaching him. The shield was clearly visible, and I wondered if I could only see it because of my new senses. It looked like a spider web, only rectangular and translucent, stretching in front of David.

"The full-body shield. A useful spell which can protect not only you but those around you if the range is broad enough." David explained. "Of course, it doesn't hold for long, and a powerful opponent can breech it, but it can still slow them down, giving you a chance for a counterattack."

A couple of hours later, I learned not only how to cast the shield but also to throw attacking spells off their course, and to turn the curse against the person who cast it, so that it rebounded. It became easier to concentrate on my anchor emotion and gem flavour; I was so used to the garnet that it lit up the moment I thought of using it. Most of the time, I used happy moments with Ivan as my anchor emotion. Sometimes it was the growing hope in the positive outcome of the upcoming rebellion. Trying to avoid negative anchors, I kept anger at Tanatos and sadness at the loss of my grandparents out of my mind as often as I could.

My arsenal consisted only of basic fighting spells so far, but I was satisfied. I could cast a mean kicking curse, and that alone was a valuable skill.

"You're an incredibly fast learner," Natasha said to me one day, "which isn't that surprising considering you're a Panmage."

The next phase in my training was learning how to use all the other gemstones. According to Tomislav, it was best to take smaller steps. Using all twelve gemstones at once would make the learning process too difficult, he explained.

"Just because you collide with all the gemstones, it does not necessarily mean you have to *use* them all. This is pretty much unchartered territory since no one has dealt with a Panmage in centuries, but I'd imagine that you'd still find some gemstones that suit you better than the others. You're a young mage, still learning and attaining skills, and using all gemstones straight away could only confuse you and possibly harm your progress."

I nodded in understanding, relieved I wouldn't have to master all twelve gems at once.

"What do you suggest I do?"

"Perhaps she should try one by one, see how they suit her," Natasha suggested. She joined us in the training session today. "We don't want her to pass out again, like the last time; using them all once again might be overwhelming," she explained, looking at her husband.

Tomislav agreed, and so we started the testing. The two of them were like excited scholars with the new lab project, fetching all the different stones for me and watching my reaction to their flavour.

Only after trying out every single gemstone, I understood just how much my own birthstone suited me. I soon discovered I could channel my magic through every one of them, but not every gemstone *felt* right. Some took more of my effort to be controlled; some had almost uncomfortable flavours that didn't match with me. The pearl had unusual energy around it. When using it, I felt discomfort, as if something massive was pushing down on my chest. I was able to channel magic but couldn't wait to free myself of the gemstone.

"You, as a mage, have an energy about you. That energy is moulded by your motivations, hopes and fears. It is shaped by your personality. Pearl doesn't suit you, which is why you feel discomfort," Natasha explained. "At least you can use it if you must. A regular mage wouldn't be able to channel magic through an alien gemstone, none at all," she added, her face glowing with pride.

After a whole hour of testing, I've found out that, apart from garnet, the gemstones that suited me best were ruby, diamond, turquoise and topaz.

"That makes sense," Tomislav said, unsurprised. "Turquoise is your family gemstone, so it'll suit you; it's genetic. Ruby is similar to your own garnet in properties and flavour. Topaz could agree with you because of Ivan. It's his birthstone, and it often happens that romantic partners share gemstones." He winked at me before continuing, "And diamond... it's just pure strength — an explosion of positivity. Very suitable for a Panmage."

He attached the secondary gemstones to the bracelet Ivan gave me. A small piece of his topaz was already on there, so the other three were added. It was a pretty piece of jewellery, a thin silver band adorned with blue-green turquoise, golden topaz, deep-rose ruby and white-hot diamond. I never was much into jewellery but somehow couldn't take my eyes off the pretty bracelet.

I couldn't fall asleep for a long time that evening. Ivan was on marble duty tonight for the first time, and, having gotten used to sleeping next to him every night, I felt extremely restless. The schedule Tomislav worked out was doing its job well. Each evening, one member of the League would deliver new marbles to Vesna through the portal by the Promenade. They'd cross into Velesh through the portal in Kairos Café to meet up with Vesna, who waited in Nocturno. Sometimes it took a while because Vesna's schedule depended on Helena's whereabouts that day, as Helena and her family were her primary responsibility. It could take hours to deliver the marbles Vesna needed to be able to protect Helena against Tanatos.

Just as my body started to relax, and I was falling asleep, my eyes flew open. A sharp pang of pain went through my every muscle, entrapping my mind, immobilising me completely. I could hear myself scream but didn't understand why. As soon as the pain was gone, I sat upright on the bed, staring around the dark room, alerted. At first, I thought someone cast some sort of pain-inflicting curse on me, but no one was there. Who could have done it? Is it possible to cast curses from a distance? Could Tanatos be doing this to me from afar?

215

Then, a vision came, so clear in my head as if I were watching a film on my own, inner television. I was strapped, my arms and legs tied so that I couldn't move a centimetre. My back brushed against the cold wall behind me. A tall, handsome man with a pointed chin and sleek dark hair stood in front of me, grinning excitedly, his arms outstretched as he was casting a spell.

"That should have done the trick. If you two are indeed *an item* now, Ms Filipov should have gotten the message. All you and I need to do now, vilenak… is wait. Your soulmate shall come to us."

My eyes regained their focus, and the vision was gone. Every cell in my body hurt, terrified, fearing for his life. I jumped out of bed, grabbing the bracelet and the garnet ring. I had to go; there was no time to waste. Tanatos has Ivan.

Chapter 26
Kalemgrad

I dressed quickly, grabbing the first pair of jeans and a shirt I could find. Taking a small metal box out of the desk drawer, I searched for my satin caste band and put it on. Best to have it with me; at least that way, I'd avoid unnecessary questions. Going back into nemage Danubia was the last thing I wanted to do, but I had no choice.

Stepping into the empty hallway, I heard faint voices coming from downstairs. It can't be that late yet, I thought, if League members were still here. I rushed down the stairs, noticing all the gemstones I was wearing — the garnet and the secondaries — were brightly lit. Alerted, ready to fight. My fear was so palpable I didn't even have to make an effort to summon an anchor emotion. Going down the stairs in what seemed like one giant leap, I burst through the bar door, knocking it down to the floor with a loud thud.

"Sofija? Is everything okay?" I heard Tomislav asking. *Just the person I need,* I thought with relief.

Walking — no, *jumping* over the knocked-down bar door, I approached him, stopping abruptly just centimetres from where he was sitting. Natasha was sitting at the table with Tomislav, Maya, David, and his wife, Sandra. All were staring at me with puzzled expressions.

I had eyes only for Tomislav. He is the leader; he can help. When I spoke, my voice wasn't urgent enough. It didn't convey the panic brewing inside me.

"He's keeping Ivan imprisoned. I have to go; I have to save him. He took him to get to me, Tomislav. I have to—" My voice broke as I pleaded with him. I could see comprehension dawning on Tomislav's tired face, and he started pacing, running his hands nervously through his curly hair.

"Tanatos has captured Ivan? That would explain why he's not returned yet," he said, still pacing.

"Why don't you sit down Sofija, we'll figure out a plan?" Natasha said, her concerned eyes looking me over.

"I — can't — sit — down!" I grunted through my teeth, doing my best not to start shouting.

"There's no time! Don't you understand, he's torturing him as we speak!" I could hear my voice tremble, feel the tears running down my cheeks, but I didn't care. They wouldn't change my mind; I was going to cross into Agram. Tonight.

Maya approached me, her amethyst gleaming brightly. Carefully, she put both her hands on my shoulders and said, in a calm voice, "Sofija, please tell us what's happened first. How do you know all this? Please, just have a seat for a moment."

Something about her calming voice spoke to me, and I took a deep breath, attempting to calm my insane heartbeat. Trying not to dread, not to fear. Unspeaking, I took the nearest empty seat. All eyes were on me, watching me with worry.

"I saw it. It was like I was in Ivan's body; I could see through his eyes. I was... *he* was strapped against the wall, powerless, and Tanatos was using magic to torture him. When he did that, I woke up. Ivan had said earlier that I can now feel what he feels and see what he sees. Perhaps that's how the vision happened. And then, Tanatos said that I'd come to him." I said all this in a rush, my eyes glued to the floor. It took a lot of effort to concentrate on the vision, which was rapidly fading from my frantic mind.

"You'd come to him?" Maya asked, surprised. "To rescue Ivan. But anyone of us can do that; what makes him think it'll be you?"

"Because she's his soulmate. She has to help him, or Tanatos will keep on torturing Ivan until she complies. She can feel what he feels, so it wouldn't take long because she'll suffer too. It's ancient vila magic," David explained, speaking for the first time. I looked up at him, terrified.

"You're his *soulmate*?" Maya asked me, surprised. "So that explains the speed at which the two of you got together." Something in her tone made me think she didn't approve of the idea. I didn't have the time to ask for an explanation; it wasn't important right now.

"I have to go; there is no time to waste," I said, standing up. Tomislav grabbed my arm, stopping me.

218

"Sofija, we don't have a plan yet. You cannot go alone. If you'd just wait a few hours until morning, when the curfew is over, then we can go together." I could see the pleading in his eyes. He wanted me to be careful; I knew that. But right now, I couldn't care less about caution.

"You don't understand; I cannot just sit around and do nothing," I protested.

Tomislav sighed, rolling his eyes at the ceiling. "For once, just once, Sofija," he said, his voice strained, "*please* don't be so stubborn. Listen to us."

I could see there was no arguing with him, not when he had all the others on his side, too. So, I sat back down, doing my best to appear calm. "Okay. Let's work on the plan."

Relieved that it didn't take long to persuade me, Tomislav and the others got to planning straight away. I didn't listen because it didn't matter anyway, not to me. Natasha was in full-on motherly mode, bringing me tea and food, and I took it without comment as I didn't want to worry her. I sat there, quietly, for a whole hour, thinking up my next move. There must be a way to leave here without having to argue again. I knew very well I'd just lose once more.

Maya approached me, sitting down.

"Are you all right? Don't worry, we've done these things before. You know, rescuing people from Kalemgrad. Ivan will be okay; he's got decades of fighting under his belt." Her dark eyes scrutinised my face, no doubt worried about my silence.

And then an idea struck me.

"Come to my room with me. I need your help with... something," I whispered. Maya looked confused but stood up and followed me to the bar exit, nevertheless.

"I'm just going to change into something better; Maya's coming with me," I said. No one paid much attention to us, as the conversation about Ivan's rescue mission was in full swing.

Passing by the knock-down set of doors, we rushed up the stairs. A moment later, I was sitting on my bed, Maya looking at me with her eyebrows raised.

"So? What's all this about?"

"Teach me to shapeshift," I said, my voice steady and confident.

There was a pause as Maya stared at me as if I'd lost my mind.

"You can't just teach a mage to shapeshift, Sofija. You either have it in you, or you don't."

"Not just any mage. A Panmage," I said, waiting a few seconds before continuing, "please, help me, so I can get out of here unnoticed. There must be a way for me to change my appearance. It'll help me get into Agram without raising flags with the Armiya, too. You can tell others what's happened when I'm gone, but I need a head start. I cannot just sit here and discuss plans and strategies while Ivan's in pain."

Maya seemed to struggle with her thoughts for a minute. Then, finally, she said:

"There is another way to change appearance, but the spell will only last for a couple of hours, at least here, in Tayna. In Danubia... well, it's unpredictable; every spell behaves differently in a place without magical supplies. You won't learn to shapeshift, but this is close enough. The only problem is... it isn't exactly light magic. You see, taking on someone else's appearance, unless you're a natural shapeshifter, is in sort of a grey area. What it means is that this piece of magic will come with a price you'd have to pay. Are you prepared for that?"

"Yes," I said without stopping to think. Nothing mattered but saving Ivan.

Maya still seemed undecided but nodded, nevertheless. "Who do you want to pose as? It needs to be someone from the League, or the others will be suspicious."

I had the answer ready. "You."

I rushed down the stairs, feeling strange in the new body I'd acquired. The dark locks were jumping restlessly around my face, something I wasn't at all accustomed to. Maya's clothes were unfamiliar but comfortable — just a pair of jeans and a button-down shirt. Getting to the hotel entrance door, I lifted one of Maya's cigarettes so that Tomislav could see. "Just going to smoke this quickly, outside. Sofija is coming down soon; she's changing."

Tomislav and the others barely glanced my way, occupied with planning Ivan's rescue. Not daring to believe my luck just yet, I opened the hotel door. As soon as the warm summer night embraced me, I broke into a run towards the Promenade.

The streets of Tayna were as deserted as ever, and I found the opening between cypress trees quickly enough. Heading for the gap between them, I followed a narrow pathway stretching in front of me, leading into a park. A few seconds later, the dark seaside town was gone, and the tall trees disappeared. Instead, I walked into the Kairos Café, the all-too-familiar back door with the brass knocker behind me.

Lydia, the waitress looked my way from behind the bar, alarmed. The café was utterly deserted; she was alone, doing the final clean up by the looks of it.

"Maya! What are you doing here this late? Something happened?" she asked, rushing over to me.

"No, all is fine. I'm on guard duty in Agram tonight," I lied, hoping Lydia trusted Maya enough not to ask any more questions.

"All right then. Be careful," the blonde waitress said, her eyes narrowing. She seemed suspicious but didn't question me further.

I smiled widely at her, waved, and walked to the door. Utter silence welcomed me as I stepped onto the deserted streets of Agram old town. Curfew was usually in place until six in the morning, and now it couldn't be later than midnight.

I walked quickly, almost running, not paying much attention to where I was going. I knew how to get to Kalemgrad; that was not what concerned me now. Maya said she wasn't sure how long the disguise would last, especially in the non-magical environment. Passing the Armiya as myself would be impossible, and I hoped beyond all hope that the spell would hold at least until I got to Kalemgrad.

It crossed my mind several times that I should perhaps start running the mage speed. That way, I'd get to Ivan within a few minutes at most. But then a sudden realisation hit me: I was in a non-magical environment, stripped of all my powers. Speed and strength wouldn't work here, neither would my gemstones. I did not have any marbles with me, unfortunately. If I'd asked for them, Tomislav might have guessed what I was up to.

I was surprised at how little time I put into considering my own safety. For all I knew, my plan won't work at all; my powers wouldn't be enough to keep Tanatos at bay long enough for Ivan and me to escape.

I might be marching towards my own doom, I realised as my whole body shivered with fear. Perhaps my self-preservation urge was dampened; perhaps it was never very strong, for the fear didn't paralyse me or make me turn around. Instead, I pressed on, more decisive than ever.

I walked down the narrow, cobbled street lined with deserted shops and bars, passing the open-air market and the cathedral. Ahead of me, I saw the dark stairs leading to the mountains. Cursing the lack of magic in nemage Danubia, I ran as fast as I could. *Humans are so slow, so weak. How did I ever live like this?*

Finally, I reached the stairs at the foot of the mountain. Clenching my fists tight at my side and listening to the loud thuds of my heart, I started climbing. There was no single soul in sight, not even a stray cat; the eery silence chilled my bones to the marrow. *Think about Ivan*, I told myself. *Don't be afraid.* His smiling face lingered in front of me, emerald eyes gleaming with happiness. Hope surged through me, shining brightly like a beacon in the impenetrable night that engulfed me.

I must have climbed over five hundred steps but didn't tire much with adrenalin rushing through my veins. The city grew ever-smaller below me, stretching as far as the eye can see in all directions. Ahead stood the mighty Kalemgrad, Tanatos' headquarters. Every soul in Danubia knew where Kalemgrad was and how to get there, but no one I knew ever visited. It was not a pompous palace that offered sightseeing tours or a friendly residence where the political elites held negotiations with the commoners. No, Kalemgrad was an unapproachable and formidable fortress, built high over Agram, overlooking the city and everyone who lived in it. I thought Tanatos had quite a flair for theatrics. He personally chose the location right after claiming the presidency for himself and abolishing the rotational government. The message he was looking to send is a simple one — *your place is at my feet; you have been conquered.* The fortress could not be more intimidating, tall and built of dark marble, standing atop the highest hill above Agram. The never-ending stairs were there to test the visitor's resolve.

I was almost at the entrance now. Dark figures dressed in black, the Armiya agents, were stationed at both sides of the fortress's tall iron gates. Not allowing myself to be encumbered by fear, I walked on, my heart thumping hard in my chest.

Just keep going, Sofija, I kept on repeating to myself. *You've come this far; there's no turning back now.*

Clenching my fists and bracing myself for some sort of attack, I climbed the last three steps and faced the guards. Well aware my gemstones weren't going to work here; I forced the panic out of my mind.

Then, suddenly, I was hit by a rush of energy. My gemstones lit up instantly, all apart from one. Topaz was still unlit, but I didn't think much of it at first. Perhaps it would light later; maybe I need more practice. After all, I just started using magic. The other four gems gleamed brightly: garnet on my silver ring and the rest on my bracelet.

Tomislav was right — Tanatos stores magic at Kalemgrad, and I've just walked through the barrier. I felt something heavy on my back and shoulders. Looking down, I saw my long, chestnut hair instead of Maya's curls. A single, turquoise strand was visible even in the dark. The disguise was lifted, and I regained my appearance. Suddenly, Maya's jeans and a button-down shirt felt a little loose, but that was the last thing that mattered. I was back to myself. *Just in time to meet Tanatos.*

Feeling braver now that my gemstones worked again, I approached one of the guards. The man glanced sideways at me, not showing a particular interest even though it was the middle of the night, and I was probably the most wanted person in Danubia.

The guard was tall and entirely bald, with thick eyebrows that looked menacing above his tiny, grey eyes.

"He's been waiting for you," he said mechanically, glancing away from me. The gates opened with an ear-splitting creaking sound. Prepared for whatever was coming, I walked through the gates, finding myself in the middle of a stone square. I could see the fortress entrance just across from where I stood. As I walked over to the marble door, my every step echoed loudly against the stone tiles, in perfect synchronisation with my loud-beating heart. A giant, round symbol stood engraved on both sides of the dark marble entrance: a zero with a horizontal line stretched across the middle. I distantly remembered seeing it before but wasn't sure where. The double doors opened; no one was guarding the entrance, which made me very uneasy. This wasn't typical of Tanatos, usually always surrounded by a battalion of Armiya agents. I looked down to my right hand and saw four of my gemstones, all apart from topaz, still gleaming. Best not to think twice, I thought to myself, or the ever-growing fear, now the size of a mountain in my mind, will claim me completely. Taking a single deep breath, I walked into Kalemgrad.

Chapter 27
The Truth

A long, dark corridor stretched before me. The tall walls were covered in paintings, all depicting episodes from Danubia's history — or, as I was now aware, the *official* version of Danubia's history, modified in the Wipe. Battles against the Eastern Empire were featured on most of them, glorifying Danubia's victory over its oppressors. Then the Liberation March through every city across the country as the First Danubian Federal Republic was created. One partition of the wall was dedicated solely to the depiction of Danubia's caste system, showing all seven groups working and living in harmony with each other. The people in the paintings were all smiling, happy to contribute to their community, wearing their respective castes' colours. Even the Siva members seemed content with their place in Danubian society.

No one is content with being an outcast, I thought, disgusted. But here it was again, that twisted notion that one should be happy with the artificial position given to one by the state. One should not question the way things are. Tend to your own corner, don't look over the fence, was what we were always told. Above the paintings showing the seven castes of Danubia stood large letters, reading the familiar mantra I knew all too well: *No progress without unity. No unity without order.* Suddenly I felt a stab of longing for Tayna, and I hoped my plan would work. Otherwise, I'd have to stay in this wretched place, possibly ending up in the RC, if I didn't get killed that night. Suddenly, death seemed like a more favourable option, a friend even.

I came to a halt, reaching the end of a dark corridor. The only way forward was up the stone steps. I stood there, listening for any signs of Tanatos, Ivan or Armiya agents, but heard nothing. The silence was so deep, so eerie, it reverberated loudly in my ears, sending my heartrate through the roof. Climbing up slowly, I had my gemstones ready for the attack, my anchor emotion in the back of my mind, waiting. I went for anger this time — anger at everything Tanatos had done to my family. Everything he had done to my friends — to Natasha and Tomislav, and to the love of my life whom he'd been keeping here, inflicting great pain on him. I thought anger would be a more suitable anchor emotion for the kind of magic I planned to use on Danubia's President.

And then, as if I walked through yet another barrier, voices surrounded me. As I reached the last step, a scene unfolded before my eyes, and two things happened at once.

Ivan, strapped to the furthest wall but otherwise looking unharmed, yelled, "No!" his eyes wide with panic as he saw me walking into the room. Sharp, white light blinded me for a second, and I found myself standing in a closed-up, round container. It was a human-sized cylinder hovering above the stone floor. I tried to get out, commanding my gems to burst it open, but nothing happened. It was as if a strong, plastic film were stretched over my gemstones so they couldn't work through it; the magic just wouldn't come out. I stared around, bewildered, realising the strange cylinder was now moving. The room was dark, just like the corridors, but devoid of any paintings or ornaments. The only source of light came from tall lamps stationed in the corners.

A tall figure with the familiar pointed face I loathed so much stood only a few centimetres away from the cylinder, smirking maliciously. The man was wearing the usual Biela uniform, impeccably clean and adorned with war medals. Tanatos' arms were outstretched in front of him as he controlled the round container I was trapped in, positioning it in the centre of the room. I noticed he had no gemstones, no vessels at all. Searching, my eyes darted over his hands, arms, his belt, all the places he could've kept the gems, but there was nothing. Then, with a shock, I looked into his eyes. They weren't of the familiar, cold onyx colour. Instead, they gleamed in deep blood-red. The colour of the garnet. My birthstone.

"That will be enough, Angelov. You must be pleased; I told you Miss Filipov would join us eventually," the man said in a lazy voice, looking up at Ivan with a grin stretched across his face.

"Let — her — go," I heard Ivan grunting through his teeth. It sounded like he had trouble speaking as if his throat was stifled by an

226

invisible hand.

Tanatos laughed loudly, looking from Ivan to me. My eyes locked on Ivan's as I was trying to feel what he was feeling. It didn't seem he was in pain, but it was difficult for him to speak. Tanatos was keeping him quiet by magic so that every word cost him dearly. He couldn't move a centimetre though he struggled stubbornly to free his hands so that he could fight Tanatos. I gave Ivan my most reassuring look, trying to calm him. If I were to go head-to-head with Tanatos, he shouldn't be in the way. With my abilities running wild at the moment, I didn't want him in the line of fire, especially when he was so weak from whatever horrors Tanatos had put him through.

Looking up at Tanatos, holding my head high, I said in a clear voice, "I'd like to speak with you. Alone."

Ivan stared in disbelief. I saw a trace of pain on his beautiful face but didn't have the time to dwell on it — I'd explain everything later. Hopefully, when we get to Tayna and to safety.

Tanatos looked at me, his eyebrows raised in surprise. "Alone? But why? Wouldn't you rather have your soulmate by your side? After all, you are an extraordinary being, Sofija. He should see who you *truly* are."

His voice had a sleek, velvety quality to it. Every word reverberated against the dark, bare walls, making the hairs stand up on the back of my neck. Tanatos' handsome, young-looking face was distorted in malicious glee, wiping out all attraction he would otherwise have.

I pressed my hands to the round edges of the container, eyes locked on Tanatos. He stood there, cruel satisfaction emanating from him nearly palpable. A grin never left his features as he examined me, revelling in my apparent cluelessness. *What was he talking about? An extraordinary being, me?* There was even a hint of pride in his voice, something I couldn't explain. Didn't he lure me in here to kill me? To eliminate the dangerous promised child. Come to think of it, why was I still alive? He could have killed me by now. But then, some killers liked to play with their food, I thought in horror. Perhaps that's what this was? A sick performance to bolster his murderous appetite.

Unsure of what to say, I just stood there, staring at Tanatos' cold, blood-red eyes. He still seemed... proud. Even excited. Could he be that twisted? Did he get some sort of pleasure from torturing his victims?

"I don't want him to see this. I know why you asked me here," I managed, glancing at Ivan apologetically. He'll have to find it in him to forgive me, I thought in resignation. *Though I won't be around to know that he ever did.*

Tears swam in my eyes, and every bone in my body hurt to the breaking point. I was hoping to buy some time to get a chance to attack Tanatos by asking to speak with him. Perhaps if he'd let me out of this blasted cylinder, my gemstones would work once more, and I would have a fighting chance. I was planning to negotiate Ivan's release and Helena's safety in exchange for my death. But now, being here, I suddenly realised just how foolish my plan was. It was never going to work; I should have listened to Tomislav. Promised child or not, Panmage or not, I was too inexperienced and too weak to counter this monster of a man standing in front of me. And now I'd even lost one of my gemstones, somehow. Topaz remained unlit, still. As if reading my mind, Tanatos said in a half-fascinated voice.

"Oh my! You've dabbled in dark magic, Sofija." His eyes gleamed excitedly as he came closer to the cylinder, examining the gemstones on my bracelet and ring. "Topaz… I suppose that connects you to him." He indicated Ivan with a wave of a hand. "Interesting. Not only are you an Alfa Immortal, but you also have a backbone, the guts to do what it takes. What did you trade it for, I wonder? Was it your little disguise?"

I looked up, shocked. How could he know?

"Did you think I wouldn't know you entered *my* Danubia disguised as somebody else? Nothing escapes my notice, at least not here, dear Sofija." Tanatos said proudly. "So that must be it. You traded a valuable gemstone — a connection to your soulmate no less — to come and save him, thus giving up the status of a Panmage. How *touching*." His voice was full of badly disguised irony, sending shivers down my spine. "A scapegoat, just like your dear *mother*."

I felt a stab of anger, running so deep it could've gone straight to the bone marrow.

"Don't you mention my mother!" I said through clenched teeth. "You murderous maniac!"

Still looking amused, Tanatos cocked his head, looking me over. "Oh, is that what you think I am? A murderous maniac?" He grinned at me, and I wanted to chop his head off, the anger levels rising in me like a storm. My four remaining gemstones were shining so brightly now, I could barely see through the cylinder.

"Yes, that is exactly what you are," I answered, trying to remain calm.

"Well," he started, now pacing slowly and pausing for dramatic effect, "that's fair, Sofija, but perhaps you should collect all the pieces of the truth before judging me so harshly." Then, he stopped, looking at one of the Armiya agents standing in the corner of the dark room. I hadn't even realised they were there before.

"Bring her in," I heard Tanatos saying to the guard in a softer tone.

I didn't have the time to think about what he said or wonder who he'd sent for when my heart nearly stopped. At first, I thought I was having some kind of an out-of-body experience or that Tanatos put me to sleep for whatever reason. Because what I was seeing, *who* I was seeing in front of me couldn't be there. It must be a hallucination.

A slim, middle-aged woman, with chestnut hair — *my* chestnut hair, a single turquoise strand streaming down one side of her face, walked into the room. Or rather glided into it, the way I did when using my mage speed. She wore a large necklace, lined with gemstones of all colours and shapes, around her neck. All her gems were unlit, and I wondered for a second why that was. She stood there, still as a rock; her hands tucked into her overcoat pockets. Underneath it, I noticed, she wore a long, regal-looking dress that reached the floor.

"Oh, how I love moments like this," Tanatos said in an almost singsong voice. "Meet your mother, Sofija." Theatrically, he moved out of the way and pointed to the woman standing opposite my cylinder, her caramel-brown eyes showing no emotion as she looked at me.

There was a long silence as I stared at the woman, my mind in complete disarray. Somehow, Ivan regained the power of speech as I heard him saying:

"Alina? But this is impossible; we buried her!"

Tanatos' face gleamed with malicious triumph. He enjoyed withdrawing information and toying with us, waiting for the right moment to achieve the desired dramatic effect. He was, I realised then, a supreme showman.

"Whoever you buried, Angelov, wasn't Alina Bayamonti. She is standing right here, in front of you." Looking at the woman, he said, his voice unusually soft, "Should you take it from here, dear? It is essential that Sofija learns about her history."

"It is quite all right if you continue, Boyan," the woman replied, her eyes still impenetrable as she scrutinised my face. The moment she spoke, a horrible scene came to mind as I recognised the cold voice. This was the First Comrade, the vicious woman who hurt Mila and burnt down Tomislav's and Natasha's house.

"This is not my mother! My mother is dead. I've been to her grave!" I yelled, unable to stop myself as my body shook with anger at First Comrade. I wasn't sure whom I loathed more, her or Tanatos.

"Actually, Sofija, the President here is telling you the truth," was all she said, her voice still cold, like that night when she came to Tayna looking for me. I forced myself to meet her eyes, noticing they were caramel-brown like mine. She was telling the truth.

I gaped; my mind utterly devoid of every other thought but one: how is she alive? What happened that night, twenty-five years ago? Is my father still alive, too? Have I been lied to this whole time? And then, a horrifying thought struck me as I locked eyes with Ivan, who was watching the scene with a shocked expression on his face, too. Was Ivan in on all this? What about Tomislav and Natasha?

But before my thoughts could spin further out of control, Tanatos started pacing again, delighted at having added one more person to his audience.

"Twenty-five years ago, I crushed the feeble attempt at rebellion, killing your scoundrel of a father and most of his accomplices. Your mother, however, had more sense in her. I always knew that she never truly believed in their cause, never wanted to mix with their kind. She offered me a deal I couldn't reject. I spared her life, and instead, she gifted me with the most valuable possession," Tanatos ended the monologue with a gloating smile, his index finger pointing at me: "You, Sofija".

I stared, wide-eyed, clenching my fists still, ready to attack. Cold showers went through my body, and I felt as if the whole world around me were suddenly crashing down. Tanatos must be lying, I told myself.

He must be... he *is* lying.

"You were just a small child then... *his* child," he went on, sauntering around my container, relaxed. "I never liked your father, and the feeling was mutual. After all, we were after the same woman for so long." He glanced at First Comrade, who had her gaze glued to my face, still.

"But I won in the end, as you can see. Your mother agreed to put you into a procedure that would eventually make the most powerful mage that ever existed out of you. And what's even better, you'd be completely and utterly devoted to *me*. You see, Sofija, it isn't a coincidence that you are — well, *were* — a Panmage, nor that you learn to use magic so quickly. Even most skilled mages have trouble controlling their powers at first. But not you."

There was another pause as Tanatos paced the room, relishing the undivided attention. Then, he stopped, pointing his long, bony finger at me.

"You must wonder how I know all this. Our contact — the silly woman the League so naively stationed in Velesh to protect your loved ones from me — she told us you've mastered every spell at once. She also helped us capture your soulmate here, telling us about the clever exchange of marbles the League has organised for the past few weeks. Your powers aren't accidental. You are who you are because *I* made you so. You are *my* Alfa Immortal, and I finally get to take advantage of creating you. You see, I had to wait for so long, biding my time in the Duma, pretending to be one of the filthy nemages. All this for one reason — because I was in this for the long haul. My plan was coming to fruition, although slowly. I was waiting for you to develop your powers, to attain magical adulthood so that I could put you to the test. So far, all your skills have evolved just as I anticipated — you are extremely powerful, and you came into the role most willingly, which is precisely how it had to happen."

"What are you—" I started, but Tanatos lifted his right hand, stifling my throat so that I couldn't continue. I choked on my words, both my hands flying to my throat instinctively.

"Patience is a virtue, dear. You'll get all the answers in time. You see, I needed to create not just a skilful but also a passionate mage out of

231

you. And what makes us passionate better than anger and despair. That is why we sent you to the nemages, the most dreadful, most abominable place one could grow up in. That is why I ordered Alina to kill your grandparents. You had to be beaten down to want for my blood; otherwise, my experiment wouldn't have worked. Of course, there was a minor glitch in my plan. I didn't count on your mother getting overprotective and trying to hide you from me, disobeying my direct orders." He glanced at Alina, who was standing still, her eyes impenetrable.

"But we overcame that particular hurdle," he added in a light voice, smirking. "So, you see why I say you're extraordinary — you are one of a kind, you are my masterpiece. With your help, I'll create my very own Immortal army, which will allow me to govern across the ages. The mages will rise again, rise from the ashes after all these years. They say revenge is best served cold, and that is precisely what you're going to help me achieve. But this time, only the worthy, true mages will have another chance. I'm afraid your League friends just don't make the cut."

Frustrated that my gems still wouldn't blast the cylinder I was trapped in, I let out a horrifying scream, my eyes boring into Tanatos'. He just stood there, a satisfied smirk on his face. The countless medals pinned to his impeccably white uniform glittered against the yellowish lampshade. Rewards for his unspeakable deeds, for murders and looting, for tearing families apart and stealing futures.

"You sick, perverted man! You'd better be lying!" Ivan yelled at him, seemingly free from whatever spell kept him from talking until now. His eyes were deep-gold, ready for a fight, but to no avail as he was still bound to the dark wall.

"So many wonderful compliments are being thrown at me these days," he crooned, smiling still. "The Supreme President, the Benefactor of Danubia. Those clueless nemages are grateful for their pointless little lives, grateful to *me*. Yet, the two of you just don't seem convinced... not yet. Not to worry, I am nothing if not patient. Your mother knows that well, Sofija." He inclined his head towards Alina, who smiled back at him.

I then noticed a long scar running from the edge of her mouth to her ear. I wondered what happened to her. I was not yet convinced that she really was my mother or that any piece of the story Tanatos just told us was true. This woman — the First Comrade — deserved whatever caused that ugly scar, I thought in disgust.

"But let's move on to why we're all here. Time to see what's become of my masterpiece," he said, rolling up his sleeves and getting ready to cast a spell. His pointed face gleamed with an almost childish excitement as he moved several steps away from the cylinder, standing next to the woman. Her eyes never left my face, but I ignored her now, trying to get my gemstones to cast magic and blow up the cylinder. Whatever Tanatos planned to do next couldn't be good news, and I needed my magic back.

Chapter 28
Alfa Immortal

Hissing sounds surrounded me as white steam appeared from thin air, filling up the cylinder I was trapped in. Through the thick clouds, I saw Tanatos, mumbling incomprehensible words to himself, his hands outstretched before him. He was casting a spell. As he did so, the cylinder kept on filling with scentless steam, and soon I couldn't see anything at all, as if a white sheet of thickest linen were draped over my eyes.

Then, my head was suddenly full of countless images of people I've never met. Most of them were asleep; others were chatting and laughing. Men and women, all around my age, filled my mind so vividly I could swear I'd be able to reach out to them, to wake them from slumber, if only I tried. They were right there everywhere I turned, inside the steamy cylinder, with me. After a while, I noticed their numbers duplicating as the seconds passed. Now, their images filled almost the entire room, stretching outside the confines of my cylinder. I stared around me, bewildered, trying to understand what was going on, but nothing I came up with seemed plausible enough.

"What a glorious sight!" I heard Tanatos exclaim, his voice ecstatic. "Don't worry, dear Sofija, the steam won't hurt you. It is a potion made of hallucinogenic magical herbs. It brings up your Alfa Immortal to the surface and shows us the other Immortals out there. You can command them with the lift of a finger if you'd like. And I command you, so in fact, this is my Immortal army. My masterpiece, one I've been waiting to put to use all these years."

Tanatos strolled around the room, his hands behind his back, beaming at all the different shapes and faces, admiring his work. "Sleep, my dear soldiers. For soon, there will be no time to rest. Soon, we'll be fighting for what was lost a long time ago; we'll be restoring the proper order, one that was so unjustly taken from us."

He spoke in an eerily low voice, but there was a loving, almost caressing tone in it. It was as if he was talking to his pets. The sound made my stomach turn, and I suddenly felt sick. Then the headache came, so intense I started losing vision. Scared of fainting, I sat down on the cylinder floor, my head in my lap.

"Let her out!" I heard Ivan yelling, "she's not feeling well; let her out now!"

"Oh yes, that would be the impact of the potion. It mustn't be used in such a high dosage without practice. Sofija's body will get accustomed to it in time. And then, just by using my Alfa Immortal, I'll control the whole army. Do you know why they're called Immortal army, Angelov?" Tanatos asked Ivan in an almost quizzical tone. He wanted to play a game.

Ivan stared at him with loathing but said nothing.

"I see you're not in a talking mood," he commented, sighing as if disappointed. Then, shrugging his shoulders, he said in a mocking voice, "All right, all right, I'll tell you. It is because I used the vila genome to prolong their lives. Only I made them even better, stronger and more durable than the vila kind. See, my Immortals will live forever, as the name indicates. Unless killed, of course, but given their extraordinary magical powers, that's very unlikely."

I couldn't listen to Tanatos anymore. As much as I tried to stay awake, my whole body was longing for sleep and rest. I could feel my eyelids droop, and, as they did so, the countless faces around me started disappearing. The last thing I remember before closing my eyes was intense light coming from the entrance, but that might have just been the steam still rising all around me.

"So weak, so human. You'll grow into your role soon enough, my dear. Now wake up. It's time for you to leave us, for now." Tanatos' sleek voice woke me from a dreamless slumber. Hoping it was just a bad dream, I kept my eyes shut for another few seconds. Then, bracing myself, I opened them, looking up at the face I loathed so much, grinning at me. Ivan was still strapped to the wall, still struggling hopelessly. The First Comrade stood still as a rock, unmoving, where she was just before I closed my eyes. The steam was gone, and so were the faces of countless people — the people Tanatos said were his Immortal army.

"Davor, please escort Sofija to her cell. Who better than you to show her into her new home?" Tanatos crooned, beaming happily at someone behind me. I was so exhausted, my mind floating somewhere between waking and dreaming, that I didn't register what he'd said at first. A tall man dressed in Armiya uniform appeared in front of me, and the cylinder door opened. He stepped in, grabbing my forearm, pulling me out of the round container. The moment he touched me, my every cell started fighting, screaming for release. Looking up, I recognised the grey eyes — the scruffy beard. The stench of alcohol on his breath, so painfully familiar, every part of me wanted to run far, far away. I never thought I'd see him again, not after the last time, after I was found at the Sopot Train Station, beaten nearly to death.

"You're not taking her anywhere!" Ivan yelled, attempting to free himself from the chains that held him. "Lift the spell, Tanatos, and fight like a man!"

"Such brave words from you tonight, vilenak. I will free you, but not before sharing an interesting piece of information about your newfound soulmate. See, Davor here and Sofija have a romantic history. Am I correct?" he was looking at Davor, waiting for confirmation.

He didn't respond for a while, his eyes focused on a spot somewhere above Tanatos' head. Still clutching my forearm tightly, he gave a short nod.

"See, Sofija, Davor joined my guard a couple of months ago, sharing all his personal history with us. Unfortunately, he couldn't tell us about your whereabouts or where we might find you, but we did learn a lot about your nemage life. And thanks to your friend in Velesh, we finally found you when you were so foolishly trying to escape into Agram on an illegal travel permit. Of course, then the League interfered, and we lost you again for a while, but it all worked out in the end, my dear. Now you are reunited with your long-lost love and have a chance at burying the axe."

Ivan's eyes darted to mine, and I saw understanding dawning on his face. I told him once about the horrible relationship I had with Davor, but I didn't mention the name. It wasn't hard to guess.

"She's going nowhere with him! Over my dead body!" Tanatos turned to Ivan, facing him fully for the first time.

"I've had enough of your pointless shouting, Angelov. I have no problem killing you, but it would be such a waste spilling your extraordinarily magical blood. Perhaps a little torture would bring you to your senses and finally shut you up."

His eyes gleamed blood-red again as he prepared to cast a spell. Davor was towing me toward the exit, but I resisted. Surprised at my own strength, I realised he couldn't do anything to me any more, for I was much, much stronger. My gemstones worked again as I left the cylinder, and my reflexes were back. In one swift move, I threw Davor off, and he flew all the way across the room. I watched in shock, not daring to believe my own strength. It was as easy as brushing an annoying fly off my shoulder. A massive surge of strength swam through my body and I revelled in the sudden wave of energy.

Just as I was about to throw a kicking curse at Tanatos, he turned around and yelled, "No, you don't!" as an unfamiliar curse came flying at me. Amber light left his outstretched hands, and long ropes entrapped me, materialising out of thin air. I couldn't move, noticing in horror that my gems lost their light again.

"Ropes imbibed with yantar oil. Yantar immobilises even the most powerful of mages." Tanatos explained in a calm voice as if giving a lecture. I stood there, motionless, tied by indestructible amber ropes. My eyes darted to the First Comrade — to Alina Filipov, I thought with a painful stab. She didn't move a centimetre, helping neither side, only watching, motionlessly. It was as if she was in a state of shock or perhaps trying to decide what to do. I noticed all her gemstones — at least six or seven of them — lay unlit on her necklace.

"Davor, you can take her now. She won't be able to do anything while tied by the spell," Tanatos said, turning back to Ivan, his eyes gleaming blood-red again.

The door behind me burst open, hitting the floor with a loud thud. Alina gasped, losing her composure for the first time.

"Oh, good. I was hoping you'd join our little gathering, Antich," Tanatos commented in a lazy voice, turning around to face the newcomers, "sorry you missed dinner."

Waves of relief and new-found hope washed over me as I watched Tomislav, Natasha, David, Sandra, Goran, Marko and Maya enter the dark room. Tanatos took a few steps towards them, his back to Ivan, an evil smirk dancing on his face.

"You didn't have to demolish the door," he said, looking at Tomislav.

"I'll demolish a lot more than a set of doors if you harm Sofija," Tomislav retorted in a cold voice, so cold it was almost unrecognisable. Natasha stood by his side, the rest of the League behind them. Their gemstones gleamed brightly, ready to attack or defend.

"Always so theatrical, Antich. I've missed dealing with you, I have to admit. Whatever happened to your other friends from the League? Oh — that's right. I killed them the last time you challenged me. I'm guessing you're hoping to avenge your friend, Luka Filipov?"

Tomislav let out a hiss through his teeth, staring at Tanatos under his dark eyebrows, his muscles strained with rage, jaw clenched. He was fighting against the urge to throw himself at Tanatos, to choke him with his bare hands, I knew it. It was exactly how I felt ever since I first spoke to the monster.

"But enough of this chit-chat. We have work to do, and I don't fancy having unannounced guests." Tanatos' smirk disappeared as he stepped towards the newcomers. He was ready to attack, to kill. With one swift motion, he cast a kicking curse at Tomislav, sending him flying across the room. He landed with a loud thud on marble floor, unconscious. Tomislav attempted to cast a shield before getting hit, but the translucent web fell apart mid-air, too feeble to counter Tanatos' magic. The bastard was at his most dangerous, I realised in horror. All I could do was watch, motionless, tied by the amber ropes and Davor's tight grip. Once again, people I cared about were getting hurt, and it was all my fault. I chanced a glance at Davor. He seemed to have lost his resolve to tow me out of the room, watching the battle unfolding before us instead. *Was he waiting for Tanatos' orders to join the fight?*

Curses flew from both sides, but everything the League attempted seemed to bounce off Tanatos. "Someone lift the curse off me!" I bellowed in vain, over and over again. My voice was lost in the noise and racket of the battle, the League too busy fighting for their own lives to pay attention to me. As she was trying to get to still-unconscious Tomislav, Natasha was hit by blood-red light. Falling to the floor, she let out a horrifying scream. Clutching her stomach, she rolled to her side, writhing in pain. A deep, long cut, as if by knife, was clearly visible as blood spilt on the marble floor.

Then, utter chaos ensued, and everything became a blur. Loud, terrifying screams, gasps and explosions filled my ears; curses flew from all directions, bouncing off the walls. The room suddenly filled with people as Tanatos' Armiya agents joined the fight. Not being able to use magic as they were nemages, they threw marbles at the League members. Tanatos conjured a massive shield around them, keeping the League's spells away. Horrified, I noticed the translucent shield moving and stretching with the agents, carefully bending and curving around their black-clad bodies to keep them from harm. I couldn't see if anyone else was hit or understand where the screams were coming from. The League was losing; that much was clearer by the second. Tanatos had numbers and the impenetrable shield on his side; his agents kept on swarming into the room, dozens of them. Anything the League attempted would just evaporate into thin air. David's spell didn't even reach the shield's barrier before dissolving into nothingness. I'd never seen a shield this strong and, by the shocked expression on the League members' faces, neither did they. What kind of magic does Tanatos have? What *is* he?

Struggling to break free and desperate to help, I willed my gemstones to light up, begged them to cooperate even though I knew it wouldn't happen, not while I was bound by the amber ropes. I didn't dare look up at Davor again, knowing my anger with him would only make me lose focus. Instead, my gaze fell upon Tanatos, who was sauntering around the room, watching his agents fight the League. His eyes were glued to Tomislav who regained consciousness and was struggling to get up, all the while staring furiously at Tanatos. But the President of Danubia showed no sign of fear. He revelled in the murderous atmosphere; he was a beast ready to pounce. This was it; there was no escape. *At least I tried my best, even if my best wasn't nearly enough.*

Tanatos approached Alina, giving her a sickening, loving look. She was still standing at the same spot as before, watching the battle unfolding before her eyes. She didn't even bother to light her gemstones, I noticed, and her hands were still hidden in her overcoat pockets. Perhaps she thought her lover wouldn't need her help, that it was too easy to defeat the League. My stomach turned in disgust. If this were really my mother, I'd rather she'd died twenty-five years ago. I'd rather have no parent than the one standing by this evil creature, looking at him with such admiration. For the first time since she appeared in the room, Alina reached out for Tanatos' hand as if encouraging him to finish what he'd started, to kill Tomislav. He seemed surprised at the gesture but pleased, nevertheless.

Then, I saw her lips moving as the cold voice I loathed so much spoke in a calm, almost bored tone:

"Boyan, I believe it's been enough of this. You're not taking Sofija anywhere. You'll let Tomislav and the rest of the League leave here in peace." As she spoke, Alina still held Tanatos' hand tightly. Unsure I've heard her correctly, I stared, bewildered, at Tanatos. Understanding dawned on his pointed face, and I could see shock rising in his eyes.

"You sneaky bitch," he said in a disgusted voice, staring at Alina.

The two of them stood next to each other, hands still touching. Neither of them could move, and Tanatos' eyes regained their natural, onyx colour. Amber ropes, like those that were still entrapping me, tied around both their hands and wrists.

"It's an oil made from yantar wood resin, strong enough to incapacitate even the most powerful of mages, as you said before. I saved some for a rainy day." Alina spoke in a calm voice as her body became immobile.

Chapter 29
Alina

More spells were thrown, and more screams came. Suddenly, I could move again, the amber ropes ending up on the floor below my feet. The moment my arms were free, I threw Davor off me, but he didn't fight. Instead, he let go of me and disappeared through the door without a single word.

Tanatos' impenetrable shield vanished, and his agents lost their protection. Panicked, some of them darted for the exit, fleeing the scene.

Ivan was free of his restraints and fighting the agents' side by side with Tomislav, David, Goran, Marko and Sandra. Once his powers were back, it was almost too easy for him to defeat the Armiya agents; all he had to do is get a hold of them, and they would instantly obey. I watched in awe as Ivan moved with captivating grace among the enraged, armed agents so fast they couldn't catch up with him. He didn't have to use spells to defeat them. One pat on a shoulder was enough to make each one of them kneel at his feet, surrendering. This was the first time I had seen his extraordinary powers at work, understanding for the first time how odd it must have been for him that I was the only one who could resist.

Maya crouched on the floor next to Natasha, who was still bleeding, using her healing magic. Absurdly, Tanatos and Alina stood, frozen, on one side of the room, watching the Armiya agents being defeated. The agents had no actual magic, only marbles that were quickly running out, and the League had no difficulty throwing them off.

Soon, the battle died out as every single Armiya agent lay on the floor, motionless, bound by magic. Tomislav scooped Natasha in his arms, and I noticed with relief that she wasn't bleeding any more. Maya's magic has helped once again.

"Let's get the hell out of here, before another battalion of agents arrives," Tomislav said, "Sofija, are you okay?"

I nodded, unable to speak as I struggled with a sudden dilemma. My eyes kept darting to Alina, still incapacitated, unmoving, from the impacts of the yantar oil she willingly used on herself to trick Tanatos. Her earlier stillness made sense now, for she used the oil on herself before showing here, knowing all along she'd try and trick Tanatos. Suddenly I thought I understood where that ugly scar, stretching across her cheek, came from. Tanatos said she tried to protect me before, that she disobeyed him. He must have been punishing her. And now she cost him not only a victory against the League but also me, his Alfa Immortal. After this, he will kill her. Eventually, the effects of yantar oil will wear off, and Alina — my mother, I thought with a sinking feeling — will die.

I glanced at Tomislav, then at Alina. He seemed to understand what troubled me.

"Sofija, it's too dangerous. They're bound with the spell. If you free her, you might release the bastard also. We don't want to risk that, not now," he said gently.

"Sofija," I heard the cold voice, realising it didn't sound as malicious as before. It was, somehow, softer. "Sofija, please go. I'm not worth it, trust me."

Torn, I stared into my mother's caramel eyes — my eyes. Could I really do this? Could I leave here, knowing that she'd die? This was, after all, the woman who ordered the murder of my grandparents, the woman who burnt Tomislav and Natasha's home, who hurt David's daughter, Mila. A person like her doesn't deserve mine, or anyone else's, mercy. I should leave her here with Tanatos.

Then another voice spoke to me, the voice I tried to ignore. If I left Alina here to die, wouldn't I be just the same as her, the same as Tanatos? I didn't know a lot about magic, but I knew that I wanted to stay in the light. Looking down at my bracelet, I eyed the topaz, still unlit. It would remain unlit forever because I chose to dabble in dark magic. Maya called it a 'grey' area, but we both knew what it was. And now, my topaz would never work again. I had to remain in the light, that much was certain.

Approaching Tanatos and Alina, I cast the best shield I could muster in case he attempted to break free from his restraints. Tanatos stared at me with utmost loathing in his onyx eyes but said nothing. Concentrating on Alina alone in my mind, I lifted the spell, and the amber oil disappeared from her hands, removing the ropes.

Free of the amber ropes, she looked up at me, eyes wide in surprise.

"You released me. Why?" Alina asked, genuinely interested in my answer.

"I'm not a murderer," I said briefly. Then, turning on my heel, I followed Tomislav and the others out of Kalemgrad and back to Tayna. Behind us, in the dark marble room, Tanatos stood defeated, fuming with anger.

The journey back was smooth, the streets of Agram utterly empty in the middle of the night. Tomislav and Ivan used the remaining marbles on the few agents we came across on the way back, freezing them on the spot. We'd just started the next war, so there was no need to keep the charade and refrain from using magic in Danubia any longer.

Upon return to The Bayamonti, we found Vesna waiting for us at the hotel bar.

"Please let me explain. Tomislav, Ivan, I beg of you", she pleaded the moment we stepped through the door, her hands flying up in surrender. "For the sake of all we've been through, just give me a chance."

Vesna said Tanatos' agents found her the very first day in Velesh. They knew about the guard duty from the start. Tanatos threatened to kill her, and every single League member assigned with marble duty unless she helped them set a trap for Ivan. They somehow knew of my connection to him; they knew I'd try to save him if he was captured. So, she told them when it was Ivan's turn to carry the marbles into Kairos. She also told them everything she knew about my magical training. Even though she wasn't there to witness my progress, Vesna knew how well it was going from what others told her.

When she had no new information to share, Vesna was taken into Kalemgrad and imprisoned there. Tanatos didn't want to give her a chance to warn the League. When Ivan was captured, she was released from Kalemgrad, for she was no longer useful. By the time she reached Tayna, we were already gone.

"You had no choice, Vesna. Don't beat yourself over it; he was one step ahead of us from the very beginning," Ivan reassured her.

"You will tell us everything, from start to finish. Then we will decide what to do with you." Alina was sitting in an armchair in the middle of The Bayamonti hotel bar, bound by magical ropes. Tomislav took a seat opposite her, his gemstones gleaming readily in case she tried anything. His lip was bleeding from the battle, and he was heavily bruised but paid no attention to either as he stared furiously at Alina. "You're only alive because Sofija wanted it. If it were up to me, I would've left you to Tanatos, and you know how he deals with those who betray him."

Then, Natasha spoke in a small voice. "She did sacrifice herself to help us, Tom."

Tomislav scoffed. "I'm sure she had an ulterior motive for doing that. Be as it may, that little smidgeon of humanity still left in her bought her this opportunity to explain everything. I want to know the whole story. So, talk, *First Comrade*. I'm guessing you're a shapeshifter now, seeing as you changed your appearance the last time we saw you?"

He was livid with anger. I have never seen him like this. This was his friend, his best friend's wife. Tomislav thought she was dead; he felt guilty for letting her die, for not saving her and my father all those years ago. And now he found out she's been alive all along, standing by no other than his biggest enemy.

Alina blinked, looking at Tomislav calmly. Her gaze travelled to me, sitting in the corner of the room, Ivan's arms around my shoulders.

"Yes, I had to shapeshift through dark magic every time I left Kalemgrad because everyone I knew thought I was dead. You know I'm not a natural shapeshifter, Tom," she explained in an exasperated voice, "and I'll tell you everything, no need to threaten. It will take a while, however."

"We have the time," Tomislav snapped. But, finally, he sat back in his chair, arms crossed on his chest, and waited.

"You know well I come from an old royal dynasty — the Turquoise," Alina started in a calm, composed voice, now almost entirely devoid of the malice I heard in it before, but still cold, nevertheless. "My parents always tried to steer me towards the men of similar lineage, which is how I met Boyan Obrenovich, or Tanatos, as you know him. We were friends as children, both our families already making plans for our future together. But then I met Luka."

There was a pause as she glanced up at Tomislav, then Natasha.

"We fell in love, and there wasn't much anyone could do. Much as my parents tried to fight it, I married him and... well, you know the rest. I had spent years here, with him, fighting with the League against the man who was once my friend, even though to him I represented so much more. Boyan never forgave me for choosing Luka over him. Although it wasn't a competition in any way to me, that was how he saw it. Boyan always craved attention and love, for he fears abandonment and embarrassment more than anything else in life. You see, his father never truly cared for him. Boyan was a child Daniel Obrenovich never planned or wanted to have. I couldn't have done a greater injustice to him; at least, that was what he thought. I abandoned him for Luka Filipov, a man from a nemage family with no apparent magical skills when he first came to Tayna. It was the highest form of betrayal for Boyan, and he craved revenge."

She paused again, scanning her silent audience. Mila joined us in the bar upon return, angrily berating her parents for leaving without her. "I'm not a child, I am a member of the League. You should have taken me with you!"

All had eyes on Alina now, listening with undivided attention as she continued:

"When it was apparent the Rebellion was lost, just before the last diversion, I saw an opportunity to save myself and my daughter."

She looked up at me, her gaze tender. "I never claimed to be the noblest person or the most unselfish, but I had to do something to save Sofija. To save myself. I'm not afraid to admit that I have self-preservation instincts, no", she retorted as Maya scoffed at her last sentence.

"It's only human to try and survive. About a week before the League's diversion, a week before my husband died, I paid a visit to Boyan. I went alone. I lied like never before — I told him everything he wanted to hear. I said that I was only with Luka to spy on the League and to defy my parents; I told him I didn't even love Luka's child, but she should have a chance at good life nevertheless, for she was just a baby."

Alina's voice broke, and she let out a sob. Angrily, she removed the tears in one swift motion.

"He asked me to put Sofija into this new procedure he came up with, a combination of dark magic and science. He was to take the vila genome, adding it to an ancient spell for immortality. Of course, no one believed the spell would actually work, but he thought it might if done right. All he needed was a subject to try it on, a guinea pig. A mage young enough to have no previous memories or experiences of any significance. A blank page to write on. So… I offered Sofija, and he spared mine — and her — life."

There were gasps from all sides.

"You sacrificed your own daughter, so you'd stay alive? She could have died in the process!" David spat out in a disgusted tone.

"I did it so both of us could stay alive," Alina answered, her voice high with pride. "That was a risk I was willing to take. If I didn't take Sofija to Boyan, he would've killed her anyway," she retorted, leaning forward as much as she could with hands tied behind her back to face David. "I did it so that both of us could have a chance at staying alive", Alina went on, her voice high with pride. "What should I have done, just move aside and let him kill her and me? Because he would've done so, just like he killed Luka and so many others from the League. When I took part in the diversion, the deal with Boyan was already struck. That's how Sofija and I survived, but he made it look like I'd been killed, too. He didn't want to look like a coward for sparing my life. Sometimes, one needs to do whatever is necessary, David."

Tomislav lifted his hand up, stopping further retorts from David. "Let her finish."

Taking a deep breath, Alina continued her confession. I resembled her so much it was like looking into a mirror and seeing an older version of myself. The feeling was unnerving, knowing who this woman was and what she's done, what pain she caused the people I cared about and me.

"I didn't tell Boyan her real name, hoping anonymity might shield her a little later on. Instead, I lied that Luka and I named our daughter Amarantha. It is an old name, common in the royal families," she explained, seeing confused looks from all sides at the mention of an unusual name.

"When the procedure was over, Boyan asked me to take Sofija away. He didn't want to raise Luka's child; he was repelled by her. Boyan wasn't interested in knowing where I sent her, as long as it was somewhere in the nemage Danubia. That was when I asked you, Tom, to meet me at the Kairos and take Sofija to Luka's parents. Boyan didn't know of Luka's nemage family. I knew she would be safe with them, and the small town of Velesh was the last place he would search in. I am forever in your debt, Tom, for taking care of her. As far as Boyan knew, my daughter was taken to an orphanage and could have been adopted by anyone."

There was another pause as she tried to gather her thoughts, getting visibly exhausted from the long monologue.

"But there was one thing I had to do first. Boyan wanted an easy way to find Sofija when she comes to her full, magical adulthood. You all know well that, depending on a person, a mage usually arrives at the peak of their abilities between the ages of twenty-three and twenty-six. So, we placed a magical tracker on Sofija, imbibed it into the spell that made her an Immortal. I helped with that part, hoping to demonstrate my belief in the cause and learn how to *undo* the spell. Boyan didn't seem to suspect anything; he trusted me to ship Sofija off somewhere he'd be able to find her again. He was drunk with triumph over Luka, too arrogant to even think that I never loved him. Before giving Sofija to you, Tom, I took the tracker off, making sure Boyan wouldn't find her, at least not easily. I wanted to give her a chance at a normal life."

I looked up at her, surprised. I learned to loathe the sound of her voice, to despise the very idea of her. The things she did or executed at Tanatos' orders were beyond forgiveness, beyond any sort of understanding. But here it was, a simple act of sacrifice on her part that made my life safer. An act that showed, undoubtedly, that this woman was indeed capable of love.

"Boyan grew nervous for the past couple of years. I was punished over and over once he found out I removed the tracker. He knew I was the only one who understood the procedure well enough to remove it. Hence the scar." She indicated the ugly scar running across her face.

"I'm not looking for pity, no," Alina commented as she noticed the way Sandra was looking at her, "I'm just telling you facts. I didn't live a fantastic life over the past twenty-five years, quite the contrary."

Her voice was high with pride, and she lifted her head up, eyeing every person in the room. She was putting on quite a show to deny her vulnerability, to show that the scars meant nothing. She, like myself, wanted to appear indestructible against all difficulties.

"Boyan kept on taking random girls of Sofija's age, looking for her as I laid imprisoned in Kalemgrad dungeons for months. I lied that Luka's parents died a long time ago, hoping this would keep him off their tracks. It worked; Boyan was too busy maintaining the personality cult, while at the same time storing magic at Kalemgrad so that, when Sofija is finally found, he could test her." She paused, looking up at Tomislav. "He's succeeded, Tom; you've witnessed it yourself tonight. He restored magic in Kalemgrad, and even I don't know how when only a few of us still exercise it there. It's not nearly enough to revive the supplies."

She looked down at the floor, seemingly too tired to continue.

Natasha stood up, walking to the bar. A few minutes later, she reappeared with a fresh cup of coffee. "Here, it might help."

Alina took it from her in silence, then spoke again.

"About a couple of months ago, Armiya got a tip from Sofija's colleague, someone named Helena, from Velesh. She offered information about a carrier of an illegal travel permit in exchange for her brother's early release from the Velesh Rehabilitation Centre."

I stared at her, shocked. *Helena sold me out. Helena, my best friend? Helena, the girl I trust with my life, whom I spent nearly every happy moment of my childhood with?* The realisation hit me so hard my head started spinning. That's why she sounded so distant the last time I called. She didn't mind when I said I wouldn't be able to make it to her brother's party; she just cut the conversation short instead… because, for whatever reason, he wasn't getting out. So, she found a way to call in a favour from the Armiya. Tears swam in my eyes, more from anger and shock than anything else, and I wiped them quickly, driving the unwelcome information out of my mind.

"Boyan soon realised she was the girl he was looking for. Once he saw the surname, it wasn't hard to connect the dots. Boyan sent Armiya agents to the train Sofija boarded. But, at the same time, I sent an anonymous tip to you, Tom. I was hoping you'd get Sofija sooner than Armiya agents and help her. Once again, you did just that. Thank you." She sounded genuine, looking from Tomislav to Natasha with utmost gratitude.

"He then found out an Armiya member who recently applied to join his guard, knew Sofija in the past."

Her eyes found mine. I didn't meet her gaze, still shocked at my best friend's betrayal. If Davor sold me out, it was nothing – *nothing* – compared to what Helena had done.

Alina took a sip of her coffee and went on. "This is all standard information; every new agent in Boyan's guard must reveal his personal history. Boyan thought this man might have information on Sofija, so he was recruited immediately. A while later, Helena from Velesh gave us a letter Sofija wrote to her, which is how Boyan knew about Sofija's relationship with Ivan." There was a pause as Alina shot an apologetic glance at Ivan and me.

"Of course, once Boyan realised I'd saved my daughter yet again, I was punished once more, but it didn't matter. My goal was to protect her, and I succeeded. That is, probably, the only good deed I've done since I've lost Luka. Then, when Sofija escaped to Tayna, Boyan sent me to Velesh to talk to Irma and Marin. I was to prove myself by capturing Sofija at last, by fixing my mistake."

Her eyes found mine, and hers were full of sadness and regret. I looked away, knowing what was coming.

"I had no choice but to order their murders when they wouldn't tell us where Sofija went. If I'd spared their lives, Boyan would've become suspicious and realised I'd played him for over two decades. It was the only way to stay near him, in Kalemgrad, so that I could look after my daughter once he captures her. All my efforts only delayed the inevitable; I knew it then. I regret every day what I'd done to the Filipovs. But I'd do it again if it meant saving Sofija in the end."

Alina fell silent, her hands wrapped around a cup of coffee in front of her. Tears swam again in her eyes, and she fought them angrily.

"That certainly fills in a lot of blanks. We've been wondering who'd sent that anonymous tip. Thank you, Alina," Tomislav said, sounding genuine for the first time.

She nodded, then said, beaming up at him apologetically: "I wish I could have stopped him sooner tonight. I was afraid he might send me away or freeze me if I made a wrong move. Instead, I waited for the right opportunity to bound him with the yantar oil."

"You helped us in the end. We wouldn't be here if it weren't for you," Natasha reassured her.

"Just one more thing, then we'll let you rest," said Tomislav. "This Immortal army Tanatos created — how dangerous is it? And what is Sofija's role in it?"

Alina took a sip, putting the cup down at the table in front of her before answering.

"Unfortunately, the procedure worked. When I saw what happened when Boyan tested Sofija tonight, my heart nearly stopped. It is the most dangerous thing I've ever seen or heard of in my life. You see, after Sofija, he's put many other children through the same procedure, but there is only one Alfa Immortal, and that is Sofija. She can call them, command them. And Boyan commands her. When he conjured that odd steam tonight, it entered Sofija's body, filled her lungs and penetrated her every pore. Now he'll be able to find her, influence her for they are now connected. I'm not sure if he'd be able to command her from a distance, but I wouldn't be surprised. You have to teach her advanced mind control; she has to be prepared."

Then, looking straight at me, she said, "I'll help you, dear. He won't touch you."

Epilogue

"So, all this time, Tomislav thought Tanatos was after me because I was the promised child, a threat to him. Instead, he was looking for me because I am his deadliest weapon."

Ivan and I took a walk around the park, heading for the cemetery.

"Yes, that was quite the twist. We were convinced Tanatos wanted to destroy you, when in fact, he just wanted to... *utilise* you."

I looked up at him, worried. "What are we going to do? He's so powerful, Ivan. He doesn't even have to use gemstones to do magic."

"We figured that part out. Tanatos is a part-vilenak, like me. His father had an affair with a vila, but then, given his later position towards our kind — his hatred towards us, to be exact — he had to deny it and the child. Tanatos' childhood couldn't have been very happy." I raised my eyebrows, giving him a stern look.

"I didn't say that I care or pity him. Just that, for the first time, I can understand why he's so vile," Ivan explained calmly. "Parents can cause terrible, lifelong damage to their children if they're not careful."

"Why did we leave him there? We could have captured him, brought him to Tayna, imprison him."

I've been thinking a lot about that night at Kalemgrad, wondering why the League didn't use the opportunity to defeat Tanatos while he was at his weakest. He couldn't use magic due to yantar oil, at least not until the effects of it wore off. Once, a thought of murdering him went through my mind, but I didn't dwell on it, pushing it aside in disgust. *That's what he would do. We don't kill; I don't kill.*

"If we'd captured Tanatos, we'd now have a battalion of Armiya agents and the rest of Biela on our backs. Tomislav thinks it best to keep the new rebellion under wraps until we're ready; we've made a mistake of going head-to-head with the bastard before. He's too strong, his personality cult running too deep in nemage Danubia. If we'd captured their *Supreme* President, we'd have no chance of getting the nemages on our side. We'd be the enemy instead."

I nodded. "That would be playing right into Tanatos' hands," was all I said before we fell silent, enjoying the warm night around us.

As we entered the deserted cemetery a while later, Ivan took my right hand, stroking the place where the caste band used to be. "Your rash is gone completely" said Ivan, conversationally. "You're free of your nemage life, it would seem". Then, interlacing our fingers, he brought both my hands to his lips so he could kiss them. I pulled them away, concealing the silver bracelet.

"Stop doing that, Sofija. We've been over this. You did what you had to do." He said, rolling his eyes at me.

I looked up at him apologetically.

"I traded the topaz you gave me, a symbol of our connection, for dark magic." I spoke in an even tone, a sentence I'd repeated so many times in the past week it was getting tiresome. Why won't anybody see that what I did was beyond bad?

"It's a grey area. You didn't know what you were trading, and we'll find a way to re-collide you with topaz. I promise."

I didn't want to argue again. Thankfully, Ivan followed suit, suddenly changing the topic:

"Here's an interesting twist for you. I know Davor; I've met him before. In fact, that night I drove you, Tomislav and Natasha to Agram, I just came off the surveillance duty in Sopot. Tomislav stationed me there because we knew Davor applied to join Tanatos' guard. I was to watch him. Of course, I had no idea he was the *boyfriend* you told me about," he said, frowning, "until I saw him at Kalemgrad."

"I was wondering what you were doing in Sopot," I said, not knowing how to react to this piece of information.

We reached my father's grave and sat down on the nearest bench.

"Who did they bury here? Obviously, it isn't Alina." I asked suddenly, surprised the thought didn't cross my mind before.

"Could be anyone. Tanatos probably changed the body's appearance so we wouldn't suspect anything. That's serious dark magic, the kind he's all too familiar with."

I had no idea what to think of it. Here it was, a massive gravestone with both my parents' names on it. Yet, my mother was still alive, and